THE OTHER SIDE

BOOK FIVE IN THE UNDRALAND SERIES

MARY E. TWOMEY

Fiction
Two
9/18

For Saxon Boaz-Danger Twomey.

I can't imagine I'll be able to catch you every time you trip, but I'll happily bang up my knees trying.

CROSSING OVER TO THE OTHER SIDE

*E*motions are the strangest things. They hit us in waves, each person experiencing a different decibel of agony or elation, which makes it easy to judge others on their reactions, whether acceptable or not. Uncle Rick crossing over of his own accord into the Land of Be hit us each in varying tones of sadness, denial and confusion.

Britta turned her sadness inward, crying occasionally on our trip over to the Other Side. Jamie swallowed his reaction as best he could, displaying a supportive front to his fiancée, Jens and I. When I tapped into the psychic link we shared, I could feel his emotions swinging like a pendulum from one extreme to the other. I really had no idea how deeply men felt things until getting a peek into Prince Jamie's mind.

After a hushed conversation with his sister as we waited in a small hut that served as the office to the Other Side, Jens was quiet. He made sure our paperwork was filled out correctly, and pushed us through the turnstile with no hint of the personality I loved so much.

After the sucking sensation landed us in the creepy carnival I'd come over to Undraland in, I reached for Jens's hand. He squeezed it for a second, then dropped the connection. Though he'd forgiven me for kissing Foss, I could tell he was still nursing a pretty open wound.

Rickety organ music piped a dismal and irksome tune through the park. Cutouts and murals of terrifying clowns grinned at me, their razor-like teeth sharpened and jagged like broken glass bottles. I dropped my gaze to my toes, only to find their painted faces trying to grab at me and swallow me whole from the floor. The mirrored maze multiplied my heartrate, but when I heard a squeak, I realized it had not come from my mouth.

Britta and Jamie were pressed up against one of the mirrors, aghast at the horror that was the carnival entertainment even I could not muscle through. Jens was so distracted by the emotions he'd stuffed himself to the brim with, that only his sister's yelp and drawn knife brought him somewhat back to the moment.

"Oh, it's okay, Britt. They're fake. They won't bite you." He held my hand and Britta's, nodding Jamie forward. "Almost there, guys."

When the normal noonday sun greeted us, I breathed in the air of a world I had been missing. A hint of pavement, hot dogs, garbage cans, dirt and the rust of machines were all sucked in through my nose, filling me and pushing out the purity of Undra's natural landscape. The rides around me were in various states of disrepair, some missing carts and whole bits of track, but I didn't care.

There was nothing to be done about Uncle Rick, and I'd made my decision about Foss. My family, Nik, Tor and Henry Mancini were enough of a loss to carry. The past would be put behind me, and I would start over. With every step, I began the process of shedding Undraland from my weary bones.

I ran through the amusement park, a burst of energy hitting at the sight of civilization. It was a concrete lamppost that called out to me first. I wrapped my arms around it and kissed the dirty green beauty. "I love you, electricity! I missed you so much!" So grateful was I at being reunited with my world, I did not care about the few carnival attendees who happened to look my way, judging me as a bigger freak show than the one advertised onsite.

Jens watched me with a sad smile. It was as if something big had been at the tip of his tongue since I'd escaped the Elvage prison, but he'd been purposefully keeping his mouth shut. "Cheating on me already, are you?" he questioned, forcing levity into the shtick that just didn't suit. I could tell he was faking humor to attempt a normal disposition, but I thought it was polite not to call him on it. He was hurting.

I kissed the peeling army-colored paint again, running my finger up the slope of the pole. "Only with inanimate objects. Isn't it gorgeous? Look at it, Jens. How many people do you think have kissed this magnificent minx? I might just be the first."

"Lucky lamppost." Again with the impression of a smile.

Britta kept her head down, knowing that she stuck out a little in her Amish-style dress. Jamie's curiosity overpowered his sadness at losing Alrik. His eyes drank in the sights Jens had described to him over the years. His mouth dropped open at the enormity of it all. I checked into our link and smirked at the half-sentences that exploded in his brain in pops and fizzles. *How could that... But the lights with the... The way that moves... I... I...*

I grinned at Jamie, watching the prince come undone at the magnificence of my kingdom. "Pretty great, huh?"

"There aren't words," he mumbled, his mental musings tumbling around his cranium, knocking proper conversation out of his brain.

Jens led us to the ticket booth, where Matilda greeted us warmly. "Hey, Mattie. I need the usual, but for four of us."

Her wrinkled smile faltered when Jens did not offer up a harmless flirt. "What's got you down, James Dean?"

He cast her half a smile, but again, it was hollow. "Alrik crossed over to Be."

Confusion and concern swept over her before she produced an intelligible response. "Be? Are you sure, dear? Alrik? Our man who isn't all that fond of Pesta crossed over to Be? What about his boy?"

Jens was suddenly overcome with a wave of grief. It was fascinating to watch his masculinity suck it down by the gallon until all that was left was a despondent shrug. "Dead. He was a good kid."

I was confused, but waited until Jens finished up with Matilda to inquire about my uncle. "Why does she think Alrik had a son? He was a bachelor, big time." My hand fell into Jens's, but his grip was slack.

Jens swallowed a thick lump before speaking. "Alrik adopted a boy a while back, but he died."

My nose crinkled as I stopped walking. "What? No. He would've mentioned something. I mean, I'm his niece. I think I would know if I had a cousin somewhere, right?" A link clicked in my mind. "Is she talking about Alrik's ward? Charles Mace? Did Alrik adopt Charles Mace? Why wouldn't he tell me something like that?"

Despite the possible onlookers, Jens wrapped me in an unexpected hug, resting his chin atop my head. His heart felt heavy as he leaned some of his burden on me, so I tried to shoulder the weight with grace to let him know I was strong enough for such conversations. "Let's go find a place to sleep, babe. I need to process everything we went through in Undraland. I'll explain everything once I have more answers."

"Okay." Though I had questions aplenty, I leaned up on my toes, cupped his sad face and kissed him. "I just can't believe Uncle Rick would keep something like that from me. I always wanted a cousin. And he's really dead?"

"Please, Loos," Jens begged, and I noticed his eyes moistening. "I can't talk about it yet. Give me some time. We can talk about everything when I figure it out myself."

The sight of Jens in almost tears sent a ripple of shock through me that rocked my worldview. Jens was unshakable. Jens was ninety percent shtick and ten percent mystery. I didn't think there was room in that equation for emotion so thick, it would lead him to tears. I traced under his eyes with my finger, gathering up enough moisture to form one whole tear. "Let's get you somewhere you can rest. Undra was rough on you. I can't imagine how exhausted and sore you must be from all the saving the day you do."

People walking by us either scoffed or pretended not to see us when Jens kissed me. His lips were slow, carrying too much meaning for me to understand. I tried to interpret his affection, but the emotion was heavy, laced with confusing notes that had something to do with Alrik and the secrets my uncle always had up his sleeve. Trust was a funny thing with Uncle Rick. You trusted him with your life, but you knew parts of his truth were lies told right to your face in plain daylight.

Alrik was the only family I had. My sort of uncle and recently adopted kind of dad. Plus, there was the whole strangeness of this deceased mystery cousin.

Jens pulled away and led us to the park's exit. I tried poking around in Jamie's brain for details about Alrik's adopted son.

I don't know, Lucy.

What the crap, Jamie? What gives? Did I really have a cousin? Did I just meet my cousin in that cell minutes before he died?

I don't know. I heard Jamie's mental sigh as we passed through the park's gate. *I just lost Alrik, too. And Foss. And Nik and Tor, for that matter. I need a moment.*

I respected Jamie's space, but the questions kept building inside of me.

2

MAGICAL LAND OF COMMERCE

*I*t was entertaining to listen to Jamie and Britta rattle off all the things that amazed them about my normal universe. Britta screamed – actually screamed – when an airplane flew overhead. That took some explaining, leading to a discussion in aeronautics neither Jens nor I were qualified for.

Jens drove us for hours in a black SUV he did not have to hotwire, and finally landed at a mega grocery store. You know, the kind that has food, pharmacy, clothes, toys, hardware and pretty much anything you need to start a new life.

"Time for a breather," Jens declared, stretching as he exited the car that was on loan to Toms fresh from Undra-land. For all the seat of the pants, fly by night relocating our family did, the Undra officials were very organized.

I let myself out and was smacked in the face by a blast of slightly chilly winter air. Undra was so warm all the time. It felt strange to be cold again. We weren't far enough

7

north for the weather to really give us a good freeze, but just far enough from the south to warrant a solid shiver in the mid-forties. The parking lot was your typical vast expanse of gray, dotted by trimmed bushes that looked like they'd seen better days. Just enough nature to remind us we were outside, but not enough to where we actually had to come into direct contact with it.

I shivered, hugging my bare arms under the tall light in the parking lot that was missing two of its four bulbs. "How come you get a car? My family never got one just handed to us."

"That's because your mom's Huldra. They were exiled. You parents got fringe benefits, not full benefits."

"I think you can guess my opinion on that," I glowered. "So what kind of full benefits do you get as an actual Undran, and not the bastardized version my family is?"

"Easy, sister suffragette," Jens teased, touching his toes. "They're not my rules, and I donated many a car and more to your parents when they had to move."

"You're a saint. Does a place to sleep come with the Tomten transition package?" I inquired, hoping a bed was in my future at some point. It was twilight, but the long drive made me a mix of stir-crazy and tired.

Jens smirked. "Well, the elves filled out your paperwork as Queen Lucy, so you get quite the deluxe package. However, if we want to stay off Pesta's radar and actually have some kind of a life, we can't use Undraland's resources for long. Pesta's Mouthpieces will find out where you are, and she'll come for you again."

"Mouthpieces?" I inquired, noting the plural. "But Jamie killed the Mouthpiece."

Jens nodded. "He sure did. He only killed him because it looked like he was about to shank you or gank you. Pesta's allowed a Mouthpiece, so she'll be looking for the next person who crosses over to inhabit. It was good of Jamie to kill him, but it puts us on the defensive, because now we have no idea who the next Mouthpiece will be." He jerked his thumb over his shoulder at the giant store. "We're stocking up now. Get anything you need to start a new life. After that, we're only using the card they gave you in an emergency."

"Card?" I asked, new life lighting my eyes.

"Shop away, Cinderella. Think of the Undraland office as your own personal fairy godmother."

"How much can we spend?" I asked, making several calculations on how to get the most bang for my borrowed buck.

"There's no limit. Buy whatever you want. You're a queen to them, Loos. They want you to be comfortable after your visit. Plus, it's standard. I have one, too. Toms need money to get their charges out of jams sometimes, so I don't have a limit, either."

My mouth dropped open as I recounted all the resale shops I'd bought a new wardrobe in when we had to relocate over and over again. The only things I bought new were my shoes, underwear and like, a toothbrush and stuff like that. My parents were always on the poorer side of the Joneses, so Jens's logic of an unlimited credit card seemed ridiculous to me. "Why didn't my parents get money? My mom was forced over here. Do they know how we were living?"

Jens shook his head. "Your mom stayed off their radar

because she had the rake. She needed Pesta not to find her. Using plastic? Quickest way to track a person. We won't be using yours after we get enough stuff to lay low for a while. Plus, Huldras didn't get unlimited funds. They got a stipend for the initial crossover into the Other Side. The other Huldras didn't need to keep moving like your mom did."

"I guess that makes sense," I grumbled.

"I used my allowance to buy whatever your parents needed when she would let me. Too much pride, that mom of yours. And your dad."

I opened Jamie's door, but he did not get out. Instead, he shuddered against Britta in the backseat. "You alright, guys?" Neither of them looked like they wanted to leave the car.

Britta huddled next to Jamie. "Is your world always so cold?"

I gave her a simple smile. "Some states are colder than others. This one isn't too bad, you're just catching it at their colder time of the year. Jens, why don't we head to California? It looks like you're bent on Canada or some-where north. That might be too cold for them just yet. They're still adjusting."

Jens helped his sister out of the car and rubbed warmth into her arms. It was probably only around fifty degrees, but that was a steep drop for them. "Less wildlife for Pesta to possess in the snow, Loos. We're home, but we're still on the run from Pesta. She'll be bent on finding you, and I'm still your Tom."

My heart sank. "I don't want to move from place to

place anymore. I didn't realize we'd have to keep running from her."

Jens tried to encourage me with his steady smile. "I figured you overlooked that part. But that's why I'm taking us somewhere cold. Not much fun, but we'll have a better chance of staying in one place longer if it's harder to find us."

"Makes sense." I reached for Jamie and dragged his rigid body out of the car. He shivered as he wrapped his arms around himself, trying to keep the heat from escaping his body. "You want to go invisible or something? We can wait in the car if it's all too much."

Jamie glanced with wide eyes at the hundreds of cars in neat little rows all around us. He gulped audibly and shook his head in slow motion. "It's fine. If this is your world, it's mine now, too."

I chucked his shoulder. "That's the spirit, big brother. Let's go."

Something about my words made Jens's expression twist from business to pain.

I reached for Britta's hand and tucked it through my arm, leading the two shell-shocked Undrans into the magical land of commerce.

EATING ALONE AT A TABLE FOR FOUR

*I*t was decided we would make better use of our time if we split up. Jens took Jamie to the men's section, and I absconded with Britta, who looked like an Amish doe-eyed cutie. Well, a six-and-a-half-foot tall cutie, so we stuck out a little.

"People are staring!" she whispered through gritted teeth.

"So they've never seen two smoking hot girls at the same time before. They'll adjust. You're fine, Britt. It's probably just your clothes. The ones we're buying will help you blend, but that gorgeous face? Well, get used to being stared at."

Britta blushed, feeling the heat in her cheeks with the back of her hand. "Where your confidence comes from, I'll never know."

Without missing a beat (or considering my audience), I deadpanned, "My boobs."

Britta blushed about nine shades of pink, shaking her head at me as she let loose a guilty chuckle.

I leafed through the racks, searching for anything that might fit a super tall, lean woman. Since this was not the mall, but a superstore, our options were limited. Thank God for yoga pants. I threw in a few pairs for both of us. "I'm guessing Farmer Jens is gonna hole us up for a while when we get where we're going, so durability won't be as important as comfort. I super want to get you more dresses, but if it's cold out, there won't be much point in that."

Britta examined the different fabrics as if there might be a pop quiz on them. She studied the stitching, the hems, even the tags with utter fascination. When I asked her to try on a few things, she would not come out of the changing room no matter how much I tried to coax her forward. "I can't! It's indecent!"

I couldn't help but smile at her when she finally allowed me in the room to see what the problem was. Britta was beautiful, and thus lie the crux of her issues with modern clothing. Due to her long years spent hoeing, planting and taking dead bodies off the noose by herself, she had strong arms, lean, long and muscular legs, complimented by a tiny waist. "Um, if I looked like that in jeans, no way I would've let anyone talk me into wearing dresses. You're a friggin' bombshell, Britt." When she didn't believe me, I pressed my point further. "No joke, you're just freaking out because you're not used to people seeing the shape of your body. I'd get used to people staring, because you look like you belong at the top here." I crossed my heart. "Jamie won't know what hit him."

Britta put her Amish dress back on, and we went to the shoe department. I took Jens to heart when he said there was no limit on the card. I bought five pairs of Chuck Taylors to make up for lost time. They were beautiful, colorful, and me. Each pair earned a little hug before going into the cart just for existing. Britta got one pair of Chucks to pacify me, but preferred the sturdier shoes she could do outdoor work in.

We bought snow boots, winter gear, underwear (Britta trying to figure out modern bras? Priceless.), pajamas, fuzzy socks, hair accessories and the like until two grocery carts were overflowing. I had never owned so many new things, and the high was heady.

The toiletry section required a third cart, which we filled with too much toilet paper and everything else needed for the four of us to relocate with.

Britta was unconcerned with the details; she was too preoccupied with fitting in. She slumped her shoulders and kept her head down to appear shorter.

"How do you think the guys are doing?" I asked to distract her as I dumped four tubes of toothpaste and a handful of toothbrushes into the buggy.

"Good, I hope. I can tell Jamie's worried. Jens tells us stories about your world all the time, but to be here? It's... it's so much bigger than either of us guessed. So many people all in one place. And everything's gray. Not much green."

"How are you holding up?" I asked, placing the most expensive shampoos and conditioners in the cart. "I'm glad you came with us. I didn't want to take Jamie away from his home, but we weren't exactly having much luck setting down roots in Undraland."

Britta examined a bottle, flinching when a voice boomed on the sound system overhead. "That's normal?" she inquired, her eyes darting around for the source of the noise.

I nodded. "I'll let you know when it's time to freak out."

She put the bottle down and twiddled with a stray string on her sleeve. "Jamie and I will be fine. So long as Pesta leaves you alone, we can make any place our home. It just might take some getting used to."

"You're a trooper, that's for sure." I looked at our carts with the thrill of retail therapy flowing in my veins. "You ready to hunt down the boys? I'm not sure the SUV can hold much more."

It took us a while to find Jens and Jamie in the massive store, but when we did, Jens visibly relaxed when his eyes fell on me. His arm rubbed my back and he held my head to his chest, kissing my hair as if I was in need of emotional support.

"You okay?" I asked, his clingy nature not something I expected.

Jens nodded, but his smile was forced. "I see you took me seriously when I said there wasn't a limit on the card."

"But you said there wasn't! You said to get what we needed for a long hole-up," I protested, defending my purchases.

"I'm kidding. You did great. Got enough clothes for the both of you?"

I eyed his one cart compared to our three and frowned. "Did you?"

"Guys are funny that way."

Something caught my eye in his cart, and I scowled. "What the smack is this?" I questioned, picking up an econo pack of beef jerky. "I'll straight up clock you if you bring this into the car."

Jens produced a grin. "Food is food, Mox. That's got a decent shelf life." He looked around the aisle. "We need to head over to camping supplies."

My heart sank. "What? Why? I thought we were done sleeping on the ground."

"We are." He turned his cart around and pushed it in the direction of the outdoors section. "For now, at least. Just have to be ready for anything. Pesta's off our trail, but if she catches up to us, I want to be prepared. Plus, I lost one of my knives. I'm going to see if there's a decent replacement here."

The levity of the shopping trip crashed around me. "When will we be done running from her?"

Jens rubbed my back, but didn't answer. "Let's get the sub-zero sleeping bags, plus a spare in case anything rips. We've got the trunk space, and we'll keep most of our supplies in the car until we can settle down."

"When will that be?" My voice was quiet as I pushed my cart next to his.

He didn't answer, just kissed the top of my head and pushed forward. That same closed-off look kept him from me, and I was beginning to miss him. Sure, he was here, but he wasn't. Not really.

Jens and Jamie loaded up a whole cart with camping stuff. Every item added weighed down my spirits until the inflated high that came from shopping to my heart's content was completely absent. He was absent.

Jens suggested shopping for more food, but the response from each of us was lackluster. Plus, we were running out of carts. "There was a little deli area near the produce at the front of the store. Want to grab a bite there and refuel?" His tone was polite, devoid of sarcasm or laughter. I hated it.

The noncommittal nods from Jamie and Britta informed me that they had never been to a modern deli, so they really had no preference. "Why don't you take them, and I'll get food for the road." Jens handed me the black credit card.

"Sure. What do you want me to get you?" I asked, stuffing the card in my back pocket.

Jens shrugged. "Whatever. Something small. I'm not hungry."

I turned and left Jens without a parting word, leading Jamie and Britta through the massive store toward the deli counter. Jamie was amazed that I could order something, and someone else had already slaughtered the cow, gleaned the food and prepared it for me. Britta was just plain flabbergasted at the portion sizes.

They were starting to hit their limit on the new world, so they went behind a pillar and turned invisible so they could avoid being stared at, and could in turn gawk at my people as openly as they wished. That left me to order and carry four plates of food to the small cafeteria-style dining area and surround myself with the four carts I was in charge of watching.

"I can't eat all that!" Britta protested, eyeing her sub

sandwich with astonishment as she sat down next to me. "Do humans need to eat more than Undrans? I never noticed that about you on our side."

"No. We eat more because we can. It's all right here, so eat as much as you want." I picked the pepperoni off my pizza and placed each slimy disc on Jens's piece. After eating bunnies and fish right out of the carcass, sliced pepperonis swimming in grease lost some of their appeal. I started to understand why my mother had become a vegetarian.

Jamie and Britta gazed around as they ate, people watching and taking full advantage of the fact that no one could see them. Jamie was holding Britta's hand so they could see each other, and the two talked animatedly about the many strange things I could not begin to see the fascination of.

They entertained themselves while I sat at the table for four seemingly by myself. I sat in silence and ate slowly, my stomach not used to the heavy oils and grease, but my taste buds appreciating it all the same. I'm sure I looked how I felt. Alone.

Too much time with only my thoughts for company was a dangerous thing for me. Alrik left me for the Land of Be. I didn't understand why, nor did I care as much as the others. I loved him, but the trust part was always tricky. When my family died, he left me alone that very next week. I would miss him, and I still didn't understand his reasons for crossing over into Be, but I'd wasted enough of my life wishing he would come back and wondering why he was always leaving.

I got used to the loneliness and the occasional curious

stares that found me, questioning why the pathetic girl was eating alone, surrounded by overflowing carts. I was still the girl with no friends. I had no home and no family. The hope that Alrik would pop up for his monthly visits was gone now, and I guessed there was no use trying to figure out why he left me so abruptly.

I finished my pizza and just stared at my plate as I tried to avoid the dark thoughts I knew were right around the corner.

I missed Foss. Plain and simple, I'd gotten used to having him around. I had no one to fight with, and my problems were compounding now that I had nothing to divert my attention from them. I worried he was struggling in Undraland. I worried he had no one to take care of him. I worried that I missed him, and what that said about me.

"You look sad, Lucy Kincaid," Jens observed as he sat down across from me, purposefully squashing Jamie, who "oof"ed and relinquished his chair.

I pushed his pizza toward him. "I'm fine. Bathroom," I explained. "Didn't want to leave these two alone." I pushed my chair back and left the table with no further discussion on the matter.

I shut myself inside the restroom stall, threw my mental wall up to keep Jamie out and hugged myself, willing the growing hole inside of me not to expand any further. Something felt wrong in my soul, but I had no idea which horror to blame for it.

Uncle Rick was gone. That was part of the hole, for sure. Foss was wandering the outskirts of Undraland, nameless, homeless and without a friend. He was without me, and I'd chosen that fate for him.

As much as those two things tore me open, there was something nagging in the back of my head that felt... missing. A filled void that was suddenly gaping wide open again. My hand rubbed over my heart, spackling whatever it could into the hole.

I'd thought my problems would be over if I could just get back to my normal reality. I didn't realize Pesta would still be hunting me.

That was it. It was the promise of a real life in one place with a white picket fence, and then the sudden loss of all that hope. That must be the thing that devastated me. I was homeless. I let myself out of the stall and stared into the mirror, wondering if that's how I'd always be.

I was thinner than when I'd left for Undraland. I had bags under my eyes and a haunted look I didn't think any amount of makeup could cover up. I looked older, and not in the good way.

I looped my finger through Foss's ring around my neck, and whispered my hope into the empty lavatory that he was safe, and that he'd find a peaceful new home soon.

As I had every morning before starting a new life in a new school, I practiced smiling in the mirror. It was fake and reeked of sadness, but it was necessary. The more the corners of my mouth lifted in an attempt to pretend happiness into being, the more depressed I became.

It didn't used to be this hard.

4

NIGHTLY HABITS

*J*ens checked us into a hotel. Not a motel, a hotel. It was a big difference, trust me. The main concern I had was that the room produced a bed I could pass out in. Jens's main concern was the parking garage. He passed up three hotels because they did not have a parking garage we could hide the SUV in.

His eyelids were drooping as we took the elevator up to our adjoined suites. I had only just enough oomph in me to attempt an explanation at the mystery that was elevator to the overly-stimulated Undrans.

Jens did his best to explain to them the different functions of their room, ending with a tired, "It's probably best you just don't touch anything."

I rolled my eyes at him and covered the basics of the bathroom and the wonders of modern plumbing. "Don't touch these. They're light sockets, and unless you know how to use them, don't. And the phone? Don't bother with it. Or the A/C unit. Or the coffeemaker." I sighed. "Jens was right. Best not touch too much just yet."

Jamie and Britta were holding hands in that wistful way lovers do before they have a meaningful night together. Though I knew from Jamie's errant thoughts that they were not having sex, sleeping in a bed together was a new high for them.

Their sweet gazes toward each other only made the distance between Jens and I all the more vast. Neither of us spoke as we moved around the room, settling in, showering, and tearing the tags off fresh pajamas that were so snuggly and clean, the luxury felt mind-blowing.

The bed was everything I dreamed it could be. It was a king-sized wonder with white linens and a fluffy down comforter so I could revel in my modern luxuries. I crawled under the covers and climbed atop the pillow like a cat, giving it a genuine teddy bear snuggle. Despite the awkward vibe Jens was sending out, I was grateful we were back in my country.

Jens joined me in the bed, smelling of aftershave, soap, sugar cookies and man. I hadn't seen him clean-shaven in a while, and wished we were in a better place so I could stroke his cheek. He lay on his back, staring up at the ceiling with that same far-off expression that made me think he was really somewhere else.

Enough, already.

I took matters into my own hands and rolled atop him, my knees straddling his hips. "Alright, you. You've been in a funk since Alrik skipped town. Talk." I pointed my finger to his chest, demanding action.

Jens placed his hands on my hips and traced the bone

with his thumbs. "My funk is your funk. Just processing everything, I guess."

I narrowed my eyes at him. "It's more than that. You know something, or you're hiding something. What gives?"

Jens rolled his eyes to keep them from me and moved me off his lap, clearly annoyed. "What gives is that I'm tired. You're my charge, Loos. I've always got a million things on my mind. New territory. New threats. I'm preoccupied because I'm trying to keep us all alive."

I spoke slowly, taking in the sudden shift in his mood. "Okay. I guess you just seem unhappy, and I thought you might want someone to talk to about it. If not to me, then Jamie or Britt."

"Yup. I'm gonna get some sleep, alright? You tired?" He turned on his side away from me and settled into the sheets, punching his pillow to get it to behave.

My answer was inconsequential, so I didn't offer one. Instead I lay down, careful not to jostle the bed too much. I hugged my edge of the mattress, leaving a Foss-sized hole in between us so that all the things unspoken had a place in the bed to rest for the night.

An hour later, I was no closer to sleep, but I had not moved for fear of disturbing Jens.

"Loos?" he whispered.

I didn't want to answer him with any emotion in my voice, so I waited a few beats before opening my mouth.

Before I made a sound, Jens slipped out of bed, slid on his jeans and boots, and sneaked out the door, leaving me alone in our bed.

5

HOTEL MISERY

I had never been much for paranoia, but Jens sneaking out of the hotel room brought a myriad of unanswerable questions to my mind. When he returned three hours later, I had to fight myself to remain silent and feign sleep like an opossum. I would not be the where-were-you wife. I would not fight stupidly or waste my life reaching out to someone who couldn't be bothered to sleep next to me for one whole night alone.

Jamie had poked into my worried brain a few times during the night, gently beckoning me to go to sleep so he could escape into my subconscious. Apparently my mouth could close, but there was no turning off my mental motor.

Jens insisted on room service the next morning because it would keep me hidden, but I couldn't stay in the room with him and the building tension any longer. "I'm fine. I highly doubt Pesta frequents hotels. It's a big friggin' country, Jens."

I didn't wait for his response, or for him to put on the

boots he'd taken off when he'd sneaked back into the room at four in the morning.

Jamie's door opened, and he came bounding after me, fresh from a night spent snuggling his fiancée. "I'm starving," he informed me, pressing too many buttons in the elevator. "May I join you for breakfast?"

I nodded, and then pressed the only button we actually needed. "Wilderness Jim send you to babysit?"

Jamie gave me an affectionate grin, wrapping me in a half-hug. "Oh, *liten syster*, you're too hard on him."

"Says the guy who actually got to sleep next to his significant other. I got to pretend to sleep in an empty room half the night." I held up two sarcastic thumbs. "Super. He wants space, so I'm giving him space. He just didn't know how to ask for it. Feels really good when your boyfriend literally runs away from you in the dead of night. You definitely picked the right sibling." I guess I could've played it cool, but it was Jamie. He'd go poking around in my head for the answers eventually if I wasn't forthcoming with them.

Jamie's grin faltered a little, but he was too happy having spent some uninterrupted time alone with Britta to truly participate in my portable rain cloud. He was clad in dark jeans, a green polo, a zip-up blue hoodie and black Chucks, all of which made him look oddly right for my world. That coupled with the shave and shower made for a handsome and happy Jamie. "Jens loves you," he reminded me.

"Yup. I'm hungry," I said, changing the subject as the doors finally opened up to the correct floor. I led the way to the breakfast area and loaded up my plate with the standards: bagel, eggs, bacon, sausage, orange juice, a banana and a bottle of water.

Jamie was fascinated with the waffle iron that didn't need a fire under it to cook the batter in. He made seven fluffy Belgian waffles before the line behind him started to pile up.

Jamie was amazed by the difference in produce and baked goods, but unimpressed with the quality of our eggs. "I had two dozen chickens back home, and those are not eggs," he declared, pushing them toward me in disgust.

"Hate to break it to you, pal, but they are. Your food tastes different than ours. Yours is pure, fresh from the source. Your water's not polluted. Your air's perfect. Ours is industrialized, so it takes the quality down a notch." I forked a bite of his eggs and shoved them into my mouth. "You get used to it."

Jamie fired off a string of questions about my world, shocked that I was, as I'd insisted, not Queen of the Other Side.

"Nope. Just a regular person. Less than that. I'm technically dead, so I'm more like a ghost of a person, or someone else entirely."

A woman with curly red hair approached us and addressed Jamie with a sheepish expression. *Oh, brother.* "Are you and your girlfriend using this chair?" She leaned on the chair next to him, giving him her best flirty eyes and seventh-grade stance.

Jamie shook his head, appalled. "No, ma'am. She's not my girlfriend." Jamie was insultingly quick with his response, so I kicked him under the table.

I smiled up at her, wiping my hands off on my napkin.

"He's my brother. His fiancée's coming down in a minute, though, so you can take that chair." I pointed to a spare one at a nearby table.

The red-head wilted appropriately and slinked away, taking the chair she didn't really need to a table with her girlfriends.

"Is this married in your culture?" He motioned between us uncertainly. "You and I eating together? You were always so casual on our side. I just assumed men and women ate together all the time here." Jamie worried at our public torrid affair.

I picked at one of Jamie's many waffles, which didn't have much flavor. "They do. You're fine. Don't worry, you're spared from the horror of people assuming you're with me. That was just her clever way of fishing to see if you're single. Ginger wants to jump your bones."

Jamie turned beet red and focused on his plate. "I'm sure you can't be right. Women aren't like that. They don't have the same desires as men."

I lowered my voice. "You've been in my head, so you know that's not true. I'm telling you," I said, chewing on the waffle, "bone-jumper. Nothing wrong with her seeing if you're single."

"I should get back to Britta." Jamie pushed his plate toward me. It was clear he could not get away from me fast enough, lest someone think we were together, and he was a man who ran around on his woman.

"I'm still hungry. See ya up there."

Jamie was torn between watching over Jens's charge and fleeing the scene of his non-adultery. "You'll come right back up when you're done?"

"Yes, Dad." The word was meant to be sarcastic, but it faltered on my tongue. Pain slashed across my heart at using the precious word so callously.

Jamie's hand flew to his chest as if my ache caused him physical hurt. "Wow. That was powerful." His panic shifted to pity, and now it was me who could not get rid of him fast enough.

"See ya, Jamie." I waved him off.

He looked down at me with brotherly love in his eyes. "I wish I felt one tenth of that for my own father."

"Bye, Jamie," I said, not caring that I sounded rude.

Jamie kissed the top of my head in that same non-sexual way Jens started doing, and I wanted to puke. "See you upstairs, *liten syster.*"

I waited for him to leave before folding my arms on the table and resting my head atop them in a big huff. I was tired from the fake sleep, sure, but gearing down for a lifetime of Brother Jamie and Watchdog Jens was taxing. Thank God for Britta.

Jens was MIA when I made it upstairs half an hour later, so I ditched Jamie and Britta to go swimming. They could not have been happier to gain more alone time.

My new bathing suit was pale blue with gold straps. Totally cute on anyone else. Unfortunately I had Foss's crest burned above my breasts and various bruises peppered all over my body from the guards wrestling me into the cell before they killed that emo guy with the crazy eyes. I had a burn mark on my lower back from the fire at Foss's house, and many deep cuts that had healed poorly from my adventures in Undraland. I looked like a battered wife or something. Awesome.

I took my towel down to the pool area and just sat on the side with my legs in the water, pushing out thoughts of the Nøkkendalig. I really had no desire to swim, but knew I couldn't let myself become afraid of the water. There was too much fear in my life as it was. This was on my terms, and there were no mermen anywhere in my world to molest me and drag me down to my death. When a flirty couple came into the pool room, I plunged myself into the water to hide my body from them.

Panic. Pain. Suck it up.

Laps.

I took my fear, frustration and creeping depression out on the surface of the water, chopping my hands through with precision developed from my half a semester taking swimming for gym class. I completed seven laps in the long pool before I realized I was winded. When I stopped to look around, I noticed a dozen or so more people had entered the pool area.

The familiar set of eyes locked on mine, but the thrill of having Jens nearby fell flat when he had that business face on instead of the boyfriend smile. I saluted him with two fingers, and he reciprocated the gesture.

I'm pretty sure Jamie looked more like my boyfriend than Jens, and I really hated that.

He motioned me toward him, so I swam forward and clung to the edge of the pool where he knelt down. "I've got to go out for a bit. Jamie and Britt are holed up in their room, but could you check in on them when you're done? Make sure they don't stick their fingers in any light sockets or anything like that?"

"I was just about to get out," I said, pulling myself up out of the water.

Jens helped me to stand and gasped when he saw the state of my body. It was the first actual reaction to anything he'd had in a while, and it was a mixture of disgust and horror, all aimed at me. He turned and snatched my towel, banding it around me as if to cover up his crime. As if he was the one who'd beaten me and burned me. As if I was gross.

I felt gross.

"Let's get you upstairs." One arm curled around my back to move me forward, and the other held my towel in place so no one else would be exposed to the awfulness that was my body.

"I'm fine, Jens." I wriggled out of his grasp and snatched up my shorts, t-shirt and shoes.

"Something interesting written on my girlfriend's ass?" Jens barked at someone in the pool.

I had no words for Jens, only a snarl. It's hard to leave in a huff when you're soaking wet, but I managed.

6

COMING TO BLOWS

"I'm not done talking to you about this," Jens said as he stomped into the hotel room after me.

I hadn't said a word, and I wasn't about to fall into the trap of arguing with a two-year-old. I shut myself in the bathroom and locked the door so he couldn't follow me inside. The overwhelming white of the tiles and counter yelled at me that I didn't belong in the perfection, but I ignored the feeling, as I already had someone yelling at me on the other side of the door that couldn't be so easily discounted.

"Fine, you can just listen," Jens snapped. "I need you to be more careful when you're out in the open. All it takes is for someone in Pesta's pocket to see you, and she's on us. I want you to be able to stay in one place, Loos. I mean it. No more wandering off in your bikini."

My cheeks burned at how he made me sound. He'd had naked women riding him in a group orgy, but I wasn't allowed to go swimming by myself. Too bad the superstore didn't sell burkas.

I turned on the water so I didn't yell at him and take us down a road we couldn't return from. After I disrobed, I looked in the mirror at the marks covering my naked body. The wide mirror had gold edges and not a fingerprint on it. I, on the other hand, had plenty of marks on me, and was far from beautiful.

I vaguely recall being cute. Maybe on the verge of almost pretty on a good day. Those days were long gone. I'd been through too much. The Nøkkendalig. The fire. The fights. The Weres. The farlig. Thomas Jefferson. Piece by piece, they sucked the youth from me. There were too many bruises. I had fresh scars I could barely remember acquiring. I placed my hand on the mirror to cover up my face that looked so worn, I could scarcely take ownership of the tear-stained image.

My heart sank almost audibly. *I'm ugly.*

No sooner had I thought the words did Jamie's voice echo in my brain. *No, Lucy. You're not ugly. You're very desirable. Look at you.*

I shrieked and jumped back from the mirror, scrambling for a towel to cover myself with.

"Lucy? What? What's wrong?" Jens called from the other side of the door. "Are you hearing anything I've been saying?"

I shrank to the floor, my hands on my ears, trying to shut out both Jamie and Jens. It was confusing to have someone talk to you out loud and a different guy speak in your mind at the same time.

I'm sorry! I'm so sorry! I'm coming over there. I didn't mean to look. I'm sorry!"

"Go away!" I screamed at both of them.

I heard Jamie and Jens talking, and then shouting at each other. I could feel heat from Jamie rising up in the bond, and wished for just a little space.

Before I could despair any further, an invisible force socked me in the cheek, whipping my face to the side and banging my head into the wall. I let out a shocked sob as blood trickled out of my mouth. The stars were blinked away, but the pain drummed like a heartbeat in my face.

"Lucy? Lucy!" Jens yelled, banging on the bathroom door, shaking the built-in blow-dryer on the wall. "That stupid bond! I meant to hit Jamie, not you! Let me in, baby. Let me look at it."

I wished for a double lock, but the one was holding up well enough. The water was still running, and luckily hid most of the emotion from my quivering reply of, "I'm fine. Just taking a shower."

My jaw cracked horribly as I crawled into the tub, hoping if he did manage to break down the door, that he would respect my privacy and let me take a shower.

I lay in a ball on the floor of the shower and sobbed silently as the water fell, washing away the blood in ethereal ribbons that would have been pretty if the whole situation wasn't so doomed. I checked my teeth with my tongue to make sure none of them were loose and bit down on my knuckle as I cried my way through the echoes of pain that just kept on coming.

It's okay! We're okay, Lucy. Are you alright? Oh, sweetheart, Jens would never do that to you on purpose.

Jamie's concern only compounded my emotional imbalance. "Get out of my head!" I screamed like a crazy person.

I stroked the glass heart around my neck. Linus would never have stood for anyone hitting me, even by accident. Now I had no brother, no family to comfort me and no one who understood. My tears were fat as they shoved themselves down my cheeks, and I wondered if I would ever have something that resembled a normal life.

Foss's ring hung just below my Linus heart. I made the decision to let myself despair for that small slice of time, poking my finger through the ring and bawling through a wish that wherever Foss was, he was safe. If I was being truthful, I would admit that I wished he was here, that he would hold me as he did after the attack from the Nøkkendalig. We'd slept together many nights, and he hadn't left me alone in the bed. He'd spooned me, holding his knife to my breasts in his strange way that somehow made me feel safe while teetering on the edge of danger. I missed him, and desperately wished that gnawing ache would go away.

I ran through seven different escape plans in my head, all of which failed when the bond was factored in. I was doomed. It seemed Jamie's curse had been transferred to me somehow.

Jens finally broke open the door, tumbling in like an apologizing rhino. "Lucy, I didn't mean it! I forgot you were tied to him and just lost my temper." He tore open the shower curtain, but shut it again when I screamed.

"Get out! What makes you think you're allowed to

barge in on me in the shower? Can't a girl get some privacy? I'm still a woman, Jens!"

"I'm sorry! I wasn't thinking. Could you please come out? I need to look at your face."

"I told you, I'm fine. It'll heal, just like everything else. Go run your errands."

There was a pause, and then a plea. "Please, Lucy. Tell me how to make it right."

"We're fine," I lied. Then I dug for the truth, which was buried beneath layers of hurt. "I know you wouldn't knock me around on purpose. Just be more careful next time, and maybe don't punch your best friend in the face over something he can't always control." I swallowed and sat up in the shower, pulling myself together as best I could. "Laplanding is hard enough without you turning all possessive boyfriend on me. Don't make life harder."

"I don't like that Jamie saw you naked," Jens confessed, but his tone was still repentant. "I have every right to punch someone who's creeping on you."

I stood and turned off the water, reaching around the curtain for a hotel towel that was never big enough. Stepping out, Jens caught my elbow and helped me so I didn't slip. It was sweet. I was his ninety-year-old grandmother. Sex on a stick.

"Jamie and I are working on it. You have to chill. Yelling at the guy in the pool you think was looking at me? Not cool. I need zero of that in my life. I'm twenty years old. I can handle it." I shook my head at him, but couldn't look directly into his stricken face. "Socking your best friend over a mistake? That's not like you."

Jens nodded, taking his scolding like a repentant child. I hated the sight of it. "I'm sorry."

"You punched Linus's sister. You told me you two used to be close. How do you think he'd react to this?"

Jens gulped, ashamed. "He'd murder me where I stood, no question."

I nodded at his assessment, my skin cold and my hair dripping down my back. "I don't know what's gotten into you since we left Undraland, but whatever it is, it's changing you and taking us from each other. If you don't want to be with me, just say it. Don't ruin what we had and go down in flames like this. It's insulting."

Jens's eyes grew wide, horrified at my assumption. "I'm not going anywhere. I don't want out."

"Then why are you sneaking out at night?"

He flinched that he'd been caught. "You saw that, did you?"

"Trusting you isn't exactly easy with our track record. I wouldn't bother putting any more lies atop what's left of us right now. Out with it."

"I've been scouting out the area to make sure we haven't been followed. Pesta could have us surrounded in a second, so I don't want to give her that edge. I need to keep you safe. It's my only job, and I can't fail this time." He ran his hands through his thick hair, and I could tell he was tempering his words. "Something happened in Elvage before we left, and I haven't been able to shake it. You know that guy they executed? Charles Mace?" He winced when he spoke the guy's name.

"Yeah. Did you know him?"

Pain hit Jens anew, washing off all cockiness and coolness. "Yes, and I wasn't all that great to him. He... he deserved better from me, and he died alone. He was a hero, but he went out a villain. I was supposed to protect him, to look after him. I didn't do my job, and he died."

Out of nowhere, the dam broke and Jens slumped down to his knees.

"Oh, Jens. There was nothing you could've done. He was controlling people with his whistle thing. It's against the law. That's got nothing to do with you." He clung to my thighs and buried his head in my stomach. I was very aware that I was naked under the towel, but tried to push past it for the moment. "It's not your responsibility to keep everyone you know alive."

"It's breaking me, what happened. And I can't really talk about it. The whole thing is so awful. I've seen dozens and dozens of dead bodies, but when they brought out the head? Mace's head? With those dead eyes that looked up, begging me to find a solution? I can't shake it. He didn't deserve that, Loos. And he deserved a lot better from me."

I combed my fingers through his unruly black locks, wondering if we'd ever get it right. "I'm sorry your friend died. For what it's worth, he seemed nice." I didn't even know if that was true. So little of that whirlwind made sense to me. The guy admitted to controlling me, but I was pretty sure that wasn't true. I'd made those decisions to follow Alrik on the crazy rake mission when I first got to Tonttu, long before I met Charles Mace. "So weird that Charles Mace was my cousin."

Jens stiffened.

"I mean, it's fine. I didn't know him. It's not like I lost a brother or something."

Jens muffled a heart-wrenching moan into my stomach, gripping my thighs so tight, I worried he might bruise them.

"Hey, it's alright. Take a breath." After a few beats of pause, I stroked the golden diamond tattoo on his cheek with my thumb to soothe him. "I wish Alrik would've told me he'd adopted someone. I don't know why he never mentioned that he'd taken in a ward, and that he'd adopted him. Seems like it's worth a conversation."

"He... he had a friend, and I can't imagine how devastated she'd be if she knew. Mace loved her a lot, and she was oblivious. Treated him like family. Mace didn't always understand her, but man, was he loyal. To the death." Jens's voice started to quiver, so I hugged him tighter.

"Baby," I cooed. "You can't save everyone. You weren't even there."

"I really can't talk about it," Jens said, stuffing his emotions back to that place I wasn't allowed. "But that's what's been up with me." He relinquished his hold on my midsection and stood, examining my face with his prodding fingers. "I can't believe I did that. I should be locked up."

I jerked my face away, not willing to display it. "I'll keep that in mind when you start turning into a bad eighties movie again. I mean, seriously, you were classic jerk jock back there. Go apologize to Jamie."

"No. He shouldn't have looked at you naked like that."

"My body. I'll deal with him about it. You're acting bipolar. Get ahold of yourself. Be sad, but don't take it out on Jamie or me. We're both jacked up enough."

Jens nodded, contrite and appropriately morose. "That's fair."

There was a moment's pause, and I realized how very much I wanted space. "Right, so I'm like seven kinds of naked under this towel. Could I get a little privacy?"

The hint of the old smile I adored teased his full lips. "If you lose the towel, it'd be eight kinds of naked. That's my favorite kind."

"Nice try, smooth talker." I held the towel tighter around me and jerked my thumb toward the door. "Go play nice with Jamie. Braid each other's hair and leave me the smack alone."

"Hey," Jens said, wrapping me in a brief hug. "I really am sorry. About everything. When you get out, let's start over. Is that in the realm of possibility?"

"New realm. New possibilities." I pressed a kiss into his chest. "That sounds good."

When he finally left, I glanced at my face in the mirror, the red mark of my boyfriend's fist swelling up atop my cheekbone. I knew I'd have a shiner soon, and wondered how that would change things for us.

7

ROAD TRIP

*W*e stayed in the hotel four days before Jens insisted we move along. My eye was nice and black, as was Jamie's. The only person who apologized more than Jens was Jamie, who took full responsibility for everything, wagging his tail between his legs long after everything was forgiven.

I clung to Britta, knowing this whole laplanding business was harder on her than she let on. When she went out on patrol at night so Jens could sleep, I missed her and worried for her safety. "You're sure you're alright? Nothing fishy?" I asked, hefting her bag into the trunk.

"No fish at all, actually. There's shockingly little nature around this area." She smiled at me, adjusting her pink fitted long-sleeved shirt under her light jacket. "But no, nothing to speak of at all. We're completely hidden." I loved her two braids without the bonnet hiding her from view. So did she, I could tell. She had her dagger tucked into the waist of her jeans, but other than that, she was a normal girl.

Jens switched out the plates on the SUV again with another car in the parking structure, and loaded up our vehicle with the few things we'd taken in with us.

"Can I drive for once? You look exhausted." I held out my hand for the keys.

"I'm not tired. And I'm the Tom, so I drive." He was a different kind of distant now. He was more present, but he could barely look at me, my black eye too horrible for him to take.

I didn't feel like a fight, so I wrapped my arms around him in a hug, discreetly lifting the keys from his jacket pocket. I slid past him and hoisted myself into the driver's seat, starting up the car with authority. "In the back, Jennifer." When he tried to remove me, I shut the door and locked it, jerking my thumb toward the back. "Don't make me arm-wrestle you for it. It'll only end in your humiliation when I smoke you."

Britta rode shotgun after I won the argument. "Jens has never been good at letting someone else lead."

"Really? You don't say. Buckle up, boys," I reminded them, playing the role of the soccer mom. "Does anyone have to use the restroom before we leave?"

"Just go," Jens grumbled, pretending to be mad at me. "And don't get pulled over. You can't use that innocent face of yours to talk yourself out of a ticket." He leaned his head against the back of the seat and groaned up at the ceiling. "Because I bashed it in."

"You're absolved, Jens." I shook out my arms and readied

myself, adjusting the seat from Jens's gigantor legs. "It's been too long since I've driven. Which one's the break again?" I teased, fondling the steering wheel affectionately. I missed the feel of being behind the wheel. So much of everything was everyone else's choice. This was mine. I would be in control of the giant vehicle, and everyone would be cool about it.

Britta laid her seat back and took a nap while I drove us across Missouri. We stopped in Illinois sometime after midnight because the lines on the freeway started to run together, and I realized we might not want to have escaped Undra only to die in a stupid car wreck.

I pulled over at a rest stop and let us all out, everyone stretching and groaning at finally being able to move around.

Britta retracted from the outdoors. "It's freezing! What's wrong with the air?"

It was getting colder, that's for sure. Goose bumps stood out on my arms and I shivered as I watched my breath float out in front of my face. "We're driving north. The further up we go, the colder it'll get." It was just below forty degrees.

"Colder?" Britta gasped, floored at the possibility. "How could it get colder than this?"

"Wait till we hit Michigan." I chuckled at her growing concern. "Those winter jackets I got us are no joke. How much further?" I inquired of our fearless leader.

Jens touched his toes and then went around back to dig a blanket out of the trunk for his sister. "We can stop soon. Let's get a hotel room for a few days."

I was looking forward to crashing, but I didn't let on that I was tired. I was afraid Jens would take the wheel, and

I was enjoying the boss seat. The cold air woke me right up, but my smile faltered when I noticed Jens watching me with that same tortured expression. *Stupid black eye.*

"Quit it with the bedroom eyes," I teased, forcing levity into the air. "Your sister'll get the wrong idea about us."

Jens regained a modicum of his former self and grinned at me. "Or the very graphic right idea."

"Jens!" Britta scolded as she hoisted herself back into the car and slammed the door shut behind her.

8

STINA'S NEW PET

*W*hen we checked into the hotel, Jens was unhappy. "There's no parking garage," he stated, sliding the key card into the slot and letting us into the room. "I don't like our stash exposed like this."

"You set the alarm. I don't know how much farther we can go before we all need some sleep. We've got a hefty distance on the gate to Undra. We should rest while we can."

He kissed my forehead, but turned away when the lamplight fell on my face. "I'd argue, but I'm beat. I didn't know you had it in you to drive that far."

"I'm amazing," I bragged in monotone. "Driver gets first shower," I commanded, instating a new rule.

"Have at it, Jeeves. I'll do a once-around the perimeter and then come back up." He set his red bag on the drab comforter, looking at the king-sized bed forlornly.

"Oh, you with the sexy talk. Say 'perimeter' again."

"Perimeter," he breathed, steaming up his tone and

licking his lips to make me laugh. "Get in there, Mox. I don't want to work you up too much."

My shower was hot and long, just how I liked it. My pajamas were clean, purple and warm – my specialty. I could've opted for something more attractive than a pair of fuzzy pajama pants and a fitted thermal shirt, but given that my boyfriend could barely look at me, I didn't think sexy times were on the horizon anytime soon.

I brushed my teeth and crawled under the sheets, turning on the TV to keep me company while I waited for Jens.

And waited.

Two hours later, I was biting my nails. Another five minutes, and I knocked on my buddy's mental wall. *Hey, is Jens with you?*

Huh? Um, no. I thought he was with you. I could hear his internal thoughts searching for his shoes as he tried not to wake Britta.

You're worried. I should've told you sooner. He said he'd go check the grounds and then be right up. I pulled on a pink Chuck and a green one, shoved my arms into a blue sweater and tied up my hair. I met Jamie in the hallway. "Did you leave Britt a note?"

"Pens are amazing," he remarked, holding his elbow out to me, always the constant gentleman. I looped my arm through his and walked with him to the elevator. "I wouldn't worry," he said, covering over his own concern poorly. "Jens disappears all the time. I'm sure he just got carried away scouting out the area. He's very strict about your safety on this side."

"You're sweet to lie to me." We walked out of the building and glanced around for Jens.

What I saw nearly stopped my heart. Standing next to the SUV was Jens, accompanied by that Huldra girl who flirted with him eons ago when I first met him and left my world for Undraland. The tiny skirt girl he'd punched in the face. Stina.

It was not her I was concerned about, though.

Standing off to the side was a figure I would recognize anywhere. He was hulking and brown-skinned with a constant air of looking for a fight.

"Foss?" I choked out, my voice barely breaking the night ambiance. "Foss!"

He looked uncertain of me as he revealed himself more fully in the moonlight and the faint illumination wafting off the hotel. He stepped forward cautiously, regarding me like the disobedient animal he was.

I didn't think. I didn't hesitate. I ran to Foss, my heart bursting at the sight of him. It was dark, and so was he, but I felt lighter than I had in days.

His cagey expression lifted at my immediate acceptance of him, and he opened up his arms just before I crashed into him. "I had to come," he explained by way of an apology. "I couldn't stay in Undraland. Not after everything fell apart like it did."

"You're here," I breathed, releasing him to take a step back and get my fill of the surly face only I could make smile. "I missed your mean face."

He grimaced at my appearance and cupped my chin, jerking it toward the light. "What happened to you?"

Without waiting for me to answer, he barked at Jens, "What happened to her?"

Jamie trotted up next to me and shook Foss's hand. "I see you couldn't stay away." Both men were visibly freezing, but at least Jamie had a proper coat on. Foss was clad in pants and a t-shirt, his muscles tensed against the bite in the air.

Foss looked from Jamie's black eye to mine and nodded in understanding. "Who'd you get in a fight with, Jamie?"

"Who else?" Jamie motioned to Jens, who returned Foss's glare.

Jens shoved his hands into his pockets. "Don't give me crap about it, Foss. I already feel bad enough as it is."

Foss tsked Jens, enjoying his brief moment of not being the bad guy. "High and mighty Jens the Brave smacks his woman around like the lowly Fossegrimens. Welcome to the bottom of the barrel."

"Shut up," Jens spat through gritted teeth.

I held up my hands. "Excuse me, could we back up a second here? How did you find us? What are you doing here? And where's your coat?" I almost threw in a "young man", but thought that might be pushing it.

"I picked him up just outside the gate," cooed Stina, who leaned back casually against the SUV, watching the exchange with much curiosity.

I wished I could get a peek at her tail. I'd never seen a real Huldra tail before. Stina no doubt had it tucked away to fit in with regular earthlings.

"Bent on finding this one here." Stina pointed to me with disgust, and I tried not to bristle. "Nice shiner. Let me guess, you breathed wrong and Jens lost his temper? He always takes such good care of his women."

"Shove it, Stina. You were trying to mind-warp me with your whistle. You deserved that punch, and you know it. It's my job to protect her."

"I'm Lucy," I said, sticking my hand out to her. "We've sort of met before."

"I know. Jens's girl. Foss's wife. Prince Jamie's laplanded pal. Queen Lucy from the Other Side." She scoffed at my mismatched apparel. "If only they could see you now. Shall I ready my curtsy?"

"Nice to see you again," I lied. "Come inside, Foss. We've got a room you can warm up in."

"Let him freeze," Stina suggested, her light and airy tone was laced with cruelty. "One of the four chiefs, reduced to this." She motioned to his shivering form.

I scowled at her and rubbed Foss's arms, which were freezing to the touch. "He's frozen over! How long have you had him for? He could catch his death out here, dressed like this! You should've at least gotten him a proper coat."

Stina giggled at me, a high-pitched, nasal sound. "Well, I brought him here so you could warm him up. Skin-to-skin's the best for that, you know." She winked at me, and I fought to control my temper.

I blew on Foss's fingertips, which were so cold, he could barely move them. "Come on. Jens has a few extra sets of clothes I'm sure would fit you."

Foss came willingly, without the stubborn streak he used to be married to. Perhaps the cold had chased it out of him.

"That curse is nearly gone," she said to Jens. "Been peeling it off in layers. That halfy did a decent job. Who knew?"

Jens shook his head, communicating with his eyes for her to shut up. "We can talk about that later. Loos, take Foss up to the room. Jamie, you need to see this."

"What?" I asked, but I knew they would be tight-lipped about whatever was going on.

"Nothing, babe. Go on. I'll be up in a minute."

Stina called after me. "Have a great night on your honeymoon, Queen Lucy. I'll keep your boyfriend company while you warm up Foss. I know how you work. Your hubby told me everything."

I cringed, but Jens spoke before I could get lured into her fight. "Don't pay attention to her. She's just jealous. Knock it off, Stina. Seriously. Do you have any friends?"

"Not like Lucy has, no." Her cat-like tease was evil, and I wanted to retaliate with fiery words, but Jamie shooed me toward the hotel.

9

FOSS'S NEW PERSONALITY

I made quick work of finding Foss some clothes from Jens's pile. He was only half listening as I walked him through the shower, turning the spigot on so he could enjoy some heat. He was too tall for the shower. He was too tall for everything. I felt for the poor guy.

"How did you find us?" I questioned, not willing to leave him alone just yet.

Foss pointed a shivering finger upward. "The stars. I told you; I can always find you. Even in your strange sky, I could still see your star. Stina picked me up outside the gate, and I led her to you." He took off his shirt, and I was glad to see most of his wounds from fighting the Circhos were healed.

I rubbed some heat back into his arms, relishing the feel of Foss. "It's good to see your face, however surly."

"Speaking of faces, yours looks terrible. Maybe I should give your boyfriend a black eye to match yours. I owe him one, anyways."

I shook my head, but I couldn't stop smiling. "You found me. You came back."

"You're not mad?" he asked tentatively.

"Not mad. A little dazed, but not mad." He gazed at me as if there were many important things he wanted to say, but none birthed from his tired mouth. I patted his arm. "Wash up and warm up, soldier. We can talk when you come out."

When Foss finished washing and dressing twenty minutes later, he emerged in Jens's navy hoodie and flannel pajama pants. It was shocking the difference modern clothes made. He looked like a true human. A body builder, sure, but a human nonetheless. Though on closer inspection, he was a broken, besotted human who was a shell of his former Viking self.

I led Foss to sit on the bed and stood in front of him, the lamp giving just enough illumination for me to see the haunted look I wasn't used to finding in his black eyes. "Are you hungry?"

He looked up at me, lost and confused by the question. "Hungry? Um, maybe. Your world is... Do you have food here that's normal?"

I picked up the phone and ordered three burgers, fries, some fresh fruit and a cheese platter. "Food good enough to fill your belly will be ready in twenty. Now, talk to me. You were supposed to stay in Undraland. What happened?"

He shook his head. "I don't know how to talk to you about it."

My nose crinkled. "What are you saying? I'm the only one you talk to about stuff. You're like the Fort Knox of useful information, but I'm the only key. Be real. What's going on? Did Olaf find you?"

"No." He glanced uneasily around the room. Short carpet, big bed, two paintings of fruit on the wall – it was your average four-star hotel room. "What's that?"

"That's a telephone. It's how we communicate over long distances. What happened to you over there?"

He pointed to another object. "Why do you have a big box in your room? What does it do?"

"That's a television. Best save that one for later. I don't want to blow your mind. It's our own portable Land of Be. A perfect waste of time." My joke fell flat.

Foss stared up at me with lost eyes. "I don't like it here."

"I told you that you wouldn't." I closed the foot of space between us and hugged him, bringing his head to my chest. He relaxed in my arms as I scraped my fingernails over his scalp. "There, there. It's okay, puppy. It's not so bad on my side. Just overwhelming at first."

He wrapped his arms around my middle, holding me as if I was the one with the strength. "I'm glad I found you. The cars go so fast. Your star moves fast, too. You're here." He exhaled, and then pulled back, fingering the ring around my neck. "You're wearing my ring," he observed, looking up at me like I was the answer to all the questions he was too stubborn to ask.

"I told you I would."

Then Foss did something so unexpected, it took a solid seven seconds to process it. He leaned forward, gently pulled down the neckline of my thermal shirt and planted a kiss on my scar. His lips caressed the perfect crest of his tribe that was burned into my skin.

At first, it was a nice kind of confusing. When he dragged his lips from side to side across my chest, burying his face in my bosom, I pulled back, unable to conceal the fluster that colored my cheeks. Suddenly the room felt hot and cramped. "Um, that's really not kosher. I'm with Jens for good now. Just Jens. You know that."

"But I love you."

Alarms that had been gently dinging now clanged at full blast in my mind. "No, you don't. You hate me. On a good day, you mildly tolerate me. That's our thing."

His lost expression was too much. He was him, but not. "I do, Lucy. Lovely wife. I love you."

I kept my mouth shut and shouted into the link. *Get up here! One of you get your butt up here now. Foss is... not Foss. Something's wrong with him.*

Jamie's reply came a few seconds later, after Foss reached out and held my hand with his icy one. *What do you mean, Lucy? Foss is fine. Let him get some sleep.*

I'm telling you, he's different.

Lucy, calm down. I'll be up when I'm finished here.

I huffed as Foss put his freezing hands on my hips and pulled me forward again. He kissed my neck, and I was torn between slapping him and relishing the guilty shiver of indulgence that raked up my spine.

No. I was with Jens. Only Jens.

I decided on distance. "Foss, what happened when you crossed over? When did you start feeling all this?"

"I've always felt it. It was just buried. Stina helped me see."

"Stina," I stated, the name tasting dirty on my tongue. "That sounds about right. She's mighty helpful." I took his skull-smashing hands off my hips and held them. "Your hands are cold, and your pupils are the size of saucers. She messed with your brain, darling husband. Trust me, you don't love me. Not like that, at least."

As usual, Foss paid my words no mind. "Did you miss me? Do you regret sending me away?"

Words were dangerous now, so I stuck to nodding. The truth was that I had missed him. As much as I wanted to dismiss all dysfunctional parts of myself and leave them behind in Undraland, I did regret abandoning him. I regretted all sorts of things.

He squeezed my fingers, and then brought them to his mouth, dragging them across his parted lips in a way I tried not to feel. "I knew you did. We belong together." Then he did something so unexpected, my knees nearly buckled. Foss sucked my ring finger into his mouth, giving me a clear shot of his bedroom eyes.

My lashes fluttered, and my eyes rolled into the back of my head. Before I could stop myself, my mouth let loose a filthy curse word as my knees turned to jelly. "I... you... we can't do that," I murmured, my voice breathy.

His lips trailed to the inside of my wrist, sucking on the tender skin. "We've got a bed and a whole room to ourselves." He pulled me closer to him so he could bite my earlobe. "We can do anything you want." Then in a deadly low tone, he whispered. "What do you want, Lucy?"

"Not this!" I protested feebly, not pulling away from him with any real conviction.

"After everything, you're the only one I keep coming back to."

I finally managed to jerk myself away from the spell he

cast on me. "That's the thing about bad habits. I don't recommend you take up smoking." My shtick fell flat, and I gulped. *Jamie, get the smack up here! It's getting freaky.*

Jamie had the nerve to sound irritated with me. *Lucy, I'll be up in a few minutes. I just need to you watch Foss a little while longer. We're taking care of something.*

What could you possibly... I peeked through Jamie's eyes and caught a glimpse of something that startled me so bad, I cried out and threw myself backward into the wall.

In a burlap sack, Jamie was holding the head of the emo boy they had taken away. It was my sort of cousin, with the black and silver eyes that were so haunting, I had a hard time forgetting them.

Staring up at me was the face I did not expect to see again. Though he was a stranger, it triggered something in me so strong, my stomach lurched and I started sweating. I yanked myself out of Jamie's brain. "Ah! What's Jamie doing with that guy's head? Why's he carrying it around? What the crap, Foss! Did you bring that over here?"

Foss leapt to his feet, and I flinched when he cleared the distance between us. I let out a noise of alarm when his hands came up near my face.

"Don't!" I shouted, terrified of his mood swings.

"I won't hurt you," he promised. He retracted, but stayed too close. "You weren't supposed to see that. Jens is taking care of it."

"Taking care of what? It's a friggin' head!"

Foss palmed the back of his neck uncomfortably, searching for the right words. "The boy's bones were... important. I couldn't leave them lying around, so I took the head for us to destroy. I crossed over as soon as his body disappeared."

"Disappeared?" My throat was dry, and I felt claustrophobic with him so close. I could feel his breath on my face, and my back was pinned to the wall.

"I stole the head, but only just escaped. Pesta can't have his bones, Lucy. You have to trust me. It's important we destroy the boy's head."

"That's Charles Mace, right?"

Foss paused a few beats before answering, his careful study of my face causing him to speak slowly. "Yes. Do you know him?"

"No! Of course I don't! I was in the cell with him one minute, and then they were dragging him out to… to…" The air felt impossibly thick, like I was sucking it in through a straw. My chest heaved, so I pressed my hand flat to my sternum to keep it from jumping. "Why is your world so graphic? I don't want to see a severed head!" I started hyperventilating against the wall. "Do you know what other girls my age are doing? Shopping! Going to school! Working at a Starbucks! Come on! Why can't I just have a piece of normal for one second? You brought us a severed head?"

In a move that always managed to deepen our relationship, Foss brought me into his arms and held me, stroking my back and playing with my hair. "We sent you up here so you wouldn't have to see it."

"No! All that stuff was supposed to be left behind in Undraland! None of that was supposed to follow me here. I don't want severed heads and Pesta's minions trying to find me. I don't want any of it! I just want a normal life and a white picket fence! I want my fence, dammit!"

His chest was firm, and in that moment, comforting. "I'll get you your fence. Be patient. You only just got back." He kissed the top of my head, reminding me of our predicament.

I shirked away from him, fighting with my fit to regain some composure. "You're right. I just hate that stupid siren. Sorry." I took a deep breath and tried to push the horrid image out of my mind. "I'm cool now."

"You look tired."

I pushed my hair behind my ear. "That's the thing about the middle of the night. You're not exhausted?"

"I am." He reached out for my hand and pulled me toward the bed. "Lie down with me."

I shirked away from him. "I don't think that's the best idea."

"We've slept together dozens of times."

"Sure, but not like this. Not when you actually liked me."

He cupped my chin. "Love you. Boys like. Men love."

I gently extracted my face from his grip before I swooned too noticeably. "Oh. Um, well, I suddenly have buckets of energy. You go ahead and lay down."

The room service arrived, and I could not have been more grateful for a burger in that moment. I made Foss sit at the desk and eat while I sat in the far corner on the floor. When he tried to get up and eat closer to me, I chastised him, sending him back to his side of the room. "Not till you know what you're doing," I said with a mouthful of hamburger.

Foss mustered a sly grin at me. "Oh, I know exactly what I'm doing. I can show you when you're ready," he said, jerking his chin toward the bed.

I crossed my arms over my knees and rested my head atop them to hide my blush from my enemy. My almost friend. My husband.

10

CRAZY TOWN

*A*fter another hour of "you're more beautiful than I remembered" and a rendition of an actual song he'd written about my "golden eyelashes", I finally convinced him to turn in. It might've been humorous if it was happening to someone else, but I just found it unsettling. That Stina could change his personality with a whistle worried me. I didn't want Jens near her, or Jamie for that matter.

"Jens blacked your eye," Foss pointed out with a giant yawn as he lay down on the king-sized bed.

"I don't think you're one to talk. You gave me a concussion. Jens did this by accident. He didn't actually touch me." I tucked the covers up around him as he'd done for me when Jamie had accidentally gotten me drunk. He took up most of the bed. Sharing the space with Jens was okay, but I could not imagine trying to fit in beside Foss.

"The concussion was by accident, too." He reached around behind my leg and grasped the back of my thigh, running his thumb up and down a sensitive spot I didn't know existed.

I shivered, and Foss smirked at the effect he had on my body.

Jamie chimed in with his two cents. *Lucy? What's going on up there? I felt that. It was... pretty strong through the bond.*

"Knock it off," I insisted, worming out of Foss's grip. "That was a cheap move. It would work on any girl." Then to Jamie, I yelled, *Get the smack up here!*

"It sure worked on you," Foss said, brushing his fingertips with mine. The way he looked at me made my heart clench in my chest. It was filled with adoration and something that actually looked like the love he was proclaiming. It was heady and addictive.

And cruel. I didn't know Stina, but I really didn't like her in that moment. To give me a Foss that wasn't real smack in the middle of when Jens and I were getting back together cut me to the bone. There was a part of me that wanted...

You know I'm not finishing that sentence.

I called out to Jamie instead. *Get. Up. Here. Now! I don't know how else to say it. Foss is cracked. Send Jens up here and the Huldra he rode in on. Get away from Stina, Jamie. She did this to him.*

The pause before his response left a clear implication I did not appreciate. *Are you certain* she *did this to him?*

I let go of Foss's hand, which I did not remember reaching out for. He rolled onto his side, settling into the mattress that was nothing like anything he'd ever slept on before. "Goodnight, Foss."

"Kiss me, Lucy. I've missed the taste of you."

I bent down and kissed his forehead just to keep him from whining. "Now shut up and go to sleep," I whispered as politely as I could.

When Jens finally came back upstairs, Foss was asleep on the bed and I was clear across the room, sleeping on the high-traffic gray carpet with my knees pulled up to my chest.

"Baby, you don't have to sleep on the floor." Jens's tone was sweet, but I could tell he was upset about the skull burning they'd had to do.

"I'm glad you're back. You get to sleep with Foss. I'll take the floor."

"You're so chivalrous." Jens slumped next to me on the ground and kissed my cheek. He smelled like bonfire, but I sensed it was the bone-burning kind, and not the s'mores kind. "You look mighty cute in that top."

"That's a popular opinion today." I stretched, resting my head on Jens's lap. "I told Jamie to bring up that Huldra. She messed with Foss. She's got to undo it."

Jens rubbed his hand over his face. "What's the problem? Foss being his usual charming self?"

"Foss thinks he's in love with me. It's your girlfriend, Stina. She whistled him into Crazy Town."

Jens gave me a fleeting smile as he combed his dirty fingers through my hair. "That's not Stina. Foss is in love with you, babe."

"Don't piss me off. If he was awake, you'd see. His hands are freezing, and his pupils are ginormous. She messed him up right good."

"She told me she gave him a whistle to calm him down on the ride over. First time in a car and all."

I was a little miffed he didn't believe me. "I'm telling you, you're wrong. But whatever. Believe her and not me, fine. Just don't leave me alone with him. I'd like some form of groveling when it turns out you're dead wrong."

"I'll ready the kneepads for a proper debasement." He leaned his head back on the wall, indulging in the silence for a few beats. "Could we fight about your biggest fan tomorrow? I'm beat. I need you to do that sexy thing you do and kiss me before I pass out."

"Where are we sleeping?"

"I got us a king-sized for a reason, Moxie. Foss is big, but we can scoot him over."

"I'm telling you, he tried to kiss me earlier."

Jens grumbled under his breath about it not being the first time. "I can't leave you alone, and I can't leave him alone. He's new in the world, and I don't want him electrocuting himself or something. We're stuck in this room together."

"Fine. You can cozy up to your bestie in bed. I'm fine on the floor. I got enough problems."

Jens kissed me and hopped in the shower. I passed out shortly after the valet dropped off the cot for me to sleep on. I shifted uncomfortably on the thin, springy mattress. The dynamic was strange in the room with the three of us, but I made do and gave in to my drooping eyelids.

11

FLIGHT, NOT FIGHT

*T*he next morning, I was roused from my dream by Jens's hand tracing the slope of my cheek as I lay on my side. I kept my eyes shut and delighted in his cold finger dragging down the length of my neck, the luxurious feeling of leisure finally introducing itself into our world of peril. "That feels nice." When he shifted my shirt to touch my shoulder, I could feel how much he loved me, how deeply he savored every inch of my skin. "I've missed you so much. You're always so busy keeping us safe. I started to wonder if you still wanted to be with me."

His warm lips stroked my bare shoulder and a shiver ricocheted through my body. I reached for his head to bury my fingers in his thick mane, but landed on short hair instead.

My eyes flew open and I gasped to find not Jens, but Foss making out with my naked shoulder. The heat in my veins turned to ice. I recoiled and sat up, shifting my shirt back into place. "What are you doing?" I whispered, furious. My cheeks burned, embarrassed at how much I was savoring the moment – the wrong moment.

Foss smiled in that dilated pupil adoring gaze that was not his. "I was watching you sleep."

I tried to keep my voice pleasant. "Jens? Hun, we've got a bit of a situation here."

Jens was gone. The bed was empty, and my heart sank. He was always gone when I awoke, but this time felt like a new blow to our relationship.

"He went out with Stina." Foss pointed to the spot next to the bed where Jens kept his stuff. "Took his red pack and snuck out not too long ago."

"With Stina?" I sat up and tried to shake the confusing encounter off me as gracefully as possible. "Alright. Why don't you go back to sleep? It's only six in the morning. Not a decent time to wake up."

"I can sleep anytime. It's not often I get to watch you sleep, though. I never thought I'd see that again."

I checked in with the bond, but Jamie was dreaming some surreal montage of a chicken trying to peck his eyes out while yelling at him in his dad's voice. I kicked the chicken for good measure and left the dream so he could have a better night's sleep.

Foss was gazing at me in that unsettling way that made me wish for a mile of space between us, but yet some small part of me wanted to get closer. I hated that part of me, so I shoved it down.

"You love me," Foss declared, sensing what he wanted and ignoring the rest.

I sat up and leaned away from him on my thin cot with my back against the wall. I pulled the blanket up and used it as one more thing to keep us separate. "I guess I do. I love Britta, Jamie, Jens, Nik, Tor, Alrik – the whole mess of you. But I'm with Jens. You shouldn't watch me sleep. You shouldn't kiss my shoulder like that. I'm not your real wife, and you don't really love me. Stina just made you think you do." I touched his chilly fingers, and he laced his through mine so he could place delicate kisses on my knuckles. "Cold hands. You'll regret this when it wears off."

Foss took that to mean the cold made me uncomfortable, so he blew warm air onto my fingertips. He looked up at me through his lashes like a boy that wanted to be scolded and also a man who wanted to romance his woman. "I think you want me."

"I think you're nine buckets of crazy. And you don't want to do that," I protested. The tension in the room was building the longer he blew on my fingers. When he lifted my ring finger and sucked it into his mouth as he had the night before, my jaw dropped open and my heart nearly exploded out of my chest. "Foss, n-no!" I said, but my protest was weakened by my obvious desire I could not control.

He saw me waver. He sucked harder, making my eyes roll back and my bones feel like jelly. "You want this just as much as I do," he said, taking a break from turning me into a pile of goo to tease me.

I yanked my hand away and rolled off the cot, grabbing my overnight bag and locking myself in the bathroom. "I said no!" I shouted, but my voice quivered with uncertainty. "I'm with Jens!" Who wasn't here. Who was never here anymore. Who I'd begged not to leave me alone with... my husband.

Foss leaned on the bathroom door, just two inches of oak between our pounding hearts. "Lucy, come out. We can just talk, if that's what you want."

"You just had my finger in your mouth!"

"And you let me."

My cheeks burned. "When's Jens coming back?"

"He used to fool around with Stina. You know that, don't you? He's out with her now, and he'll be back when he's good and finished with her."

Tears pricked my eyes, but I tried to keep the dread at bay. "Okay. I'll be in the shower until then. Let me know when you're ready to calm down."

"Let me in, Lucy."

"Go back to sleep, Foss. Out of curiosity, how long do Huldra whistles typically last?"

"A few days, give or take. It depends on how powerful the Huldra is, and how susceptible the subject is to him."

"You mean her. There's no such thing as male Huldras," I corrected him, recalling Alrik's fairy tales with crystal accuracy.

There was a pause before Foss answered. "Right. I meant her, not him."

When Foss started messing with the bathroom door's handle, I turned stern. "Knock it off, Grimen. I mean it. You bust in here, it won't turn out well for you. Go back to sleep. I'll be out when I'm done."

I turned on the shower to stave off his protests, undressed and hopped inside, drowning out whines I never dreamed I'd hear from Foss. It might have been flattering if it wasn't all forced and fake.

It was the longest shower of my life, but I figured my

lack of showers in the past… however long I was missing from my world, made up for the excessive water use a little. My skin was pink from the heat. I'd scrubbed myself from head to toe four times when I heard a fist pounding on the door.

I tried to sound pleasant. "Not now, Foss. I told you, we can talk when I'm done."

The pounding stopped, so I relaxed. I decided to face the music and finally shut off the water. When I stepped out, I heard Jens's voice. I shoved a clean set of clothing on, but by the time I'd run the brush through my hair, the two had devolved into yelling. I ran out in my jeans and black fitted t-shirt to referee.

What I saw made me shriek and shut my eyes, retracting backwards. "Put some clothes on, Foss!"

"This? This is what you're up to while I'm out patrolling the area to keep *you* safe?" Jens motioned to a very specific area on Foss's anatomy. "This is the thanks I get? Nice to know I can't leave you alone with him for a second before you're off doing whatever you want." He threw up his hands before I could get a word in. "But it's all my fault, right? I cheated in Bedra – accidentally, mind you. But I cheated, and now you can just do whatever you want with whoever you want until we're even." He crossed his arms over his chest. "Well? Go ahead! He's right here, Loos. Get even. I had sex with at least two of the Mares while I was high. Foss is a good start to level the playing field. Go on. I'll sit here and watch while you rip my heart out!"

I was shocked, and equally torn between shouting back and bursting into tears. Though the situation looked damning, it was clear there would be no room for explanations or benefit of the doubt.

Instead of choosing either, I opted for flight. I waited for Foss to garner Jens's attention again and stole my moment. With my bag hoisted over my shoulder, I kifed the keys from the nightstand Jens had thrown them on in his rage at being greeted by a very nude Foss and me in the shower. I really couldn't blame the guy too much, I guess.

But I also didn't have to stay.

I checked in on the bond, seeing that Jamie was still asleep. As loudly as I could, I screamed *Wake up!* in his brain. This gave him five seconds to rouse enough to hear my light knock on his door.

He ambled to greet me, clothes rumpled and curly hair askew. "Morning, Lucy. What can I do for you?"

I scrambled for a lie. "Breakfast. There's a big breakfast once a month on the other end of town. It's the only meal we'll get all day, and if we want to eat at all today, we have to run now. Can you two shove everything into a bag and be ready in like, a minute?"

"Only meal? That's strange. What about all the food stores?"

"Closed. One day a month. Weird, right? I know. I don't get it either. Humans with their strange customs." I forced a smile up at him. "Let's go." Stepping in, I called through the room. "Britt? We gotta jet if we want food at all today." I started rudely shoving everything into their bags, knowing Jens would only be distracted by Foss for so long before he came after me.

Britta was in her just awake haze and moved through the room like a zombie while I whipped through like a tornado. I had them all packed by the time Britta and Jamie had fresh clothes on. "Let's go, campers!" I sang cheerily. "Jens is taking Foss and Stina, and they're meeting us there. Out we go." I kept my mental wall in place to ensure Jamie didn't see my endgame.

Jamie's brow wrinkled. "Jens is okay with us taking you?"

I waved the car keys in front of his face. "He gave me the keys, didn't he? Of course he's okay. It's not far. Plus, I have the two of you to watch me tool around in my little old world. Nowhere safer." I linked my arms through each of theirs and led them forward, my heart pounding. We made it into the elevator, and I began to exhale, but I wasn't truly free until I jammed the key into the car's ignition and peeled out of the parking lot.

12

STEALING MOMENTS AND CARS

$\mathcal{I}$ drove for half an hour before the telltale "how long do you think the drive will be" started. Another hour passed before Jamie started poking around in my brain for answers. I blocked him by blasting a fantastic eighties hair band song on the only decent radio station I could find, singing to it at the top of my lungs. That bought me another ten minutes before Jamie figured out how to turn off the music so he could talk to me.

"We're not going to get breakfast, are we?" he asked, his voice annoyingly calm and big-brotherly.

"Sure we are. It's just a little farther than you're used to. We'll eat."

"Pull over," Jamie commanded in his kind, but firm voice. "Lucy, what happened back there? Where's Jens?"

Britta had her head bowed and her face in her hands, and for a second, I felt guilty for taking her away from her brother.

"Jens is fine. He's fighting with Foss, and he's happy to

70

do so. I don't need a guard who yells at me for taking a shower. In fact, now that I'm in my world, I don't need a guard at all. Wanted a boyfriend, but he's not into it anymore." Even the vague sum-up was painful to say, but I kept my chin up to prove how little I cared.

"But what actually happened, Lucy?" Britta asked, her tone mournful. "What did Jens do this time?"

I couldn't tell who she was more exasperated with, me or her brother. "He didn't believe me that Foss was bewitched by that Stina girl to fall in love with me. None of you did. He left in the middle of the night, like he's done every time we could have slept next to each other. Foss told me Jens went out with Stina last night."

Britta hissed, and I echoed the sentiment.

"Call me superstitious, but if he's hanging around his ex in the middle of the night, I'm thinking they're not having platonic chats about the weather."

"That's why you split us up?" Jamie questioned.

"No, Negative Nancy. I was going to let that go, just like I've let everything go. I'm the queen of shutting up about things that should be discussed." I took a breath and accelerated to five miles over the speed limit, not wanting to get pulled over, but also not wanting Jens to find us. "Jens thinks I was getting it on with Foss."

There was a short pause, and then Jamie said in a quiet voice. "Well, were you?"

"Jamie!" Britta scolded, her braids swishing from side to side.

I almost punched him, but I knew that would only hurt me. "No! Of course not, you jerk!"

"Okay! I'm sorry."

71

"You know what? You should be." I gripped the steering wheel, ignoring the scenery of evergreens and bushes that whipped by us on the side of the four-lane highway. "Jens left, and Foss woke me up by kissing my shoulder and telling me he's in love with me. I finally shook him off me and darted into the bathroom. When Jens came back from his fun time with Short Skirt Stina, I guess Foss was waiting for me... naked." I flinched. "I had nothing to do with that, and no knowledge of it. Jens flew off the handle, accused me of every stupid thing you can guess, so I bolted." I didn't realize I'd been grinding my teeth, so I flexed my jaw. "I want a white picket fence, not Jerry Springer." My voice hitched on the last bit, so I cleared my throat to cover over the indiscretion.

Jamie sighed. "He's out every night searching the area for Weres."

I scoffed. "Yeah. That story's a little more believable without the memory of the Mares riding him in Bedra. Jens sneaks off and does what he wants. Now he's free to do just that." I glanced in the mirror at Britta. "I shouldn't have taken you away from your brother, though. As soon as we can find someone to un-lapland us, you guys can go wherever you want. It's a big world. Time we all had some space in it."

"Pull over," Jamie ordered, his tone stern now. "You wished you'd stayed in one place growing up? No one's forcing you to run now, but here you are. You lied to us to get yourself out of there." He held up his hand to quiet my protest. "I know Jens has his problems, and I'm not defending him. But you can't take Britta and I away from him just because you decide you're finished. We're all in this together."

A red glimmer overhead caught my eye. It was the small tracking light on the roof of the car blinking down at me. My heart sank. "How long has that been on?" I questioned, my tone sharp.

"I don't know. We don't know how cars work, Lucy. Pull over."

I obeyed, but not for the reasons he wanted. "He found us. He's tracking our car. We've got to switch."

"Switch what?"

"Cars! We need a different car! When I find a new one, I need you two to help me put our stuff into the new one. Can you help with that?"

When the response did not come, my grasp on the situation began to crumble. I pulled off the exit into a giant mall's parking lot, where I pretty much had my pick of vehicles. I motored past one that had two hours of quarters in the meter and just enough trunk space for our stash. I pulled in next to the rusted green station wagon and set to work.

It had been awhile since I'd broken into a car, but it turns out it's like riding a bike. Once I was in, I pulled back the panel and tried to remember the song Linus taught me about which wire needed to be disconnected and which one connected to make the spark necessary to start the car. He'd set the instructions to the tune of Safety Dance so I wouldn't forget.

When I successfully started the station wagon, the rush of adrenaline was curbed only by the sight of the two passengers still sitting in the first vehicle, unwilling to move. "Come on, guys!"

Jamie waved me back to the car and addressed me in a voice reserved for conversing with children or crazy people. "Sweetheart, Jens isn't running around on you, but you're right. He isn't patrolling the perimeter, either."

"I don't care what he does with his life anymore. It's his. He and Foss and Stina can have each other for all I care." It was a lie. A bad one, but Jamie was kind enough not to call me on it.

"Come inside, Lucy. There's something we need to talk to you about."

13

THE CIRCUS

"*B*ut we're done with Pesta!" I argued inside the SUV. I'd fixed the wiring on the station wagon per Jamie's request, but I knew I could redo the damage in a heartbeat, should I need the escape. "Sure, we're running from her, but it's a big world. She'll never find us."

Britta could not look at me, for she'd been in on the lie. "That's the thing. She'll never stop looking for you. And let's say you do escape her for years, even. Let's say you and Jens make up, get married and have children together. Those children will also be targets. Pesta needs your family's bones. Just because she hasn't found them yet doesn't mean she'll stop. She took Mace's bones because we were too distracted to put it together that he's your family, and his bones are just as valuable."

My brain tripped over too much information. "Wait, what? Charles Mace? The guy from my cell with the head? We're not blood related."

Britta pushed the answer at me quickly, like reciting the response from memory. "But Alrik adopted his ward, right? That means Alrik's blood is in Charles now. And since Alrik put his *arv* on you, that put Alrik's blood in you, too. Not a traditional relation, but enough for Pesta to make use of both your bones and his. She needs yours, so Jens can't slow down. He can't just run, either. He's a fighter. You know that, Lucy. He wants you safe for good, not safe for now."

Jamie looked out the window, sizing up the gargantuan shopping mall in front of us. "He's out every night trying to find the portal she's assembling. Why do you think he's been so specific about where we travel? Would it really matter if we were just running haphazardly?"

The new information churned in my mind. "That's a good plan, but I don't want things to be like this. We don't get to be together hardly at all, and he doesn't listen to me anymore."

"He's exhausted, Lucy!" Jamie pointed over his shoulder at Britta. "She's been helping him, and that's why she's so tired all the time. I can't hold that against her."

"Does she leave you in a room with Foss, and then accuse you of sleeping with him?"

Jamie's expression soured. "Of course not. Jens is an idiot. We all know that. But he's a well-meaning fool. You have to be patient with him, especially when he's so sleep-deprived."

"And Stina?"

Jamie shifted in his chair, so Britta answered for him. "Make no mistake, you're right about Stina. She's one in a long line of women who want to be with my brother." She tugged on her brown braid. "But he's only ever wanted to be with you."

I shook my head. "But he's not with me. He doesn't know how to be with me unless our time together is coated in danger. That's not a relationship. It's an action movie, and I didn't sign up for Vin Diesel."

Jamie reached out and placed his hand atop mine. "You're overreacting."

I glared at him. "Really? Really? Should I have stuck around after everyone ignored me and just left me with a bewitched Foss? Should I have just up and let him kiss me? If Jens hadn't come back, I would've finished getting dressed and come out to a naked Foss. Is that a mental image you want to savor?" I conjured up the memory of Foss I'd been subjected to that morning and thrust it forcefully into Jamie's mind. I relished his blanch and shudder.

"That was unnecessary," he scolded me. Jamie whipped his head from left to right like a dog trying to rid himself of fleas. "Yes, we should've taken you more seriously, but you're still overreacting on Jens. He loves you, and he's doing the best he can on the little he's got to work with." Then Jamie had the nerve to scold me. "Be gracious, sweetheart."

I bristled and retracted from him. "It's a good thing we're laplanded, or I'd be running from you, too!"

He shook his head at me, lowering his voice as a few pedestrians happened by the car. "You'll never get your white picket fence if you run from everyone who challenges you."

I said nothing to this, lest he know he'd won a point

there. "Fine. I'll take us back. But I'm putting you in charge of keeping Foss away from me until the magic wears off."

"I'll do my utmost."

I started up the car with a scowl. "I'm serious, Jamie. He was watching me sleep this morning. I woke up, and he was inches from my face. He wrote me a love song last night!"

Jamie managed to keep his laugh to a few notes before he swallowed the rest of it. "I should like to have seen that. You know, Foss does care for you."

"I don't want to hear it," I snapped. Then I nearly jumped out of my skin when something loud and hard banged on my door.

"Lucinda Stella Kincaid!" Jens shouted, banging his fist on the window, rattling the glass.

I turned and recoiled from the door, glaring at him. "What?" I called, pretending I couldn't hear him at all.

"Don't you ever do that again! You almost made it out of the state without me!"

"Huh?" I cupped my ear and mimed that I couldn't understand him.

"Don't you play with me. Get out of this car!" He banged again, so I locked him out with a click of a button. His eyebrows raised and nostrils flared as he tried the handle (which he should've done in the first place instead of hitting the car like a gorilla).

"I'll talk to him," Britta offered. She got out and walked around, placing her hand on her brother's shoulder as he fumed. She led him away from the car, beauty that she was, jamming sense into him wherever possible.

"She'll calm him down," Jamie assured me.

I yelped when I turned to talk to Jamie, and caught a glimpse of Foss sliding into Britta's vacant seat. "You were right to leave Jens. He doesn't understand what we have."

I cast Jamie a look of warning before answering. "Hey, buddy. Whatcha doing here?"

"I came to get you and take you home. A home for just the two of us. We've lived in a group long enough. It's time we started our married life together."

His normally harsh voice was gone, and in its place was a poet. A true softy had replaced Foss, and it was so unsettling that Jamie could only gawk, mouth agape.

Thanks for all that help, big brother. I said to Jamie bitterly.

I, um. I'm sorry for not taking you seriously. Then I heard him laughing in his head and letting slip a verbal chuckle.

Foss reached up and stroked my arm, cupping my elbow with gentle fingers. "You shouldn't have run away from me, though. I'm ready to be with you now. Stina helped me see how good we are together. I think I made it clear in the hotel back there that you can have me anytime you want."

Jamie choked on his laughter, his face turning red. "Ho! Okay, friend. Let's you and I go for a walk." Jamie finally decided to be helpful, so I shot him a look of gratitude.

"I won't leave her," Foss vowed.

"Oh, I know. I just want to properly congratulate you on your marriage. Lucy is like a sister to me. I want to hear all the things you have planned for your life together. I want to help however I can. You two are such a sweet pair."

Foss beamed at finally being taken seriously. He accompanied Jamie outside in the biting cold, but not before kissing my hand and my cheek, assuring me he'd only be a moment.

Stina tapped on the glass with a wicked grin. "Hello, Tribeswoman. Are you enjoying having the best of both worlds?"

I unlocked my door and slammed it into her, knocking the cocky grin off her face. She banged into the car next to us as I hopped out, ready for a fight. "What's your damage, Heather?" I shouted. "What's your glitch? If you've got a problem with me, deal with me. Leave Foss alone. He's been through enough, and he's going to remember this whole thing. He doesn't need you messing with his head and forcing him to feel things he doesn't. No one asked you to tag along."

Stina righted herself, but I'd had enough. I'd long forsaken the peaceful teachings of Martin Luther King, so I felt only marginal guilt when I shoved her hard against the car, her tiny skirt shifting in the scuffle.

I'd never seen Stina's cow's tail before, but at the jostle, the foot-long oddity slipped out from the tuck job she'd done under her skirt.

It was the fight she'd been looking for from me. "Oh, honey. You shouldn't have done that. Your adoring fans aren't here to save you this time."

Since the day we'd met, she hated me. Shoving turned into slapping and body-checking, but I got tired of that quickly. My conscience tugged when I threw the first punch, and before I knew it, we were a brawling mess of Jerry Springer theatrics in the parking lot. I was grateful Foss made me learn how to deliver a decent blow. My rage made up for her know-how, so we were pretty evenly matched.

"Break it up, you two!" Jens shouted, running over to us with wide eyes.

"She did this! She messed with Foss's head!"

Foss's arms were suddenly around me, yanking me back.

Jens was on Stina, launching her away from me, shocked at the intensity of our hatred for each other.

Her words came back at me with vengeance. "I didn't bring out anything that wasn't already there! You can't have one of the four chiefs, plus Jens following you around like a dog. Now Jens can see you for what you really are!"

"You're insane!" I shouted. "I've never done a thing to you to deserve this! And what's Foss done?"

"He's a Grimen. That's reason enough for me." Stina's lips pursed, and I called out a warning. Jens was on it. He cuffed his hand over Stina's mouth and knocked her to the ground, his knee pressing on her spine to keep her there. "Get in the car. Everyone. Jamie, load up everything that's ours from Stina's car into yours."

Jamie and Britta obeyed, but I seethed in Foss's arms as I yelled at my boyfriend. "I told you what she was up to, and you didn't listen to me! Then you accuse me of sleeping with Foss? I'm not going anywhere with you!"

Jens struggled to keep Stina still, her sexy clothing not the best wear for being pinned to the icy ground. "I got it. You were right. Just get in the car. You can drive."

"Thanks for your permission," I jeered. "I'm the one with the keys, you jag!" I stepped on Stina's bejeweled hand as I got into the car, ignoring her rage-filled howl. I started up the ignition and turned on the radio to drown out the sounds of everyone else. I watched Jens look over his shoulder for witnesses, and then stuff Stina into the trunk of her own car, but the sight gave me little satisfaction.

He climbed into the backseat between his sister and Foss and pulled out his phone. He called a guy named Tucker, gave him our location and asked if he could let Stina out of her trunk in an hour. Very chivalrous.

The classic rock song ended, and the gravel-voiced DJ came on. "Hey, next up we have the newest from Static Neverland. That should warm you up on this chilly November morning. Here's hoping we stay above freezing a few days longer."

My mouth dropped open at the DJ's mention of the month I had not expected to come so soon, and I froze before I could put the car into gear. The next song started, but I didn't really hear it. Everything was noise. Even Jens yelling at me was just a blur of sound.

I suddenly forgot how to drive. My heart was so heavy, I felt like napping to ease the burden of it. "Somebody else drive," I insisted, climbing past the console and switching places with a befuddled Jens so I could sit in back. Let Jamie ride shotgun next to his foul mood. Fine by me.

"Well, it's no fun to yell at you if you're not going to yell back," Jens conceded, buckling himself into the driver's seat.

I squeezed myself between Foss and Britta, staring down at my hands to see if they looked any different. September 3rd had come and gone without a thought. Though it had been true for weeks, in that moment, I felt it.

"What, Loos? Did Stina get one in on you?"

I shook my head. "Let's just go. Sorry for running. You found me. You win."

Jens scoffed and pulled out of the parking spot. "No one won this." He sighed, exhaling his crazy and breathing in fresh perspective. "I should've listened to you about Foss. I thought you were exaggerating. Then when I walked in and he was sprawled out on the bed waiting for you, I should've let you explain instead of jumping down your throat."

Jens gripped the steering wheel as he navigated through the winding lot. I knew he hated having these kinds of talks in front of the group as much as I did, but was muscling through the chagrin for the sake of peace among the ranks.

Since I said nothing, Jens felt the need to fill the silence. "Regardless of how much of a jerk I'm being, you can't run like that. It's dangerous and doesn't actually solve anything. I can't believe you'd just ditch me like that for losing my temper in a pretty confusing situation. Not cool, Loos. I deserve better than that from you, and you deserved better than what you got from me." He cleared his throat, not loving having a private conversation so out in the open. "So let's be better to each other. Can we just truce it out?"

I nodded, sullen as he drove us around the vast parking lot, trying to locate an exit in the maze. "Yup. Sorry for my part of it. Next time you find a naked man in my room, I'll make sure we're having lots of sex, so when you explode at me, it'll be legit."

"That's my girl." He glanced in the rearview mirror and saw Foss's arm around me. "And lover boy should be back to his charming self by tonight or tomorrow. Stina's not all that powerful."

"Mm-hm." I wasn't really listening anymore. All I could think about was that I'd completely missed September 3rd on the calendar, and that was a crime I couldn't forgive myself for. I thought I would be different, look different when I pictured myself at the age I now was, and I guess that had happened, just not how I expected it to. I had shorter hair, a black eye and was down too many pounds to look healthy. I guess I *was* older, much older than I expected to be.

"What's wrong?" Jens pried, waiting his turn at the stop sign.

"Nothing important." My stomach was empty, but I didn't care. I felt empty all over. It really was nothing important, and I felt childish for being so sad about it.

Foss whispered in my ear, "When can we have some time just us?" I ignored him until he sucked my earlobe into his mouth, sending jolts of unwelcome heat through my weary body.

I gently pushed him away and wiped my ear off, ashamed at how readily my body responded to his seductions. "Tomorrow night, alright? Can you wait until then?"

Foss beamed a truly triumphant grin, and I felt a little guilty at putting off our encounter until after his joy juice ran out. "I can wait." He brought my head to his chest, and despite Jens's eyes on me in the rearview mirror, I sank into the comfort. Foss's thick arm wrapped around me like a warm blanket I'd gone too much of my life without. I felt like crying, but was too sad to commit to the effort, and didn't want to deal with the questions. So I let Foss be my comfort, as he had so many times before back in Undra-land. I'd missed him, but most of all, I missed myself.

Jamie did his best to distract Jens with conversation, but after a few noncommittal grunts, the prince gave up and pried into my brain. "What's September 3rd?"

Jens swerved for a second as he added up the months in his head. "Oh, shite! Just shite. A steaming pile of it." He glanced at me in the mirror. "I'm sorry, Loos. I'll turn around. Let me buy you something at the mall."

"It's fine. Just drive, Jens," I said tonelessly.

When Linus and I were small, we begged like gypsies for our parents to take us to the circus for our birthday. What kid wouldn't? The next year was the same until we had four straight years of birthdays celebrated at the circus. Sometimes Mom and Dad even drove us across the state just to make sure we could find one to go to relatively near our birthday.

When I turned eight, I asked Mom and Dad if we could have a real birthday party. They were hesitant, but if Linus and I were good at anything, it was wearing down the parentals. They finally agreed, and we were all set with invitations and everything.

Now that I understood Pesta and the whole mess, I knew it wasn't their fault we had to move two days before the party, but when you're a kid, the only people to blame are yourself and your parents, and I knew that one wasn't on me.

We had circus birthdays until our sixteenth.

For my sweet sixteen, I again wanted a real birthday party. Linus had given up on the idea of birthdays being a big deal, but I had not. I was determined to redeem the day and make it an event. I bought streamers and balloons and even got a cake with clowns on it so we didn't miss out on the whole circus experience, in case any of us actually enjoyed it still.

That's the thing about always being the new kid. No one comes to your birthday party.

I spent my sweet sixteen crying in my brother's arms. I was embarrassed and ashamed that my parents now knew I didn't have any actual friends.

I had Linus, who died three years later.

My twentieth birthday was a bleak affair. I'd sprinkled the ashes not two months prior and still couldn't bring myself to speak. Linus had programmed my phone to play a special song about farts sung to the tune of Happy Birthday that woke me to commemorate the first day I was no longer a teenager.

So I did what we would have done. I took myself to the circus.

Suffice to say, I was the only twenty-year-old woman sitting by herself at the circus that day, and probably every day before or since. I studied the clowns, desperately trying to find the best fake smile so I could practice it at home in the mirror. I cried silently through the entire show, and when it was over, an old lady who sold cotton candy took pity on me and gave me a hug. Sweet gal.

It was probably best I'd forgotten my birthday this year.

Jens was frantic. "Pick anything. Any store you want. Name the present, it's yours."

I don't think I could've felt worse as we chugged along on the freeway, but listening to my boyfriend try to pull a belated gift out of his hat definitely pushed me down further into the muck. I cleared my throat and feigned indifference. "No, thanks. It's fine. I told you it wasn't anything important. And Jamie? If I say it's nothing important, you don't need to go picking around in my brain to fish it out. Total violation."

"I'm sorry," Jamie said, though I didn't believe him.

Foss stroked my arm, and I wanted to punch him for being sweet to me when I was on the edge of bursting into tears. "What's the significance? What'd I miss?"

"There's no significance," I answered succinctly.

Jens was visibly sweating as he turned off the freeway toward a cluster of generic stores. "It was her birthday. It's a human thing. Every year, they celebrate the day they were born. They have parties, cake, gifts. It's a lot like our coming of age parties, only theirs happen on a smaller scale every year."

"That's kind of sweet," Britta remarked. "I should like to celebrate the people I love every year, not just once."

Jens cringed. "Twenty-one is a big deal, the most important birthday to a lot of people, and I forgot hers."

I pushed a curl behind my ear, and Foss held me closer. Of all the times for the jerk to sense my pain. "It's not a big deal, Jens. I forgot it, too. We were in Undraland when it happened. I was probably in that jail cell, which is how lots of people end their twenty-first birthday bashes. I just took the direct route there." I shook my head into Foss when Jens paled. "Could we just drop it?"

"Is there anything you wanted for your birthday? We'll make a stop, babe. Whatever you want." He pulled into a lackluster strip mall that had a tobacco store, a beef jerky outlet and a children's shoe store. He pounded his fist on the steering wheel. "This sucks! I swore after I sat next to you at that terrible circus you went to last year that if I ever had the chance, I'd take you somewhere amazing."

That was the punch in the gut. Worse than my parents knowing I had no friends, my boyfriend had witnessed me sobbing alone at the circus on my twentieth birthday. The utter embarrassment pushed me down lower yet. The depression was seeping into my pores, weighting my shoulders. I caught an unbidden sob in my hands, trying to stuff it back into my mouth, lest the entire car knew how childish I was being.

Jamie grabbed his chest, astonished at the devastation I felt. "I think that was the wrong thing to say."

Jens shook his head and let out a grunt of frustration aimed at himself. "I know it was." He looked in the rearview mirror at me, and I forced a smile. "The first year I get to buy you a present that Linus doesn't have to pass off as his, and I blow it all over the place."

I choked out a response that sounded light. "I'm dead, remember? Dead people don't age, so I get to be twenty forever." I pumped my fist in the air, trying to force a celebratory moment that fell like a deflated party balloon. Tears slid down my cheeks, but I kept my tone even, hoping they would go unnoticed, invisible against my pale and bruised skin. I practiced one of the clown's painted smiles to pass off how okay I was with everything. With nothing. "C-Could you just turn on some music or something? I really, really, *really* don't want to talk about it. And please don't buy me anything. I'd just rather forget the whole thing. It's not a big deal." I wondered if my twenty-first birthday was when Linus came to me in that horrible dream. Perhaps we had spent it together, as much as we were able.

Jens looked like he felt about as low as I did, so he obeyed with no taunting, turning on a station that wasn't too annoying. He drove us further north, and none of us spoke for hours as Foss stroked my cheek, keeping my few silent tears that fell onto his shirt between us.

14

BITS OF NORMAL

*W*e pulled into the next hotel on our stop just as the sun began to dip down below the horizon. No one had spoken the entire way, and I'd cried myself to sleep on Foss's shoulder sometime before we crossed states.

"There's a Huldra colony I trust not too far from here," Jens informed us as he unloaded our overnight bags, and then helped his sister out of the car.

"Define 'not too far,'" I yawned.

Jamie murmured, "Define 'trust.'"

Jens shrugged, offering up his most evasive answer. "We don't have to cross an ocean. So, you know, big plus. Can you imagine this lot on a plane?"

Foss awoke and pushed me away when he realized I was resting on him. "Get off me, Lucy. I'm not your pillow."

I stretched, ready to put the last couple days behind me and start afresh. "Good to have you back, darling husband."

I kissed his cheek just to make him mad. He shoved me, and I shoved him back. Business as usual, thank goodness.

Jens held his hand out to me, but it felt too distant to take it. Instead I wrapped my arms around his neck and my legs around his waist, collapsing into him. I was tired of the chasm between us.

"That's the stuff," he sighed, kissing me once. "There we are. We lost us for a little bit there. I didn't like it."

"Me neither. Let's never fight again. That sounds doable, right?"

"I'm nothing if not doable," he teased, waggling the eyebrows I loved. Foss pushed passed Jens in a huff. "Suzy Sunshine's bunking with you tonight, Jamie. I've seen enough of Foss Junior for a lifetime."

Foss froze. "That wasn't... do you mean to tell me... that really happened?"

Jens nodded, his laugh vindictive now that things were in their proper place. He kissed my cheek before he let me down. "You were pretty vocal about your feelings for your little wife."

"It was that Huldra woman! Stina, that stupid rat!" He shook his fist in the air. "This is why their kind was banished to the Other Side. This is why! If I see her again, she's dead!"

"How did that song go he sang you, Lucy? The one about your golden hair?" Jens was being a jerk. While I couldn't really blame him, it definitely wasn't his sexiest shade of seduction.

Foss looked like he was torn between vomiting and going on a Hulked-out rage. "Not the one about your golden eyelashes? Tell me I didn't sing the song I wrote for you back in Fossegrim!"

My head whipped to my husband. "I thought you wrote that because Stina scrambled your brains. You... you wrote the song that long ago?"

Foss growled at me not to start with him.

I wasn't starting anything. I was genuinely touched. No one had ever written me a song. Unless you count the innumerable ones Linus had composed about farts to make me laugh. This was not the same. The words had been beautiful, dripping with sincerity as he recounted the details of my face, and the nuances he took notice of that added to his love for me. I'd been the only one to hear the whole song, and the lyrics stayed locked inside my heart so I could treasure them as something precious, something beautiful. Something of my husband that was mine to keep.

Jamie slapped his hands together to relieve the tension. "So, anyone want to explain the leafless trees? Is it so cold here, they just up and die?"

I shifted my coat around my torso. "Actually, that's pretty accurate."

Britta intervened. "You're welcome to stay with us tonight, Foss."

"If you want to watch my girl sleep again, suck on her shoulder or make love to her ear, knock twice first." Jens's teasing had a bit too much bite to it for my taste.

"Let's get some sleep, guys. I'm beat. Foss didn't know what he was doing. Lay off." I slipped off of Jens and led him upstairs after he checked us in. I was grateful for the privacy the two-room suite afforded us.

"That was a long drive. You didn't touch your lunch.

How about we go grab a bite before we turn in? I could do with a little time away." He stretched after setting down our bags.

The room was like any other three-star hotel. High-traffic carpet, dresser only people planning on living there like us used, resale shop artwork, heavy burgundy draperies, big brown comforter on a giant bed, a too-small tub and various mini toiletries I liked to line up like little soldiers who obeyed my every command.

Jens watched me deflate at the small size of the tub. "What do you say we order them some room service and you and I go out? Let's ditch 'em. Go someplace nice. I'm tired of fast food and grocery stores." He hooked his finger through one of my front belt loops to lure me closer for a swift kiss. "I saw they have an Italian restaurant just down the street."

He was playful Jens again. I loved that guy. "You mean like a date?" A small smile teased my lips. I kissed him again. "No one's ever asked me on a date before."

His happiness vanished, and he pulled away. "I forgot your birthday, and I've never even taken you out on a proper date. I'm scum."

"Where would you have taken me? Tipping cows in Tonttu? Fishing in Fossegrim? It's fine. We're here now. You've asked, and I'm accepting." I grinned, rubbing his back to rally him. "I date now. I'm a dating girl."

"That, you are." He anchored his fist down into the mattress. "I really wished I hadn't forgotten your birthday, though. I had big plans for your twenty-first."

"It's fine, Jens. I don't even know your birthday. I'm not upset with you. Just the whole missing my own birthday feels kinda crappy. Talk about compromising myself."

"Undrans don't do things the way you do. I have no idea what day I was born. It was the year of the squash flower, sometime in the seventh moon."

My nose wrinkled. "When the smack is that?"

"Exactly. Birthdays are a human thing." He pulled out a nicer shirt. It was a black button-down with silver buttons on the cuffs. He shoved his arms into it as he spoke. With every modern article of clothing I saw him in, he looked less like Jens the sexy nomad, and more like Jens, hottest model in the universe. "Linus and I had it all planned out. You two were going to go to a bar, because you know, twenty-one and all."

"Sure."

"I was going to show up and buy you a drink from across the bar. You'd be all nervous and giggly, and you'd say, 'Linus, that hot guy over there bought me a drink! What should I do?'" His voice went super girly when he imitated me.

I rolled my eyes. "Your impersonation of me? Stellar."

"Then Linus would make you get up and talk to me."

I shook my head. "That's it? That's your plan? My parents make you wait to meet me until I'm an adult, and your big move is get me drunk?" I whistled. "Smooth operator."

He grimaced, pinching my side. "That's not my big move. It's the first time you meet me. I'm not telling you my big move. After that smooth operator comment, you don't deserve it."

"Oh, do you say 'Hey, baby. Is this seat taken?'"

"Yes. That's my big move."

"Do you ask me my sign?"

"I'm not big on that. That's Foss. He's the closeted stargazer. Let him wow you by telling you you'll meet a handsome stranger today."

"Do you let me win at beer pong?"

Jens scolded me with his eyes, cinching his hands around my hips and squeezing. "You'll never win at that. I can't get drunk off alcohol, and you've got bad aim when you're stone sober." He kissed me, and I let myself sink into his arms as our lips moved together. "I'm so in love with you."

"Then you should date me," I suggested, adoring the idea. We kissed, and it was a sweet relief that rode through my body. "I hate the time we were apart."

"Have I said I'm sorry about that?" he asked, sucking his toned stomach in as I surprised him by working off his buttons and tearing open the shirt he'd just put on.

"Only a hundred times." I pulled the black undershirt he was wearing up over his head. "Less chatter from you. More kissing." I weaved my fingers through his gorgeous hair as he pressed his lips to mine, grateful we didn't have to rehash all the ways we went wrong. I pushed him onto the bed, and like a good sport for pretending I was strong enough to move someone like him, he fell.

I loved the way he fell for me. It was a soft crash, but permanent. All the stories of the great Jens the Brave being such a hard nut to crack, and he was looking up at me through those thick lashes any girl would kill for.

Jens's hands were strong and large. When he looped his finger down the waist of my jeans to draw me to lay atop him, I tried not to let him see my shiver. When he cupped the backs of my thighs to move them so I was straddling him, I tried not to let my trepidation show. After months of bunking with his sister and a bunch of dudes, we were finally alone and far enough from where Pesta could track us. I could feel relief radiating off him, adding to the body heat building between us. Instead of appreciating him from afar, I got to run my hands through the hair on his chest, rake my fingernails down his stomach and squeeze his hips with my thighs. I sucked on his lower lip, and he groaned deliciously into my mouth.

Lucy! Jamie scolded me. *This is not proper!*

Get out of my head and let me have a moment, here. I don't need a third person in the room for this.

Jens's fingers crept under the hem of my shirt, and I thrilled at the sensation as I arched my back.

I don't approve of this, Jamie chided, his tone repugnant. *We're talking about this later. I can feel what you're feeling, and it's... this is not proper!*

Jens kissed my navel, and I melted all over him, dismissing the voice in my head that left in a huff. I was a pool of my former stoic self. Lucy Kincaid who never had a boyfriend, never had a date even, was losing her mind over a lick to her belly button. There was nothing else in the world but his thick, luscious lips and the magic they worked on my stomach.

I shifted atop him, and he froze with his tongue on my abdomen. He jerked his arms off me and rested his head back on the fluffy comforter.

"Why'd you stop? Am I doing this wrong?" I asked, my

chest heaving like I'd just sprinted up four flights of stairs. "You can be on top, if you want."

Jens groaned, but shut his eyes and rattled his head like a dog to shake himself out of the moment. "Your mom would whistle me off a cliff for this."

"She would not. She didn't use her whistle, remember?"

Jens's eyelids flared upward as he shook his head again, his arms stretched over his head to keep them honest. "She'd make an exception if she could read the thoughts running through my filthy mind." He stared down at my navel again, and I could see the lust in his eyes. "I'm suddenly very aware I'm doing all this to my friend's sister."

I harrumphed. "Well, all that's always going to be true."

"Sure, but this is the wrong order. We've broken up and got back together all before I've even taken you on a real date." He sat up, wrapping his arms around me so I could still straddle his lap. "You have to make me work harder than this."

I kissed him again, pressing up against him. "Harder than what we've already been through?"

"That's survival. I don't want a relationship based on that. When this is all over, I want us to last. Trust me on this. We need to cover the basics before we get lost in a sex haze."

I eyed him. "A sex haze, eh? That's awfully presumptuous of you."

He pfft'd in my face. "Please. I was two minutes away from pay day." He kissed me, and I shivered. "One day when we're not living to survive. When we can calm down, get you your white picket fence and make rational lifelong decisions."

"Okay, chief. Dinner and a movie it is." I extracted myself from him and shifted my shirt back into place.

He held up his finger. "I'll need a minute." When he eyed my form with lusty eyes, I did a little shimmy to garner the expected whimper. "What were my reasons again?"

"Sorry. Does this help?" I stopped dancing sexy and switched to the chicken dance instead.

Jens laughed, which only attracted me more to him. We were in quite the predicament. "Nope. Still hot. Sexiest chicken I've ever seen. Let's go. This room's laced with something that makes us take our clothes off. Dangerous." He shoved his undershirt and button-down back on and put on nice shoes and socks, eyeing me all the while.

I observed the difference between us and frowned. "I didn't really shop for date clothes. I think I was still in survival mode." I pointed to his black, square-toed shoes that would have fit in nicely at a jazz club or a board meeting.

"You look like you, and I like you." He kissed me again, stuffing his pockets with the essentials for leaving the room. You know, room key, car key, wallet and four concealed weapons. "We're both wearing jeans."

I wasn't the type of girl to wear skirts, but I kinda wished I was in that moment. "I look like a kid next to you. You look like the model for those clothes."

He gave me the stink eye. "Why do your compliments sound like you're disappointed? I can change my shoes, if that's what's bugging you."

"No, no. I like the look of you. It's a new side I haven't seen before. No more black boots. You look... pretty in those."

Jens rolled his eyes. "Okay, now I'm changing."

I waved my hand to excuse my choice of words. "I didn't mean that. Don't change a thing. Just give me a minute."

I fished through my bag of clothes and found a black long-sleeved fitted shirt. I usually didn't go for black, but they had a limited selection at the supermart, if you can believe it. I went to the bathroom to change and spent a few moments doing my hair. I hadn't actually put my hair up since it had been cut, so it was a new series of experiments. I ended up with most of my curls pinned away from my face, and a few hanging down. This exposed my complexion a bit more than usual, and I was grateful my black eye had faded to a sallow yellow and wasn't swollen anymore. A touch of lip gloss, and I felt like a new woman, or a woman, anyway, and less like a little girl or a dude.

I settled on a red Chuck Taylor and a black one, not willing to leave myself entirely behind to look nice next to my boyfriend. Jens reached out and took my hand as we left the room, and I realized that's all it took for us to look like we were together.

15

FIRST DATE

"So, Jamie's pissed at our improper behavior."

Jens looked guilty. "Yikes. How much did he see?"

I shrugged. "He can feel it when I get... overexcited."

"Loving that bond more and more," he groused. "So when we do finally go for it, it'll be like making love to my best friend and my girlfriend. Really not the kind of threesome any guy wants."

I shook my head, blanching. "No, no. We just have to work out a heads-up system. He was able to walk away once he stopped Papa Don't Preaching me."

"I really don't want him seeing me like that. He'll learn moves he can use on my sister." We walked through the icy air down the street toward the only restaurant that wouldn't take me too far from the tether. "Not that I don't want her to be happy, but still. It's weird."

"You've got moves?" I teased, feigning unimpressed.

"I've got moves that'd blow your mind."

I shrugged as he opened the door for me, loving the chivalry that came with a real date. "I have yet to see evidence of that." I reached up on my toes and pecked his cheek. "I love that you opened the door for me. Very boyfriendy."

"Well, I am your boyfriend. You need to raise the bar higher. Make me work harder than opening a door. Challenge me, woman!" He pretended to boss me around, knowing it would get a rise out of me.

My head started to hurt when the hostess led us an inch past her stand, and I nearly cursed aloud.

Lucy? Where are you? came my buddy's voice.

At the restaurant down the street. I sighed. *Jens and I are on a date. We'll only be an hour. Can you hold out?*

A restaurant... with food?

That's the thing about restaurants. Lousy with food.

Okay.

When his voice left my head, I relaxed.

"Is Jamie alright?" Jens inquired, sitting across from me and reaching out for my hand. The hostess handed him the menu, but he didn't give it a glance.

"You could tell I was talking to him?"

"Yeah." He leaned across the booth and tapped the space between my eyes. "You get a worried little wrinkle right there when your head starts hurting. You want to go back?"

"No," I insisted. "It's my first date. A little headache's nothing. I can barely feel it anymore."

"It's your call, Mox."

"Then I call that conversation over. On to the next." I opened the menu and perused all the choices that merged together to form one delicious restaurant. "I stinking love

Italian food. And would you look at that? No kanins anywhere on the list. My kind of place."

Jens didn't open his menu, but stood and kissed my cheek. "Be right back. Bathroom. Order me spaghetti, will you?"

"Spaghetti? That's it? Your first sit-down meal in months, and you want spaghetti?"

"It's hard to mess up marinara and noodles."

"True enough." I watched him walk away, enjoying his swagger. He must've felt my eyes on him, because halfway to the bathroom, he stopped, lifted his shirt and gave me a nice swish of his backside. Really kinda loved that guy.

A few minutes later, the door opened, and I caught sight of Jamie, Britta and Foss. My heart sank as I waved them over. They had no idea about restaurant protocol, so they kept their heads down and made a beeline over to me as quick as they could. "Hey, guys. Do you know what a date is, Jamie?" I asked, none too pleased.

"No. I assume it's going to a place to eat food, since that's what you're doing. Did we do it wrong?" He took off his jacket and sat down across from me. Britta slid into the booth on my side while Foss stood awkwardly in the aisle, not willing to look me in the eye.

I sighed. "Nope. That's about right. You guys look hungry. Have a seat." I waved the waitress over. "Could we move to a table for five? Would that be possible?"

The waitress was appropriately polite and hid that we inconvenienced her well enough. "Certainly. It'll just be a moment." She took in the beautiful giants surrounding me with a professional smile.

We scooted out of the booth and followed her to a table

near the window. "Oh, sorry. Could we have something near the back of the restaurant? I'm a little chilly." Yup. Total high-maintenance customer. I know. But I also knew that when Jens came out, he would make us move to a less visible spot anyways.

Poor sweet strawberry blonde waitress complied and even had the grace to apologize for not asking. She moved us, and I sat like a good little girl who never complains, the two of us apologizing to each other until she left for the kitchen to fill the beverage orders I put in for the table.

"That was weak," Foss critiqued me, sitting next to me with a territorial air I was all too familiar with. "She's clearly a servant. You don't ask for what you want." He pressed his fist to the dark wood table. "You tell them."

I handed him a menu and gripped the front of the shirt he'd borrowed from Jamie, pulling him down so I could whisper in his ear. "Look, rat. This is why I didn't want you in my world. You don't know crap about anything here, so don't you dare tell me what to do or how to be. You begged me, *begged* to come over to my world. I told you I didn't think you could submit to me." I could smell his manly scent I wish I wasn't familiar with, and tried to ignore the intimacy of my cheek pressed against his. "Are you going to let me be right?"

When I released him, I pulled back, but realized his body was nearly wrapped around mine just from that small encounter. His shoulders curved forward, swallowing my form in his. His knees were open, and my body had been between them. Nothing lewd, but given our history that was barely history, we both swallowed with discomfort at the feelings we wished were not there.

He kept his voice low. "I can submit. You forget my mother was a slave. I was a stable boy once upon a time."

I patted the top of his head just to patronize him. "That's a good little rat. Put your menu down. I'll decide what and when you eat. You be good, I'll feed you. You act up, and I'll pin you down and shove food down your throat when I feel charitable."

"You were starving yourself!" I could tell he wanted to argue further, but bit his tongue. In that simple action, I could tell Stina had been successful in peeling back the layers of his curse. "I can submit," he repeated, more for himself this time than for me.

The bartender came over to our table with a pink cocktail. "This is from the gentleman at the bar."

I blushed and glanced up at the bar with a grin aimed at Jens, who looked resigned to the downward turn our night had taken. He made his way over to us and sat across from me, leaning back in his chair and crossing his ankle over his knee. "So, Jamie doesn't know what a date is, does he."

"We'll go out another time. It's fine." I sipped my drink. It was fruity and packed a medium punch. A far sight better than Gar. "Not a bad move, Jens Bond."

He rolled his eyes. "That wasn't my move. It was a joke to make you blush, which it did. Mission accomplished." He put on a forced smile for his sister. "See anything good?"

Britta was studying the menu as if there might be a test on it later. "I can really choose anything here?"

"You got it, sis."

"What's ravioli?"

Jens systematically explained every single menu item

on the entrees page, patiently waiting for Britta to find something that sounded appetizing. He lost his irritation at having to babysit the others and smiled at his sister. "This world looks good on you, Britt. I mean, the clothes sure, but the independence. It works for you." He motioned around the restaurant. "Women have as much choices as men here. Give it a couple months, and you'll fit in better than you ever did in Tonttu."

Britta grinned up at her brother. "I like it here. I can see why you stayed away from us for so long."

When the waitress came back, I ordered for myself, Foss and Jamie. Jens got his treasured spaghetti, and Britta ordered three entrees for herself since she couldn't decide. "Is that okay?" she asked, handing over the menu.

"Get whatever you want, Britt. I told you, you're just as powerful as a man over here. If you want to eat three meals, go for it. I personally don't think you'll be able to, but I'll have fun watching you try."

"I'll take that challenge." There was life in Britta's eyes that Undraland had dulled out over the years. It was a beautiful thing to watch.

The five of us chatted about the difference in hotels, the drive and other such things before Jens and I let them fire away question after question about our world.

"No, Jamie. You can't drive the car."

"Why not? I'm a prince. Do they not allow princes to drive their own cars?"

Jens shook his head. "They don't allow people who haven't passed a test to show they know what they're doing to drive. I'm telling you, it's more complicated than you realize."

Lucy can do it. How complicated can it be?

"Hey! I heard that, you jerk." I kicked Jamie under the table. "I co-killed that Were with you and the Sleipnir. I drowned the Circhos and figured out how to blow up the farlig. I'm not dead weight, here."

Jamie looked down, contrite. "I'm sorry, *syster*. It was a fleeting thought not meant to be heard. You're vital to the mission. If it weren't for you, we'd certainly all be at the bottom of the sea."

I scratched my scalp. "Good thing that farlig opened its mouth right when I needed him to. If he hadn't done that, it wouldn't have worked."

Jens, Britta and Foss looked away from me at once. Jens sipped his drink. "You were amazing. I hope they have ice cream here. I didn't look. But that'll be a good thing for them to try, don't you think?"

The waitress brought our food, and I was grateful I'd insisted on a full table instead of a booth. The many entrees were spread out in the center, and we picked at each one at our leisure, mixing them and laughing as we reminisced about the different flavors kanins should come in, had we the choice.

I fed Jens a bite of lobster ravioli that Britta swore up and down she could finish, but tapped out after trying the crab cakes. Foss ate without incident, but every now and then I caught him watching me as if he had something to say.

When the dessert menu was presented, Britta groaned. "Oh, I can't stomach another bite."

"You say that now. Wait until you try ice cream, sis. I'm

telling you, it'll blow your mind." I laughed at Jens's imitation of brains exploding out the side of his skull.

Out of the corner of my eye, I saw a movement directed at me. I turned and lost all other thoughts in my brain.

"Lucy? I... Lucy?"

Brown eyes, mocha skin, tight spindly braids and a gaping mouth I'd recognize anywhere beamed at me in astonishment as if she was seeing a ghost.

For all intents and purposes, she was.

I knocked over my chair as I stood in haste, forgetting everything else. I ran to her, forsaking my friends in that moment for my one true girlfriend.

Tonya screamed a mix of elation and fear as our bodies collided in a hug that outweighed all others on the planet in terms of relief and love.

16

TONYA IN THE FLESH

*T*onya burst into tears in my arms. "But you're dead! The coroner told me you died in the fire! I don't understand!"

There was no explanation but the absurd. "Witness Protection. I wanted to tell you so many times, but I couldn't. I'm sorry. I'm so sorry!"

"Are you serious? That's so James Bond of you. You're alive!" She hugged me anew, kissing my face as we wept all over each other.

"I am. And you're... you're you. As you as you've always been." Her black spindly hair matched her dark skin perfectly, and her eyes danced with love for me as she processed all the time lost between us.

"I'm less me without you," she admitted, squeezing me again.

"That's the thing about best friends you share shoes with." I pointed down at our feet, noting that she was wearing one black Chuck and one red, just like I was. It was as if we subconsciously knew we would meet up today, and our feet were ready for the reunion.

"Oh, that's freaky! Come sit with me and Man Friend." She jerked her thumb over her shoulder to a guy in his early forties who looked creepily old next to her youthful-barely-out-of-teen-years exuberance. Had she not pointed him out, I would never have guessed they were together.

"Oh, hi. Nice to meet you, Man Friend." I stuck my hand out and shook his, feigning happiness to meet him to cover over the ick factor.

He was tall, dark and hunched with a round face not prone to smiling. One of his eyes pointed in a wonky direction while the other followed me in a way that was not friendly. "Nice to meet you."

"Man Friend and I have been together for two months."

Girl talk after so much time apart and so many monsters slain was a welcome flood of happiness and flittery flowers. I scarcely remembered the girl I used to be, but having Tonya to remind me brought me more relief and emotion than I would have ever found on my own.

I smiled through my tears. "Two months, huh? He must be magical. Should I wish for a pot of gold while he's here?"

She shrugged, shaking her head. "I tried that, and nothing." We giggled at his expense, but he gave no reaction to this. He only sighed and looked around as if he did not know us.

I kinda hated him.

Tonya clasped her hands together, getting right down to business. "Tell me everything you're allowed to. This whole being without you thing? I'm over it. So over it. You're never leaving my sight again."

My heart and posture fell simultaneously. "I can't stay, T. I wish I could, but they pulled me out for a reason. It's not safe for me to be around people not in the program."

She nodded, crestfallen. "You're here tonight, though, right? I got a place down the street from here. Come with me just for tonight. We can catch up and talk till we're all up to speed." She pinched me to test if I was a mirage. "I can't believe it's really you. I'm not hallucinating, right?"

"No more than usual."

She motioned to the booth she'd been headed toward before I'd intercepted her. "Come eat with me," she begged.

I pulled her toward the others. "No. You can meet my friends. They're in my new life, and I'm sure they'd love to meet you. They've heard stories about your antics."

"My juggling antics? Because I left my chainsaws at home."

It was the perfect bit of nonsense. She always was. I stopped walking and hugged her again. "I missed you," I whispered in her ear. "Of all the things I wish I didn't have to give up, you're the biggest one."

Tonya looked at me as if I was made of gold. "Back at you, Little L." We held hands like little girls as I brought her to the table of gawkers.

"Guys? This is my BFF, Tonya."

Tonya waved and nodded at Jamie and Britta as they introduced themselves.

I was too distracted by seeing Tonya to comment on Jens's calculating manor or Foss's steaming bull impression directed at Man Friend, who hung back like a stalker.

When it was his turn, Foss stood, towering over Tonya just to intimidate Man Friend. "I'm Foss, Lucy's husband," he said, directing his glare at Man Friend. Foss wrapped an arm around my middle possessively. I heard Jens hiss under his breath.

Tonya's hand flew over her heart. "You're married?! Little Miss too-busy-studying-to-go-to-the-clubs-on-a-Friday-night is up and married? Foss, is it?" She ignored the threat he was trying to send them and threw her arms around him, shocking the scowl off his face. "Oh, I love you already! You married my best friend? You're the luckiest man alive! She's amazing. Tell me you're a bodybuilder or something that makes sense, because I mean, holy crap. That's just impractical." She motioned to his height and musculature.

Tonya was rambling, which meant she found him attractive and was trying to hide it.

She didn't give Foss a chance to answer, which was good, since he was perplexed as to why his intimidation was not working on her. "Oo! Show me the ring!" She grabbed at my finger, but frowned when it was not bedecked in karats.

I dug the large gold ring out of my shirt and displayed it to her. "Ta-da. It's an heirloom." I explained the absence of a diamond.

Tonya grinned through her gut response of disappointment. "Well, it's beautiful." She hugged me again. "You're married, kid. Married and alive. I'm telling you, I'm so happy, I could explode all over the restaurant!" She turned to Jens. "Who's this tall drink of handsome?"

Jens stood and extended his hand to Tonya. "Jens, Lucy's handler."

I shot him an apologetic look, which he brushed off with a half-smile. Of course this is how our date would go.

Tonya mumbled something like, "I'd like him to handle me," and a "Mother may I?" when she shook Jens's hand. Clearly she and Man Friend were very close. "Let's blow this joint and go back to my place. Too much catching up to do for a restaurant. I plan on kidnapping you nice and proper."

Foss did not find this amusing. He kept a respectful distance from Tonya, lest he lose his temper and smack her.

We got our food packed up and drove behind Tonya and Man Friend three blocks down to a cute little house with white shudders and, of all things, a white picket fence.

My heart ached so badly, Jamie rubbed his chest to soothe us both. I ran my fingers over the fence in longing. A white picket fence had never been Tonya's dream. I was happy for her, but part of me felt my own dream life moving further and further away. "You live here?" I inquired of the family-style ranch. My jaw was on the floor as I took in the property – actual land – that my dear friend was the owner of. "Like, you live here. You have a house? How? How do you have a house?" I rested my hand on the picket fence. It was iconic and perfect, like I'd always envisioned. My emotions tugged at me, and I could feel Jens watching my reaction. "Tonya, how do you have all this?"

"Settlement from when the apartment burned down. Danny spent all his on a vacation and video games. Didn't think it was possible to waste that much so fast, but he rallied for the occasion." She unlocked the door to her house and ushered us in, grinning when Foss hit his head on the frame. "Watch it, Shaq. My ceilings weren't built for giants. How tall are you?"

Tonya put a kettle on the stove as she fired off a million questions in a single-file line. When she reached the end of her queries and was rummaging in the cupboards to make us all some tea, I finally breathed and allowed myself to look around the house. "T, your place is amazing! When did you turn into an interior decorator?" The caramel walls had lavender accents painted near the top and bottom. There was artwork on the walls and an adult woman setup in the living room where we were all gathered. It didn't seem like her taste, but it was nice all the same. "You have knickknacks! Tons of them! What is this?" I pointed to a ceramic cow that I could not believe was her taste. Our apartment had always been so bare and mismatched. "You're domestic!" I accused. "You've Stepforded on me! Seriously, how did you do all this? You're like a true grownup."

Tonya grinned as she came out into the living room, taking in the sight of me in her home. "I love that you're here. It's perfect now." She motioned to a side table littered with kitten collectibles next to the couch she ushered Foss and I to. "All this stuff's from my mom. She cleaned out her basement and brought it over when she helped me move. She calls to check in on the ceramic kittens once a week at least."

"Ah. That makes more sense. How did you and Man Friend meet?"

She waved off the question. "Oh, you know. Grieving girl loses best friend, runs to her shrink. They fall in love.

The rest is history." Then she gave me a seductive smirk. "Or chemistry." She grinned over at Man Friend, who was skulking behind her in a way that made me uncomfortable for her. His black eyes darted around the house, not landing on any of us for too long. "Nice try. It's you who's got the questions to answer." She rattled off seven more before the kettle sang and she jumped up to get it with Man Friend.

Jens was leaning on the wall next to the couch Foss and I were seated on. He whispered, "Can I say I hate her boyfriend?"

"No, but you can whisper it. And it's Man Friend, not boyfriend."

"No joke. Dude's like fifty."

Britta and Jamie were on the loveseat. Britta piped in with, "I think Tonya's lovely. Just as fun as you described. And to invite us all in like this. It's very nice of her."

I smiled at Britta. "Thanks for saying that. She is amazing. I miss her so much. Makes me happy you like her."

"Something's off," Jens commented, looking around the living room skeptically. "I can't put my finger on it, but we're not sleeping here, even if she offers. Got it?"

"Oh, you're no fun," I pouted.

When Tonya brought the tea to the coffee table, she switched to questioning Foss, grilling him with precision only a best friend could. "So, Foss. Tell me why you think you deserve to be with Lucy. She's only the greatest girl on the planet. How'd you win her over?"

That's my girl.

Foss looked at me, trying to hide his annoyance and shrugged. "I bought her for sixty gold coins."

Tonya paused and then burst out laughing. I cackled along as I socked his shoulder with wide eyes. "Oh, honey. Shut up. Your jokes are just terrible." Then I turned to Tonya. "You know the story. Girl meets boy, boy falls madly in love with girl. Girl tolerates boy. They live happily ever after." Tonya and I laughed together, and I could feel Britta, Jamie and Jens watching me.

"Sure, but the details. I'm sorry, I just can't believe you're married! Did you want sugar in your tea? I know you've never been much of a tea drinker, but I just started batching my own with Man Friend. Try it!" She clasped her hands together, squealing with girlish anticipation.

I knew I wouldn't escape without drinking it down to the dregs. I downed mine halfway in one gulp and grinned. The taste was like pixie stix and something flowery sweet that stung my nose almost like carbonation. At least she didn't use hot dog water. "It's delicious," I lied. "You're so talented."

Tonya motioned for everyone else to try theirs. "Drink up, guys. I'm just learning how to make it myself."

I gave Jens a brave smile, which he returned. He shook his head at me when I pointed to his cup, and it dawned on me that he probably knew more about Tonya than I did from his days spent watching me. Her terrible luck in the kitchen scared him off.

"Foss?" Tonya asked, scooting his tea cup closer.

He was surly, and had been born without the people-pleasing gene. "No."

I rolled my eyes. "You could at least say 'no, thank you.' Pretend you're a polite person for one night."

Foss looked at me from his position to my left on the couch and folded his arms over his chest. "No."

Britta drank a sip of hers and faked a smile. "It's lovely, Tonya. Thank you."

Tonya pressed Foss for more information. "No, really. Tell me more. How did you propose?"

Foss looked up at Jens and smirked. "I kissed her just like this," he said, and before I could brace myself properly, Foss pressed his mouth to mine, really hamming up the eroticism for the viewers. It was a game of chicken between him and me, and also one between him and Jens. A joke, really, but taken way too far.

Then it wasn't. Foss's lips were hot on mine, and his firm grip on my lower back tugged me closer. My eyes fluttered shut, and my heart pounded as I struggled for... for...

Surely I was struggling to make a clean break, right? I was just waiting for the opportunity to pull away inconspicuously, wasn't I?

My hands were gripping the seat and the back of the couch to brace myself, but my back was arched as we kissed beyond what was socially appropriate.

I finally came to my senses and shook my head, turning away from his kiss as two more planted themselves on my cheek. Foss straightened, but did not look away from me as he spoke. "I kissed her like that, and told her we would be married."

"Just like that?" Tonya asked. Her Cinderella sigh and smile covered over the reality that I was choking on my embarrassment and rage just a few feet from her. The euphoria I didn't want to feel pulsed through me, making me lightheaded and slightly giddy. I giggled, and covered my mouth at the unexpected indiscretion.

"Such a sweet couple," Jens commented, my odd swing of emotion trumping his rage toward Foss. "You alright there, Mrs. Foss?"

"I... I..." My breath drew in too much oxygen, and the colors in the room began to pop out at me in a wide array of sixties groovy madness. My face was flushed and I felt suddenly dizzy. My fingers felt fuzzy, and my head started lifting like a balloon floating away from my body. "Can I use your restroom?" I asked. "That kiss and the tea were a little strong."

Tonya pointed down the hallway. My vision started to tunnel, white light in my periphery edging out the caramel walls. Behind me I heard Britta say, "Jens? Something feels strange. Is this how you feel after ravioli usually?"

Man Friend followed me down the hall. By the time I made it to the bathroom, I was oddly at peace with everything in my life. The happy twinkling lights danced in my vision as Man Friend caught my elbow, lowered me to the carpet, dragged me into a side room and shoved a hood over my head.

17

PAINLESS

I awoke to chaos. Pure chaos.

The hood over my face kept the details at bay, but I could hear fists and shouts being thrown haphazardly about as I tried to care about the urgency of the moment.

Everything was so pretty inside the hood. The black was the perfect canvas for my mind to practice its psychedelics on. Spindly colors drew patterns in my mind's eye. Turquoise and pinks painted so beautifully on the black. My hands were bound, but I still tried to grasp at the pretty colors and shapes.

Jens shouted something to me, and I giggled. I knew this was the wrong response, but that's all I could do.

The laughter vanished when someone dragged my body down the hall and knocked my head into the wall. It didn't hurt at all – that was the thing that gave me pause. I could tell by the force that it should've put me in tears, but I felt oddly boneless. Nothing hurt. Not my head, not the circus, not Linus.

I was picked up and hefted over a shoulder I wasn't sure I should trust. The colors spun, but I didn't mind. They rearranged themselves so beautifully, captivating my attention as I was taken outside and slammed into a trunk.

I tried to care, but the pretty colors danced for me like a fireworks show, demanding my attention as they pirouetted and spun in their own musical motions. The car took off, and I was rattled around in the trunk, banging into hard things that again, I could tell were supposed to be hurting me.

The car was afraid; I could feel it. Okay, maybe not the car, but the driver, for sure. They drove it like they were escaping something. I couldn't remember if I was supposed to cheer them on or protest.

The colors were so pretty. They were making triangles now.

My head. That hurt on a psychic level, and I could tell Jamie was too far away. I'm sure other parts of my body stung, too, but for some reason, I didn't care so much about those. My head was unhappy, though.

I like bunnies. I don't want to eat them ever again. I want a waffle. And chicken. And pie. Not pumpkin pie. Pie with ice cream and whipped cream. I like cream cheese. And bagels. The cheesy kind with the cheese.

Foss had kissed me. That was kinda funny. Maybe one day I'd shake him and be able to just be with Jens. My marriage had caught up with me.

Now the colors were all purple. I like purple.

The colors jolted and popped as the car was slammed

by something bigger than it, harder. Suddenly the car was airborne. I giggled out a "Wee!" before it crashed down and tipped so my feet were higher than my head. The colors reappeared, and I tried to catch them with my teeth.

The car slammed back down and skidded to a halt. Something wet trickled on my face, and it made me laugh. Again, I could tell something was supposed to be painful, but I couldn't remember what. My head still hurt, but the colors were so pretty, I didn't care. It was Pink Floyd in my brain, and I was enchanted.

They sang to me. They loved me.

No one loves me like the colors do.

"Help me! Foss, grab something to pry open the trunk! I can't open it. Hurry!"

Oh, Jens. So yummy. Like warm bagels dipped in sugar.

A big metal noise happened above my head, and then I heard Foss and Jens shout in unison. "No!"

"Careful! Foss, clear a space in the car where we can put her. Help Jamie! If we can stop his bleeding, it'll save her."

Jens picked me up, and the pain was more acute. It chased away the colors I'd become quite attached to. When I heard his voice again, it was tainted with a sob. "Kill the driver, Foss! Just finish him! Where's the girl?"

My heart had been drumming in time with the song I couldn't place in my head, but the rhythm beat slower, moving at a snail's pace as my heart languidly chugged along, coming closer and closer to a stop.

The colors melted and faded, and all I saw was the black of the hood before I closed my eyes, letting the slow song lull me to sleep.

18

SNATSAFRIGGA

*T*his time the chaos I awoke to was the most intense physical pain I had ever felt. There were no words for the excruciating nature of the brutality I was assaulted with. I screamed at the assailant before it dawned on me that the hood was gone and so were the colors. I opened my eyes and took in a high ceiling with brown tapestries and sparklingly clean windows.

Oh, the pain in my arm and all over my body.

"I have to whistle her back down, Jens. She can't handle all this! She's just a child." The woman's voice was stern, but gentle.

"Fine, but nothing more than that!"

The most beautiful bird's song hit my ears, and I felt warm and snuggly. My pain was muted, and I could take in my surroundings a little more.

I was in a huge house of some sort. The mansion kind with vaulted ceilings and archways and real art on the walls.

"Bring the doctor in here! Hurry!"

An Indian man in his fifties stood over me, his composed face telling me that everything was fine and there was nothing to freak out about. Not that I could freak out if there was. A blanket of chill crept over me. When I turned my head, I saw Jamie in the bed next to me, enjoying the same contented state. He had an IV in his arm and was marveling at the liquid going into his body via the tube.

"I like the world with the this in it," he mumbled, his words slurring like a drunkard.

I tried to nod, but I couldn't really access my neck. It felt like there was a brace around it, but I couldn't figure out why. "I like the this, too, Jamie. I like the Jens and the Foss. Sometimes not the Foss." The world tilted. "I need my half. My Linus half."

"I like the snatsafrigga." Jamie's brain slurred at the same time mine did, and I turned to the doctor just before my world went dark again.

* * *

THERE WAS BEEPING, and it reminded me of when Linus was in the hospital during junior prom. He'd been super bummed because he'd finally gotten the nerve to ask a girl to the dance, she'd said yes, but he'd gotten sick the night before the big day. No one had asked me to the dance, of course, but Linus had insisted I tag along with him and Marta. The hospital had felt especially lonely that night, despite the fact that we were together. Knowing we were missing out on fun made his illness that much worse.

The beeping had been relentless. It was a good thing. It meant his heart was beating and his breathing was happening on its own, but the sound started driving us mad.

And that's how the Great Safety Dance Rally was founded. We realized that Safety Dance fit perfectly with the hospital machine beeps, so I sang and danced to the song while Linus did the robot to it in bed. We must've gone through the entire song two dozen times before my dad begged us on actual hands and knees to sing anything else.

"What's the matter, Dad? You can dance if you want to."

Then Linus would chime in with a breathy, "You can leave your friends behind."

Then it would start all over again, but this time with more laughter. It became our favorite song. Linus taught me all sorts of useful things to the tune of Safety Dance. How to hotwire a car, steal someone's alternator belt, and break into a building with the standard locks most schools came with. While the entire school was dancing a few miles away to the hustle or whatever, we had our own school dance. And let's face it, any party with Safety Dance at it is a good one, even if it's in a hospital. I bet they had to dance to something crappy, like country music.

The same beeping rang in my ears, but the song didn't hold the same joy it once had. Now I was the one confined to the bed with tubes in me.

I opened my eyes and saw Jens sitting in between my bed and Jamie's in the same strange museum-like mansion that was our makeshift hospital. Jens was leaning forward with his hands clasped, his forehead resting on his thumbs. He kept whispering, "Please, please, please."

I tried to lift my hand to comfort him, but I couldn't find the proper controls in my brain to operate my arm. "Jens?" I whispered.

Jens sat upright and whipped his head around to confirm I'd spoken. "Lucy?" He was off the chair in a heartbeat. "She's awake! Somebody grab Doctor Sharma!"

There was a fair amount of commotion, but Jens knelt next to my bed and held my hand.

"Ah. There it is," I said, my words sluggish and slurred.

"There what is? What do you need, baby?"

"You found my hand. I couldn't remember where I put it."

Jens wove his fingers through mine and lifted our hands so I could see them without moving my head. "It's here. I'm here." He leaned forward and buried the top of his head in my palm. There was a sniffle, and then the dam broke. Jens sobbed harder than I'd ever seen him cry, kissing my palm every now and then to make sure I was real. That we were real. That I wouldn't disappear out from under him again.

I tried to turn my head, but found there was a brace on my neck. The doctor explained while Jens tried to compose himself that I sprained my wrist, broke a rib and tore something I couldn't pronounce in my calf. There was talk of a concussion, whiplash and blood loss that was worrisome, but the biggest thing that told me how bad the ordeal had been was Jens in tears at my bedside.

I was confined to the bed for the foreseeable future. My leg could not be walked on, nor could my spine handle the stress of me being upright for more than a few minutes. Doctor Sharma was kind but firm, recommending bed rest, fluids and a special diet for me to get my weight up.

"What happened?" I finally asked after the doctor moved to check on Jamie, who was still unconscious.

"I didn't see it, but I should've. All the signs were there." The tears sprang afresh, wetting his thick lashes and displaying his torment across his cheeks. "Tonya. It's not her anymore. She's Pesta's Mouthpiece. I didn't even put together that Pesta constructing a portal here meant that she would need a Mouthpiece to act on her behalf. Of course she would pick someone you would trust. Pesta needs your bones to finish the portal." He sniffed and then let out a pitiful sob. "The tea! She dosed you with lavender powder. It was a nearly lethal dose. If you hadn't been tied to Jamie, it might have had some serious consequences to your brain. She doesn't need you to have brainwaves, though. She just wants your bones." He rubbed my palm on his stubble, kissing the heel of my hand with his eyes closed. "I've failed you. You could've died. They almost got away with kidnapping you, too. I had to crash our car into theirs to stop them. I tried to aim away from the trunk, but the car ricocheted into a building and messed you up pretty good."

"I was drugged?" I asked, piecing together enough parts of Jens's story to make sense of my scattered recollection. "That's what the powder feels like?"

Jens shook his head. "No. You were overdosed. You and Jamie've been tripping for a long time. Your leg got impaled by an umbrella in the trunk, and you didn't even feel it. It's dangerous at that level, especially for a first-timer. I'm so sorry. I'll never touch the stuff again!" He wiped his cheeks with his sleeve. "I almost lost my best friend and my girl in one swoop. I need you to be alive. I need it, Loos. Linus was the one who got you? Well, you're the only one who gets me!"

"You're so sad," I observed, my eyelids heavy. "I'ma sleep now. Don't leave me."

"I promise, I'll never leave you," Jens vowed. The last thing I remember before I passed back out was my boyfriend's pleas for me not to leave him, either.

19

ELSA'S BABY DOLL

*I*t was a week before I was allowed to take the neck brace off. It was two weeks until I could put pressure on my leg, and three weeks before my ribs were healed enough for walking across the long bedroom without audible groans.

I really could've used another month on top of all that before I dealt with the Huldra of Toronto.

"I can't believe you'd say that. She's obviously human. Look how short she is!" exclaimed a loud-mouthed brunette.

"But she survived an overdose. That's not normal," another Huldra argued.

The basement of the mansion was really a whole house unto itself. I sat on the plush white leather couch in the home entertainment area in front of the giant TV I wished I could just watch. Tuning out the arguing sounded like the most refreshing thing at the moment.

One giant house. Twenty-seven Huldra women, ten

men and five kids. Four Undrans. One human. No rules. It would've made a great reality TV show.

"She's clearly human – you *know* she's human – and I'm not debating this all over again. I just explained her entire bloodline to you people. She's got a little extra elf in her blood now from Alrik adopting her, so maybe that helped her pulled through. Or maybe it's because she's laplanded to a Tom. I don't really care. Moving on," Jens demanded. He was standing in front of the TV with a lanky black-haired, long-nosed Huldra named Liv who I'd never seen in anything other than skin-tight leggings and short, tight shirts.

This was hour three of everyone debating what should be done with me and how they would move forward now that I was living with them.

Jamie and Britta had locked themselves in our room to avoid the Huldras. Though we were grateful for their shelter, we were all very much aware that we could be under their control at any moment.

The source of our safety was Elsa, a Huldra who'd helped Jens on a few guard duties a while back, and Leif, her husband. Elsa sat on my other side in the basement's long rec room, leaning back into the couch with her hubby in their matching fur-lined brown hiking boots. They were the picture of repose, but I was not fooled. When any other Huldras got too near me, she tensed and pursed her lips, sending them off to occupy one of the other many eggshell-colored leather couches.

I had a hard time differentiating which men were there because they wanted to be, and who was there because they were under the influence of the Huldra's whistle. One thing was sure, all the men were gorgeous. It was a little intimidating.

Leif was the only man living in the coven I trusted to some extent. He was deaf, so I knew he was not under Elsa's control. Though as she strummed her pink fingernails on his knee, I realized she did not need a whistle to keep him under her spell.

Foss was there on principle, but he hated every second he was amongst the dangerous females. He kept securing the cotton in his ears, sitting erect on the long couch next to me, waiting for any of the women to make a false move.

I'm not sure how, but I'd convinced Foss that in my culture, the husband was the wife's servant. It was fantastic. He waited on me hand and foot, hating every second of his obeisance. When my stomach growled, he was so well-trained that he got up and brought me a bowl of beef stew that had been served up earlier that evening. "Thanks, Foss." I stirred the thick gravy and spooned out a large carrot chunk that bobbed in the brown.

Everyone debated the next point of interest and the next, but I contented myself with my stew until Jens got riled up by Liv. "I don't care what you say! We can up and leave anytime we like. We'll let Pesta build a portal on earth, and you all can just deal with her setting up camp in your world." There was much uproar to this, cow tails swishing angrily through poked holes in the backs of pants and skirts. "Or you can help us. Lucy's the only one who can destroy the portal. Elsa knows where it is, but we need your help getting there without Pesta intercepting us. Pesta's closing in on us, so we need to get outta Dodge if you're going to keep your house and your life here."

A few women debated until Elsa stood. There was something about her that made everyone shut up. Perhaps it was that she chose her words wisely and didn't waste them on arguing. She wore a knitted floppy cap and a yellow sweater to match. She was tall and curvy, like the other Huldras, but this forty-something with two black braids commanded the room with her authoritative voice like none other. Everyone fell silent as she spoke and signed for her husband. "I'll take Lucy to the portal by myself if I have to. My husband is human, so he can pose as a man trying to make his way through to Be, if the portal's already up and running. You say she might have enough bones without Lucy? That might work to our advantage. Pesta won't be expecting Leif to be against her. He's just another human to her."

A few Huldras hissed at this, and my heart grew for the bickering women. Though they took forever to agree on anything, they were united in their coven. Huldra or human, it was one for all and all for one.

Jens put his hand on his forehead. "No, Elsa. I mean, yes. Thanks for agreeing to take us to the portal, but I don't want to put Leif in danger."

"But you'll put your girlfriend in danger?" Elsa questioned imperiously, squaring her shoulders to Jens, daring him to correct her again. "We stand to lose just as much if Pesta opens a portal on earth. I won't sit back and watch what she did to Undraland happen here. She starts with a little gift, then it turns to a wager. Then it's a little power, and then more. Before you know it, we've got Werewolves, Weretigers and who knows what else." She raised her chin to Jens, who backed down under her determined glare.

"She smoked the Huldras out of Undraland. Who's to say she's not going to do the same thing here? All it takes is the humans learning they might be the victim of mind control, and we've got a witch hunt on our hands." She shook her head and sat back down between her husband and me. "No. Leif can walk your baby doll to the portal just fine."

I really hated her pet name for me. As if I didn't already feel small amongst the giants. She treated me like a toy. Even though I could tell she was on the side of the mission, I didn't look forward to working with her. I took another bite of my stew and shook off her hand that was clutching my knee.

Despite his healthy fear and respect for Elsa, Jens said his piece. "If something happens to Leif, I won't have the wrath of your coven on my head. I got enough problems without that."

Liv laughed – a cackle that sounded like a throaty witch. "Your girlfriend's married to a Fossegrimen. I'd say you're up to your ears in problems, friend." She was perched on the arm of our couch next to Foss's shoulder. He'd stuffed cotton in his ears to fend off being mind-warped, but it did nothing to relax him. Every now and then I noticed Liv brushing her fingers against him "accidentally", and each time, he tensed at the contact and moved his hand further away.

Jens didn't look at me, but Foss sneered, taking one piece of cotton from his ear so he could converse more easily. "Huldras take what they want through trickery. Fossegrimens work for it."

"Fossegrimens can persuade people using their fiddles," one of them countered.

Foss displayed his empty hand and pretended to look under the couch. "Do you see a fiddle on me? No! I bought Lucy. I worked to keep her safe. I'd marry a mule if it would end Pesta, which is pretty much what I did." He nodded to Jens, who was fuming. "Jens took a life oath to watch over her family. You have no idea what he's been through to get her here. You'll not make jokes at our expense."

A fifty-something-year-old Huldra named Gala grinned like a cat who'd just got a new ball to bat around with her long, manicured claws. "One of the four chiefs strutting around our lair. What shall we do with him, ladies?"

Elsa continued her fingernail tapping on Leif's knee. "You'll do nothing, like you always do, Gala dear. You'll be kind to one of the few guests we get around here and take what he's offering you – the chance to kill the siren who took us from our land." Elsa placed her other hand on my knee again, and I stiffened at the touch that was a little too familiar for my taste. Each time I removed it, she waited a minute and went back to the bad habit. It was unsettling. "Baby doll, when do you think you'll be ready to travel?"

"My name's Lucy," I corrected her for the tenth time. Then I shrugged. "On foot? Not for a while. If all I have to do is drive there, hobble up and give the structure a good whack with the rake, I can do that tonight." I looked up at Jens, who was none too happy with Elsa chumming up to me. "To end the wench who killed my parents and give me a chance at a normal life? I can do that, like, yesterday."

Elsa raked her long fingernails from my knee up my thigh, and I batted her hand away again, giving her the stink eye. She looked on me as if sizing me up to see how I would fit into her plan. "It's settled, then. It's a few days' drive if the weather's good to us. Pack, sleep and be ready to go in the morning." She patted my head like I was her kitten.

I cringed. "Knock it off."

Foss came to my aid and pushed Elsa's hand away from me. "You won't touch what's mine," he ordered.

Liv stiffened, while Elsa pinched my thigh and grinned like an evil wizard. "Given your luck, baby doll, I'd ready myself for a blizzard."

20

BASIL CUBBINGTON

Foss got his own room with Liv, who'd been giving him the glad eye all through the meeting. She was none too pleased with me, but I tried not to dwell on the snide comments and superior looks she cast me as she took Foss up to her bed. She'd done the "accidental" slam of her shoulder to mine as she brushed by me, and I rolled my eyes. *Have at it, sister. Good luck with that headache.*

The Huldras were kind of weird with their physical boundaries. Most of them were in their late forties or above, but every single one of them had their hands in my hair at one point or another, braiding it and unbraiding it as it suited them. It would have been sweet if only any of them had spoken to me about it or asked me first. I was the house pet, and I really didn't like it.

Jens linked his fingers through mine as we walked to the room I'd been sharing with Jamie. "Hey," I whispered as we turned down the familiar hallway. "Can we sleep in your room tonight? I'm tired of bunking with Jamie, and you need a good night's sleep. No patrol tonight, okay?"

Jens looked like he wanted to argue, but the bags under his eyes played to my favor. "Yeah, okay. That's probably best."

It was a job, but he helped me hobble up the stairs, knowing I'd hit my limit on people picking me up and carrying me places. We went up to the room he and Foss had been sharing, and I gusted out a breath of relief when the door locked behind us. "I've missed you."

"You sure you don't need your husband here for this?" he joked bitterly.

I limped over to him and rubbed his arm. "Are we really going to do this? Be pissy on our one night together?"

He deflated. "I guess not. Sorry. I just hate all the husband/boyfriend jokes. I hate the whole situation. Having him constantly around you grates on me. His smug face..."

"Oh, whatever. He's just as miserable about it as we are. It's a formality that'll be over once all this is done. He's off with Liv. Let him have his fun." I motioned to myself. "I'm here, and I don't really want to have every moment be with or about Foss."

"You're right." He slapped his hands together to start the conversation afresh. "New topic. How's your leg?"

I shrugged. "You know. It got stabbed by rain gear, so no mountain climbing any time soon."

"I mean do you need your pills?"

I sat on the bed. "It stings a little, but the pills make me sleepy. I kinda don't want to take them yet. Haven't seen you much. You've been avoiding me with work." I was too tired to beat around the bush.

Jens looked like he wanted to say something, but stopped himself. He pulled off his green polo shirt and rubbed his perfect abs. "I'm not avoiding you now."

I reached out and stroked his stomach, constantly amazed at his body no matter how many times I saw it. "You ever gonna tell me what all your scars are from?" I asked, tickling the puckered line that sliced diagonally from his right side down to his navel. I knew that one was from trolls, but he had so many others.

"Nope. It's part of what makes me mysterious."

"Seriously?" I traced a circle around his belly button, loving that he sucked in his stomach at my touch. It was nice to see that I still had an effect on him the way he did on me. "I'll bet you tripped and got yourself on a table or something. High heels are tricky."

He rolled his eyes. "Yes. That's exactly it." He knelt before me and cupped my calf, gently rolling up the hem of my jeans to expose the bandage on my calf to him. "I really hate that you have scars now. Every one of them, my fault."

I was really tired of arguing with him about this, since it seemed to be the reason he avoided me. "Oh yeah? Then what are you gonna do about it?"

His eyebrows furrowed. "I got you here. Had them mind-warp a doctor for you. I'm staying on top of your pain meds. I'm out on patrol all the time."

I shook my head and kissed the wrinkle between the eyebrows I loved to let entertain me with their constant dance. "I mean after Pesta and all this mess. How are you going to make sure we lead a boring life where the only scars I'll get are actually from slipping and catching my side on the edge of a table while wearing high heels?"

"You and that white picket fence." His smirk was genuine, and I'd missed it. There was always a hint of sadness these days that replaced the swagger I'd been longing for.

I looped my arms around his neck and drew him between my legs so there was no space between us for misunderstanding to creep in. "One day when this is all over, I want you to take me away. Like to London or somewhere. I'll change my name to Basil Cubbington or something and we can eat scones and tea at all hours of the day. They've got loads of white picket fences there. I'm sure of it."

"You hate scones." Jens gave me a look that questioned my intelligence. He gave in to our close proximity and kissed me, his thick lips stroking mine and making my heart flutter like a hummingbird. He *hmm'ed* against my mouth, and I felt his shoulders relaxing as he sunk into my body. He kissed my neck and then my collarbone before speaking into my skin. "And Basil's a man's name, you know."

"Is not," I argued, tilting my head back to indulge in the moment.

Jens tipped me back. Conscious of my sore ribs, he laid me carefully on the bed, hovering over me in all of his half-naked hotness. "Is so."

I harrumphed, trying not to let him know I was nervous being so close to him. We hadn't been alone in weeks. "Look, I don't think someone named Jens is fit to lecture me about what is or is not a man's name." I kissed him to stifle his retort, grinning when I felt him rile up and deflate as we satiated our need for attack and comfort. It was our own dance, and we did it well.

When the debate within him grew stronger than the romantic moment, Jens pulled back. "Jens is our version of John! If we were in Sweden right now, it would be pronounced Yens. Totally normal man's name."

I traced my finger down his warm chest. "Well, Yennifer, Basil is a woman's name, and that's what I choose for my fictional life in London. Deal with it."

He kissed me again, fighting me without words as our mouths battled for dominance. "I'm not calling you Basil," he insisted between kisses.

My hands ran down his back, tracing my fingers along the waistline of his jeans. "Then I'm not calling you boyfriend."

He squashed the two inches that separated our bodies and squeezed my hipbone. "I can't decide if I like you when you're like this, or if I really hate it."

I squirmed under him, relishing the feel of his hand on my hip. "You love it. You love me." I nuzzled his nose with mine and then licked him from the tip of his nose to his forehead just to poke the bear.

"Crap. I do love you." He wiped my spit off by burying his face in the crook of my neck. "So in the spirit of loving you, I'm going to take a shower. Not sure how long it's been, and you deserve to sleep next to a clean man."

I lifted up his arm and sniffed his armpit. "I'm guessing two days? Three if your deodorant's worth its salt."

Jens barked out a laugh and sat up, clamping his arms

down. "You're sick! I can't believe you'd subject yourself to that."

"I've faced a farlig. I highly doubt your pits are scarier than that."

Jens kissed me again, and with every one, I could tell he was remembering how good we were together, and that he'd punished himself enough. Now was not the time for separation. It was the time for adoring each other. We made out on the bed for a solid half hour before Jens hopped in the shower for the mere advantage of cooling off.

I hobbled down to the room I'd shared with Jamie, really hoping I wasn't ruining the mood by asking for my pajamas. Britta brought me my overnight bag and insisted on carrying it up to the room for me, lest I hurt my (Jamie's) ribs. My leg was screaming at me, begging me to lie down.

"How are you?" she asked.

"You mean how's Jamie?" I clarified. "We're fine. Sore, but fine. He could probably use a soak in the tub to ease the stiffness in his ribs. We're up for the journey tomorrow, though. Ready to get all this over with." I placed my hand on her shoulder as reality dawned on me. "Do you really think it could be done with by this time next week?"

Britta cupped my face in her hands. "Yes. It's what's getting me through. Soon, sister. Soon."

My leg felt better and my whole body was lighter as I limped into the room Jens was still showering in. I changed into pajamas and made myself comfortable in the bed, smoothing out the cream sheets with peach roses on them and fluffing the matching pillow at my back.

Just as the shower turned off, someone knocked on the door. My head felt light and a little clouded as I opened the door, casting Elsa a dreamy smile as I welcomed her into the room. "What's up?"

"Nothing, baby doll." She patted the top of my head, but I was bordering on loopy, so I didn't suppress my unhappiness properly this time around.

"I'm not a baby doll or a dog," I groused, rubbing the top of my head to show my irritation.

"Jens's baby doll. Foss's dog," she ruled. "Or is it the other way around? Whose puppy are you?"

I growled at her and barked, not sure how better to demonstrate I wouldn't engage with her. "You come here for a reason?" I asked, slurring on the last word. My focus was slipping as exhaustion beat down on me from out of nowhere. I felt like I'd taken the pain medication that was supposed to help me sleep, but I know I hadn't. I'd avoided that pill and took the pain so I could have some quality time with Jens for once.

Elsa sat down on the bed and crossed one knee over the other. "I just wanted to make sure you were all set for the night. I need you well-rested for the trip. It's not an easy one, so I need you sharp."

I snapped my finger and gave her a thumbs up. "Sharp as cheese."

She was mildly entertained by my answer and said as much when Jens entered the room wearing only a towel. His expectant expression fell when he saw we were not alone. *I feel ya, buddy.*

"What do you need, Elsa?"

Elsa pointed up at my glazed-over expression as I

leaned against the wall, the room taking an unfortunate tilt. "Your communal girlfriend's a trip. Or she's on one."

"Oh, no," I murmured, my mouth not opening all the way. "Something's wrong with the floor."

I swooned, and Elsa caught me. "How many pills did you take?" she questioned.

"None-thing." I groaned. "The Jamie has the pain and the too many pills. I'ma leg hurts no more."

Jens and Elsa covered me with a blanket after lowering me in the bed. A few minutes later, and seconds before I passed out, Jens climbed into bed with me.

"I'm in love with you," I murmured. "Your eyebrows and your abs. Yummy."

The look he gave me (from what I could make out through my haze) was filled with meaning and unfathomable emotion. "Lucy, I love you. One day I'll rescue you for real. I'll get you your white picket fence, a real dog that's not a wolf, and an address we never have to move from." He kissed my lips lightly, and my mouth went slack. "Just you and me, Moxie." He held me and kissed my face until I lost my grip on lucidity in the comfort of his arms.

21

OFF-ROADING

"I said I was sorry," Jamie explained again as he hobbled into the van. His two sweaters and winter jacket did not keep him from shivering. It was cold for me, so I couldn't imagine how the newbie Undrans were handling the bone chill. "I didn't think about the bond. My leg was killing me, which means it was killing you, and you just let us be in pain."

"Next time you have to give me a heads up. What if I'd been driving?"

"Again, I'm sorry. You know, toughing it out only hurts us both. Next time you're in pain, talk to me at least, since your pain literally affects me."

"Gotcha." I looked around as Jens boosted me into the middle bench. "Where's Foss? I thought for sure he would've beaten us down here."

Jens smirked as Foss emerged from the house with his hand on the small of Liv's back. "I think you may have lost your shadow, Loos." He wrapped a thick comforter around his shivering sister and handed Jamie a flowery blanket.

"Fine by me. Just be on time, is all I ask." I noticed Foss's pupils were dilated. When he passed by me, his cold hand squeezed mine. "No way. I'm not traveling with Foss if he's been possessed by one of them. Next thing I know, he's yanking on the wheel and pushing us off a cliff."

Jens nodded up to Elsa, who was in the driver's seat. "Fair point. Trust is pretty thin as it is. Foss, heft it into the second van."

The caravan was two vans long. One was full of us, plus Leif and Elsa, and the other was packed with Huldras.

Foss grumbled, but obeyed, following Liv to the second van.

Jens sat in the backseat and stretched, enjoying the luxury of the extra space. "That leg of yours looks like it needs to be elevated, Mox. Come back here and prop it up on the seat." He patted the spot next to him with a sly grin.

I hobbled back and kissed him. "You must be feeling pretty good about yourself, getting rid of Foss and securing us this make-out bench."

"You know? I am. You were right, I needed a full night of sleep. It's been a while." His arm went around me as he wrapped us in the third comforter, and we felt like us. The good us, not the bickering version.

I kissed him, snuggling into his side as we enjoyed the intimacy of sharing a blanket on a freezing winter day. "Say it again. Tell me who was right."

"You were, college girl." His lips stroked mine, and I nearly forgot we were not in a private room together. "This car ride could never be long enough, now that we're arranged like this."

"Too bad there's no partition," I whispered, cozying myself in his arms.

Jens wiggled his fingers with purpose, as if gearing up to pull a rabbit out of his hat. "What would you do if you were invisible?" he rasped low in my ear.

The genius of Jens's invisibility kept us occupied for a good hour under the blanket before Jamie got irritated. "You know I can't always shut you out of my mind, right?"

We smartened up when we reentered reality and looked around to find we were driving straight into a snow storm. The drifts were already piled up several feet on the sides of the freeway. The white fluff was whipping at the windshield, creating a narrow field of vision that made everyone nervous. Elsa was clenching the steering wheel like she wanted to choke it, and Leif was biting his lower lip.

Jens and I put our seatbelts on when a huge gust shook the van, veering the vehicle off the road slightly. Elsa managed to get us back on track, but the crash behind us choked a cry from my throat. I turned around and saw between the white blurs the second van smashed against the steel wall of the freeway, the entire front end crumpled like cheap foil. "They crashed! Stop the car!" I yelled to Elsa.

She pulled over too slow for my liking. My heart pounded as I ripped the seatbelt off me and made for the door.

Jens placed his hand on my shoulder. "I got it. You're barely upright. You guys stay in here. I'll get them out. Just make as much room as you can for them, alright? Their car ain't going nowhere."

Jens hopped out of the van in his snow boots and proper winter attire with Leif and Elsa. I could tell Jamie wanted to help, but the cold and his many injuries kept him in his seat. "Lucy, come sit up here with us. Let's try to give them the back."

How we were going to fit six Undrans in the back, I'll never know. I obeyed, aiming for the floor, but Britta scooted onto Jamie's lap to make room for me and Jens.

One by one, banged, dazed and frozen Huldras and their mates made their way to our car. I was in charge of letting them in, while Britta and Jamie tried not to freeze. They huddled together and shivered as a single unit. It would have been sweet, could I not feel his pain at the chill through the bond.

Inga was a darker-skinned Huldra I wasn't too familiar with, but when she came to the car on Leif's arm, my heart went out to her. She had a cut on her arm from a shattered window and was crying as I helped her inside. "I'll take a look at it once we're all settled," I promised. "Liv, could you find the green bag in the trunk? It's got my first aid kit in it."

Liv had none of her previous swagger and obeyed immediately, producing said bag a few minutes later. "It was Pesta's Mouthpiece," she choked out through her tears. "Had to be. The car was gunning straight for us."

"Well, then we should get out of here right quick." I fished through my bag and called out commands, grateful no one argued with me in their stunned state. "Liv, make room in the trunk for me and Jens. Pile up the bags on one side so we don't sit on them. There's just no room for Foss in here." I pulled out my small first aid kit and hoped there was enough antiseptic in there to help everyone who needed it. "Inga, take your coat off and give me your arm." I looked to her husband, whose lap she was sitting on and nodded. "I forget your name."

"Reg," he reminded me in his deep timbre.

"Right. Hold her arm so it doesn't move around."

He nodded. Inga had help getting her coat off, but her thermal shirt was touching the wound. "Reg, it's real deep!"

I held up my hands as she whimpered. "I got it. Close your eyes and think of England."

"What?" she asked, then she howled as I ripped the shirt off the caking blood. The gash was far bigger than I anticipated, but I tried to keep my voice light to avoid her freaking out. There was still a shard of the window embedded in her dermis. Her human husband (who kinda looked like an older version of Usher) covered her eyes with his palm and held her still as I wedged it out, singing "Come On, Get Happy" by the Partridge Family to cover over my nerves. The blood was coagulating in spots, but not enough for me to feel comfortable sewing her up just yet. I tried not to barf when she shivered and a whole mess of red and pus oozed out near her elbow.

Reg cooed soothing words to her while the freaking out around us ensued. I finally managed to clean, sew and bandage her wound, and her husband made quick work of warming her up.

"Is anyone else hurt?"

A couple complained of whiplash, a few had bumped their heads, and all were sore, but no one seemed terribly beyond repair. Thank goodness we had only been crawling along at a few miles per hour. The cold descended upon us, so Elsa started up the van when she hopped back into the driver's seat.

Foss, Leif and Jens were still not back, and I began to worry. "Elsa, what's taking the guys?"

I looked up toward the front and realized Elsa had tears streaming down her face. She shook her head, and my heart dropped into my stomach.

"Everyone, pile up and make room." I turned and spoke low to Elsa. "Is Foss very hurt? What does he need?"

Elsa wiped an icy tear away and sniffled her response. "His head was bleeding pretty badly. He was unconscious when I came back here. I think it was his head that broke the window."

I was sweating and freezing all at once, my adrenaline kicking into high gear. "Change of plans. Liv, grab as many bags as you can and shove them under seats. I mean it. I need the trunk as cleared out as we can get it." I gripped the handle and slid the door open, introducing ice and buckets of snow to the car. "Bundle up, kids. I'll be back."

2 2

STAYING ALIVE

*L*eif and Jens were trying to extract Foss from the van to no avail. He was large, which was one problem, but every time they tried to move his head, it started bleeding. Then they would release him to reposition, and the blood would freeze to the door. It was a vicious cycle, and both were too crazed on adrenaline to really see the problem.

I climbed into the second van and placed my hand on Leif's shoulder. "Get the bags," I said, motioning to the trunk. "I got him."

Leif nodded, knowing he had reached the pinnacle of his usefulness, and was starting to freeze over.

"Lucy, get back in the other van!" Jens barked. "You don't need to see this." He tried to edge Foss's head off the wall, but as soon as the blood flowed, it froze him more to the steel of the car through the broken window.

I ignored Jens and climbed as gracefully as I could to

Foss's head. I used my hot breath to add a little warmth to the frozen area, ready with my coat sleeve to catch any blood that oozed out as I pried his cranium off the steel. Inch by inch, it worked.

Jens let out a cry of relief when Foss's head detached from the iced-over car. "Careful, now," I warned, holding my glove up to him. "Watch his neck."

Jens dragged Foss gently while I positioned his head for optimum damage control. Leif finished with the bags and offered his assistance in getting Foss into the trunk, where I climbed in atop him.

Leif shut the two of us inside while he and Jens boarded the van. Elsa had no use for her rearview mirror as she drove at the pace of a snail. Everyone and everything was stacked to the brim.

They passed me my kit, but I was at a loss. The skin on the left top part of his scalp was partly missing and partly crystallized from the icy weather. There was no making sense of his head wound at my level of inexpertise. "Hospital!" I commanded. "And crank up that heat, girl. I can't get him warm."

Jamie's blanket was passed back while Jens Googled different head wounds and how to treat them. Shockingly, none that matched Foss's came up. He was unconscious, and I was in full-on panic mode. I straddled his torso, moving the bags so they were up against the trunk door for added insulation from the cold. "I need another blanket!" I sobbed when his skin was still ice on my wrist. I ripped off my gloves and felt for his pulse.

There was nothing.

My fingers were nearly numb, so I used the back of my hand instead after wrapping the second blanket around him, making sure not to move his spine.

Nothing.

"I need someone with warm fingers!" I cried, tears streaming down my face as I began CPR.

Not Foss. Not Foss. Not Foss.

"What's going on, Loos? How is he?" Jens asked, breathless from his rescue mission.

Gala offered her hand that at least had sensation still in it to feel for Foss's pulse. She shook her head. "I can't feel anything."

"No pulse!" I beat the rhythm of *Staying Alive* into Foss's sternum, crying and begging him to wake up. "Please, Foss! Open your eyes, you stubborn jerk! The one thing I ask of you! Please!" I screamed, and then I paused my rant to breathe into his mouth as I pinched his nose.

My fingers were ice, but they worked feverishly. "I told you I didn't want you here! I said you wouldn't survive in my world, but I didn't mean this! Grow a heart, you ass!" I pumped into his chest, but still felt nothing.

For six minutes, I worked on him, sobbing when Jens coaxed me with tears in his voice to let him go.

"No!" I screamed. "I can fix this! I can fix him. Just get us to the hospital!" I begged, pumping and puffing in my steady rhythm.

"We're not too far, Lucy," Elsa called back. I could tell that she was crying, too.

I gave up trying to feel for Foss's pulse. Gala tried again and again, but found nothing. "Your hands are still too cold," I reasoned. "It's there. I know it's there!" My tears splashed down onto Foss's chest. "I would feel it if he was dead."

Not Foss. Not Foss. Not Foss.

Jens, Jamie and Britta were silent out of respect for what they assumed was Foss's passing. The others did their best to look away and give me my moment of insanity as I tried desperately to birth a heart inside a man who never had one to begin with. It was my constant battle with him, and I was not ready to lose just yet.

I pumped and breathed and pumped and breathed until Elsa pulled into the emergency entrance of the hospital. Jens trotted out in a manner too slow to be urgent, but I kept my pace. My arms weary, but determined.

When Jens opened the trunk, bags fell out, but I held my rhythm. "Keep doing CPR!" I commanded the medics, stumbling out after them. I hobbled behind the gurney as we flew inside.

One of the nurses held up her hand to me as Foss was taken to a partition with paddles. "Family only," she insisted.

Without hesitation, I pushed past her and shouted, "He's my husband!" My heart pounded and my ribs felt like they might burst. I watched in horror when Foss's enormous chest jumped off the gurney when the paddles jolted electricity through him.

In the movies, I recall there being three or four zaps before the heart started beating again. I think Foss knew that my nerves could only take one burst.

His heart beat on the monitors, and I exhaled, light-headed from all the CPR.

My adrenaline ebbed as a cry of relief burst out of me,

and I passed right the smack out in the middle of the emergency room.

23

JAMIE'S SLEEPING BAG

*I*f you ever decide to pass out, I recommend doing it in a hospital. That is, unless you're supposed to be dead and flying under the radar.

I awoke several hours later in the van, which was chugging along at a labored pace, due to the incessant weather beating down on us. I opened my eyes and saw that I was in the empty trunk of the van, snuggled up next to Jamie, who was on his back staring up at the roof of the car in the blue sub-zero sleeping bag we shared. My mouth was dry and tasted funny, like I'd alternated sucking on pieces of metal and cotton. I sat up, but my whole body was cross with me over the tiniest movement. My hand was on Jamie's chest; I'd been cuddling him during my nap. It felt weird and a little dirty.

"Britt?" I called.

Britta turned around. "She's awake! Pull over."

"I'm not stopping for nothing," Jens answered. "Hey, babe. How are you feeling?"

I sat up, casting Jamie an apologetic look for cozying up to him. He sat up next to me and rubbed my back. "How long was she out?" he asked Britta.

"Six hours. That was some powerful venom, if I do say so myself." Britta grinned deviously.

Jamie smiled, cracking his neck to the side. "I've never been poisoned by you before. I don't think I'll try it again anytime soon."

"Huh?" I turned to him, our faces just inches from each other since we were tucked into the same sleeping bag. "Britta poisoned you?" Then it dawned on me. "She poisoned me?" When Britta looked unrepentant, my mouth hung open in utter flabbergast. "Why? Why would you do something like that?"

Jamie patted my back in a half-hug. "We had to. You never would've agreed to leave Foss in the hospital."

My nose crinkled in disgust. "Leave Foss?" I slipped out of the sleeping bag and looked around the van that had far fewer bodies and bags in it than when I saw it last. "How could you do that? You left him? I… but he… he has no idea what he's doing here! He'll get himself arrested for sure. Turn around, Jens. Turn around!" I shouted up to the driver.

Jens didn't even flinch. "Sorry, Mox. We've got a lot of road to cover, and Pesta's gunning for you. I shouldn't have even let you set foot in that hospital. She'll be checking that place out for sure after running us off the road like she did. I mean, like her Mouthpiece did."

"Tonya," I spat. "You can say her name."

Jens took on a more adult tone. "She's not Tonya anymore, Loos. I don't know how long she's been Pesta's

Mouthpiece, but Pesta feeds on her puppet's memories and keeps the body functional so her soul can wear the skin and be the person convincingly. When Pesta's done, her soul leaves the body, and they're always dead."

I put my hands over my ears and shouted, "I'm not trying to hear that! She's my best friend. Don't talk about her like she's not even alive!"

"She's not alive," Jens responded.

Stupidly.

It bears mentioning that Jens responded *stupidly*, and therefore deserved what he got.

I lunged toward him, ready to hurdle myself over the seat, but Jamie dragged me back down to the sleeping bag. "Have some sense, Jens," he chided his best friend. "It's alright, Lucy. Best not to think about that right now. We're safe, and there's been no sign of the Mouthpiece since the accident." He rubbed my back as I scowled at his kindness like a child. "Foss is still at the hospital. Most of the Huldras that wanted to accompany us jumped ship after the crash. They didn't realize what they were getting themselves into." He motioned up toward the middle bench of the van. "We've got Elsa and Leif, so we're good. They're the best ones anyway."

"I can't believe you left him alone. Was he even alive? Did you think to check? You just abandoned him!"

Jamie's back was against the side of the trunk, but there was not really room for the both of us to sit side by side comfortably. He moved me to sit on his lap and brought the sleeping bag up around us, unzipping it like a blanket. "Now, now. Of course we didn't abandon him. Foss was being taken to surgery when you fainted. He's alive, but they have to do significant repair to his head."

I wanted to take the hand Jamie was rubbing my back with and slap him with it. He sensed this either through the bond or through common sense and removed his hand. "You left him to go through surgery by himself?" I growled through gritted teeth.

"Foss is one of us, but he's injured, Lucy. We can't stop the mission, and we can't leave him alone, of course. Liv and most of the Huldras stayed with him. Not many places safer than with a team of Huldras protecting you. He'll get the best treatment and wake up to friendly faces."

"But he'll think I..."

"He'll be grateful to you he can think at all. You saved his life, Loos." Jens spoke up from the driver's seat. "The doctor said your CPR kept his heart moving just enough to keep his brain from crapping out altogether."

My voice came out a quiet squeak as the snow beat against the van. "How can we know he's okay?"

Jens waved his hand like it was all no big deal. "He'll catch up when he's a hundred percent. And by then, hopefully we'll already have destroyed the portal. Who knows? Maybe they'll give your Scarecrow a fresh brain while we're away, Dorothy."

"You shouldn't have poisoned me," I lectured Britta, searching for a reason to hold onto my anger.

"I'm sorry," Britta lied, doing her best to appear contrite.

Elsa and Leif occupied the middle bench. Elsa called to me over her shoulder. "Liv'll take good care of your hubby, baby doll," she assured me.

"My name is Lucy!" I shouted at her, pissed she couldn't ever just call me by my name, and that my fake marriage was yet again being thrown in my face. "And don't call Foss my husband. I'm a terrible wife. What kind of woman would just leave her husband to go through surgery by himself?" I buried my face in my hands.

Elsa's voice was hesitant, as if answering an obvious question to an idiot. "Um, the drugged kind? It's not as if we gave you a choice. And I'll call you whatever I wish. If you don't like baby doll, I can call you Mrs. Tribeswoman."

"Baby doll's fine," I groused.

Jamie brought me to his chest in a gentle hug I felt guilty for finding comfort in. He felt my internal debate and smiled paternally down at me. "Here, why don't we try invisible for a bit? Have a little chat." His hand on my back served as an invisibility conductor, vanishing us both into our own private world.

I pondered briefly the pros and cons of being laplanded to Jamie, and knew at some point I'd have to make my peace with someone being in my head and near me all the time.

We can disappear and talk privately whenever you like. Isn't this nice? he asked, tapping into my thoughts.

I guess so, I admitted, the awkwardness at being so close with him faded as I adjusted to our strange reality. The trunk wasn't a bad place to have a little pow-wow. *I don't like that we just left Foss. He risked his life to put himself back in the mission, and we just ditch him? Feels off.*

Foss will be fine. Liv said she would call Elsa once they know he's on the road to recovery.

I thought he was dead, I admitted, tears springing to my

eyes. I buried my face in Jamie's broad chest to keep my emotions under wraps. *I was so scared he... he...*

Jamie's arms enveloped me in the warmest hug. In our quiet, cold cave, I could feel the platonic affection he had for me. It was nice. Like having a much older brother.

Jamie smiled at the comfortable label he fished out of my jumbled thoughts. *Liten syster, you saved him.*

Could you be my brother? I feel like I need it. Plus, we have to have a reason we're always together and not, you know, together.

Britta will be my wife, and you're with her brother, so in a way, that does make you my sister. Jamie held my hand, weaving his fingers through mine. *My sister in Tonttu never had much time or patience for me. I should like to have had a sister like you. Would've made the palace more enjoyable.*

I'd be good in a palace, I thought to him. *We'd pay your dad back for being a foul smackhole right quick. I've got loads of tricks up my sleeve. I can't imagine them treating you like a second-class citizen.* I rubbed his tummy like he was a pregnant woman. *I won't do that to you.*

I know. And Foss knows of your love for him.

I swallowed and allowed Jamie's words to settle without a debate. *Wow, you're turning me into a big, giant mess back here. We should probably rejoin humanity before I start bawling even more.*

Take as much time as you need.

The very second the tears passed, I removed myself from Jamie and kicked him out of the trunk so he could put his arms around his girlfriend. I craved the solitude of the trunk and crept back into the sleeping bag, napping to avoid conversation and the dread of what was to come.

24

THE MAGIC OF HEADLIGHTS

*J*ens tapped out when the traffic started to thicken around the middle of the evening. "I can't drive anymore. My eyes are going cross, and the lines are all running together. Let's get a hotel."

I'd been awake for a while, but had kept to myself in the trunk. "I got it," I volunteered.

Jens shook his head as he pulled off the freeway. "No. Let's get something to eat and get a good night's rest."

"I'm rested," I argued, flipping my leg over the backseat between Jamie and Britta. "Find a drive-thru and let me take a crack at it."

"But the sun's going down." Jens looked as tired as he sounded. He had bags under his eyes and his smile was forced.

"Behold, the magic of headlights. I've got news for you all. I'm a better driver than everyone here, except maybe Leif. We were born into this world. As much as you all

159

picked up from being sent here, I can hold my own just fine. Believe it or not, I can even drive a car at night."

"Alright, Mox," Jens said, pulling into a mediocre fast food chain I had not often frequented in my travels. "Shout out what you want, otherwise it's burgers all around."

Jamie ordered Gar and roast duck, which was, well, adorable. His face soured when he bit into the atrocity that was this chain's excuse for a burger. "Oh, this is awful, Lucy. Is this really what your food tastes like?"

"The low-brow stuff," I explained, buckling myself into the driver's seat. The snowstorm was daunting, and I wondered for a second if it wouldn't be wiser to turn in for the night as Jens suggested. "I'll make you all a giant Thanksgiving dinner when this is all over. You can even slaughter the turkey if that makes you feel more at home here."

"Give me a real challenge," Jamie scoffed, his arm around his fiancée.

Jens was settled in the reclined passenger's seat with a comforter draped over him. "You're totally precious right now," I told him, earning a true smile from his perfect lips. "You should always dress in patterns with roses on them."

He glanced down at the girly comforter and snuggled it closer. "Only real men can rock roses." He held up his fist with his little finger and pointer sticking up in an imitation of a true rock and roller. "I miss your Thanksgiving dinners. You and your mom could whip magic out of cans. I don't know how you did it, but your mashed potatoes tasted incredible, like nothing else on earth. She always shooed me out of the house so I wouldn't steal her secret."

I swallowed as I remembered my mom and me dancing

around the kitchen as we listened to Ella Fitzgerald and Billie Holiday. She had a thing with the female greats and Thanksgiving. One year Linus rebelled and blasted Kid Rock (I know. I take no responsibility for his taste in music) while we were cooking, and Mom responded by duct taping his iPod to the oven and threatening to cook it with the bird if he didn't knock it off.

My mom was cool.

I reached over and kissed Jens after I situated the seat and mirrors to the reach of a normal person. "If we get outta this alive, I'll teach you how to make those potatoes myself."

"But if we don't live through this, no potatoes?" he clarified. "Then that settles it. Pesta's going down. I wasn't properly motivated before. Those are some high stakes, Mox."

"Get some sleep," I told them all. "When you wake up, we'll be halfway there."

My voice was light, but my fingers gripped the wheel as I pulled out onto the main road. Sure, driving through the night was no big thing. My family did it all the time when we relocated with no warning. I wasn't worried about falling asleep. I was concerned about the weather hazards, sure, but more troublesome was Tonya gunning for me in her SUV. Tired as they all were, I wasn't willing to stop until we reached our destination and tore down that portal.

25

CALM BEFORE THE STORM

*E*lsa wrestled the wheel away from me around noon the next day when they were all begging for a bathroom break. I wasn't trying to be a tyrant, but my father's words flowed out of me faster than I could stop them. "We'll get there when I say we're there, so either go back to sleep or think up solutions to end world hunger in your head. I'm driving." My dad was a cute old grump. That's about the time Linus would start popping his gum. The calm before the storm.

Jens sniggered at my tone. My wince at sounding like my father had not gone unnoticed by him. "Sure thing, Rolf."

When we pulled over at a rest stop, I was on high alert. The snow was several feet deep off the parking lot, but I knew Canada had elk, which could easily become Were-elk in a jiff. "Get back in the car as soon as you can, guys. I'll fill her up."

Even filling up the gas tank was rife with tension. The

usual truckers and a smattering of families were at the rest stop gas station, but I was looking for Tonya's face alone. I was getting paranoid and the drive had made me jumpy, but I was dealing. I got the biggest coffee they offered, and then a whole smackload of cream and sugar because, let's face it, coffee's disgusting. It's a necessity, and I needed it.

When everyone piled into the car, Elsa and Jens shook their heads at me when I commandeered the driver's seat. "My turn, baby doll," Elsa insisted, gloved hand extended for the keys.

"I'm good. I've got another couple hours in me, at least." I opened the driver's side door, but Jens kifed the keys from my hand. "Hey! I said I'm fine. Got me some coffee, and I'm wired anyway."

"We're taking turns. You can't drive half-cocked, Mox. You'll get us all killed."

I blew on my coffee and wished they didn't serve it so scalding, you couldn't drink it for half an hour. I needed to be awake now. "Elsa, I love ya like the crazy aunt I never had or loved, but you drive too slow. We're trying to beat Tonya there, or at the very least, outrun her. She's gunning for us, so we can't slow down."

Elsa nodded. "I'll go as fast as the weather will let me."

"Sorry, not fast enough." I grabbed at the keys in Jens's hand, but he tossed them over my head to Leif, who slid into the driver's seat and started up the car. "Hey!"

Elsa nodded to her husband. "We'll take the next shift. You two get some rest. You sped through the night and most of the day. You shaved five hours off our drive time. Well done, baby doll. We should get there later tonight, which means you'll need to be well-rested." She held up her hands to stave off my protest. "And Leif's a far more reck-less driver than me. He'll get us there in no time."

Jens went around to the trunk and moved our bags to the middle of the car, spreading the sleeping bag out on the floor of the trunk so the feet stretched under the backseat like a little hidden bed underfoot. "Get in," he said to me.

There's something about the sexy way the man you love tells you to get into bed with him when you're dog tired that makes you swallow the "shove it" you had all stored up. With my coat and boots still on, I crawled into the sleeping bag with Jens, loving the closeness the small cocoon forced us to share. Our legs were tangled and he smelled like pine and sugar cookies, which was never a bad thing. I was in his arms, and as the van hurtled down the freeway at a speed I could not complain about, I was asleep in seconds.

I'm not sure how long later it was that the van swerved, but holy crap, it did. It had to have been some amount of time, because I had to wipe my drool off Jens's arm when I tried to reassemble my bearings.

Leif was crying out, but I couldn't understand him. Seatbelts were buckling furiously, but Jens and I were still under the seat in our bag.

Jens moved his bicep atop me and caged me in, using his body as a shield for any bumps that were bound to happen. His face was serious and calculating, which made me afraid. I clung to him to protect him from being flung about and hurting his back on the seat if the car went over any large bumps.

We swerved again, and Elsa screamed. "She found us! Hang on! We can make it over the bridge! We can make it!"

Jens reached around for his red backpack and slipped it over his arms as I slid out of the sleeping bag and into the trunk.

I'm sure Jens's intention was to get us to the seatbelts. I'm sure he had a well thought-out plan. None of that mattered when the vehicle giving chase crashed into ours.

GUNNING FOR THE PORTAL

a freeze like I'd never experienced hit me when the trunk popped open and I fell out the back with the luggage. I didn't see much, but the horror and the loss on Jens's face stayed with me as I hurtled through the widely spaced rungs on the bridge, flew through the air and splashed through the ice below.

Ice. Pure arctic ice pierced me. Every pore on my body closed in protest, screaming at me in hatred and panic. I didn't dare open my eyes, lest they freeze. I fought my way to the top, my head cutting through the surface seconds before the water froze over and sealed me in. Jamie was shouting in my head, panicking enough for the both of us. He'd never experienced cold like this before.

Polar Bear Clubs. Ice fishing. Crazy frat initiations. All those people survived getting dunked in frozen water, and so would I. Nik would have known what to do.

I clawed at the ice, using my nails to grip the slick surface. I screamed, I'm not sure to what end, but the sound was good to my soul. I was still alive, and for now, that was a good thing. I clawed harder, hefting my leg up and finally breaking the surface with my knee.

Something was wrong with my other leg, but I was too cold to feel it. Small blessings.

Somehow, someway I rolled onto the ice that was just merciful enough to hold me without breaking. Every breath was excruciating, the ice permeating my lungs and every organ I needed to survive. I would freeze if I didn't move, but my leg was pretty useless, so I just concentrated on breathing.

I looked above me and saw the van on the bridge with a black SUV. Heads popped over the side to peer down at me, and I gasped when I saw Tonya smile in that evil way she did when she was about to go flirt with a hot guy who had no idea he was about to be taken down by her charm.

Only she didn't arm herself with charm this time.

She had a gun.

KILLED ME FIRST

*M*an Friend and Jens were at loggerheads with each other until Jens threw him off the bridge a little ways from me. Dude plunged right through the ice, but didn't have the wherewithal to fight to the surface.

The ice began to splinter, terrifying me to my very soul. I scrambled toward the shore, my ears ringing when a bullet burst from Tonya's gun in my direction.

My left leg was useless, so I dragged it behind me as I crawled. I heard a scuffle above, and I could only hope someone was wrestling the gun away from my BFF.

I dug my elbows into the ice in an army crawl that was not terribly effective, given my broken and frozen state.

When the second bullet zipped by my head, I let out a loud sob and hurried as best I could, my pathetic pace just above a toddler's.

Impossibly, I reached the shore under the bridge and hid there, catching what little breath I could. I still couldn't tell you how I made it without falling through again or getting shot. I can only attribute my survival to luck, adrenaline and whoever deflected Tonya's attention. When I reached the snow bank, I collapsed behind a small tundra, letting it shelter me from the wind and from sight.

My heave of relief was short-lived. I saw Tonya running toward the water, having escaped the fight on the bridge. The smile on her face was now contorted to irritation, and her shoulder was bleeding. "I know you didn't fall through again!" she called out to me. Then her tone turned playful. "You can't hide from me, Little L."

In the early months after my family died, I was understandably in a bad place. There was no gravesite to go visit, no roses to hang. Tonya insisted on getting me out of the apartment, so she brought me to a cemetery one Sunday morning. She had stayed up all night finding two grave markers with the names "Hilda" and "Ralph" on them. My dad's name was Rolf, but it was the next best thing. She couldn't find a Linus, if you can believe it. The two graves belonged to a family plot in a sea of Johnsons, but the intention was clear. I was to say goodbye to my parents, and she was to talk their ears off about me.

For hours we sat on the two stones as Tonya talked. She said all the things I couldn't in my months of uninterrupted silence. She asked my parents if they were in a better place. She told them stories about me, even admitting to our short scandal of sneaking into Danny's club a few times. She begged them to say something, to do something to let me know that I had to stay alive and try to make a life for myself. She promised them she would never leave me, and that even though I gave up on life, she would never give up on mine.

That was the first day I spoke. It wasn't so much speaking as it was audible babbling and bawling. Tonya had held me, and that Sunday, we started to move forward. Not move on, but move forward. It was the best I could do, and some days, even that still feels impossible.

As Tonya crept along the shore calling out my name in a playful manner, my heart froze over. There was no trace of my best friend there anymore. Tonya wouldn't have tolerated a fly bothering me for too long, much less try to kill me. I slunk down in the bramble and snow as she neared the place I lay in wait.

So attuned to her every movement was I that I didn't even need sight to feel her coming toward me. My leg was a handicap, for certain, but I didn't intend on using it for long.

Four more steps.

Three.

I sat up and lunged for her, kicking off the ground with my good leg and tackling her around the knees. The gun went off, but missed, hitting the underside of the bridge instead.

We screamed in unison. It would be the last thing we did together.

My hands were seasoned from climbing mountains and fighting off Sleipnir, bears and the Nøkkendalig. Pesta was ruthless, but Tonya had no skill at such things. If I guessed correctly, she had probably failed weightlifting class. I grabbed the gun and wrestled her for it, knocking us over into the snowdrifts. We rolled and grunted as we fought for what the other threatened to take from us. I fought for life, and she fought for souls.

"Lucy, don't hurt me! I'm still in here!" she shrieked. "Save me!"

I paled, but kept up my fight, punching her in the face with my free hand to show her I didn't believe a word of it.

Tonya cackled out a laugh and spat blood in my face. "Your little friend begged like a whore for me to take away her pain."

Foss's voice was in my head, egging me on and pushing me to be bigger, to fight harder, and never to let the other side gain the upper hand. I rolled Tonya in the snow so I was on top as we struggled for the gun. I was relentless in my fight as my free hand clawed at her face, drawing fresh blood.

We began to slip in the snow, so I angled us toward the ice, inching her tight, spindly curls toward the hard surface.

It was a leap of faith (or insanity, depending on if it worked or not), and I took it. I exhaled, and then released my grip on the gun, using both of my hands to slide her forward onto the ice. As she gripped the gun, I punched her skull down hard, cracking the surface of the ice just enough to give her a good scare.

Then I snatched the gun straight outta her freezing hands. Before a merciful thought could enter my brain, I turned it on her, aimed and pulled the trigger.

The bullet exploded out from the gun and embedded itself into Tonya's chest.

We both froze as I sobbed, apologetic and completely

devoid of triumph. There was no victory here. No matter who was alive now, Pesta had won this battle.

Tonya gasped and gurgled, as shocked as I that I was capable of such cold-blooded murder.

"You killed my family!" I raged, not even sure if she could hear me anymore. "You should've killed me first!"

Impossibly, she reached for me again in a last ditch effort to drag me under with her. I screamed, aimed and blasted another bullet straight into her head, right through her open mouth.

One red shoe, then one black shoe sank down into the water as the ice closed over top of Tonya's bloody, rigid corpse.

DOCTORS WITH DILATED PUPILS

*J*ens.

Britta crying, saying... something.

Water hitting my skin like pinpricks.

Warmth. Heat turning my skin red.

Then pain. Oh, the pain. Agony ripped through me as sensation hit my body in crushing waves. My voice found lucidity first, and I shouted out, reaching for the source of the unnatural tear.

My left leg was in agony. I was in a double-sized Jacuzzi tub with... Jamie?

How the smack did I get here?

I looked down, relieved that I had my clothes on. My jacket had been torn off, but my shirt and jeans were enough to give reason to the chaos.

When Jens's stricken face entered my narrow field of vision, I grabbed him like a drunkard. "My leg! It's broken or something. It hurts so bad!"

"On it," Jamie assured me in a voice that was pinched

with pain. He reached out and gripped my arm as we endured the agony together. He was chugging straight vinegar from a restaurant-sized jug as if our lives depended on it. He was shivering, as I was, but his where-withal was better than mine. Perhaps he had been awake longer than I had been, and therefore, had more time to process the shock of it all. Perhaps Jamie was just tougher than me. Perhaps it was because he hadn't just murdered his best friend in cold blood.

Jens hugged me, getting his elbows and chest wet without pause. "Elsa's whistling us a doctor right now. Hold on, babe." He held me together as I gritted my teeth through the pain. Each shiver jolted thunder and heat through my leg, but they could not be helped. "Get lower," Jens advised, shifting me further down so the water was up to my shoulders. He cupped the hot water and laved it over my face and hair.

This was not how I pictured having a bath with my boyfriend. Nothing about my life was how I pictured it. The devastation of my reality was crushing. I sobbed in his arms as I wiped water from my lashes. "I killed her!" I confessed, clinging to Jens as if he was my only chance at sanity and absolution. "I killed my best Tonya!"

Jens nodded, trying to meet my gaze and make me focus. I felt so guilty, my eyes only stayed trained on his face a few seconds before drifting off. "Tonya was dead long before she found us. It was just a shell you killed, and Pesta gave you no choice."

"Martin Luther King would've found a way! I'm nothing like who I wanted to be! I kill everyone I love!"

Jens squeezed me, his stubble-covered cheek mushing

to mine as he tried to keep me in one functioning piece. "That's not true. It's just not. Pesta killed Tonya."

I pushed at him, a wave of alcohol-like vinegar crushing my motor skills in one heavy-handed blow. "Run away," I whispered. "I love you. I can't be the one to kill you. Save y-yourslelf." My slur didn't deter him, and neither did my attempt at breaking up with him. I giggled out of nowhere. "Jamie's got big jugs." I motioned to the vinegar, giving us both a moment of ADD to detract from the horror that never seemed to leave us alone.

Jens was a good man. He simply held me through my crazy haze, and said nothing as I sobbed through my self-loathing. Jens kissed my cheek and kept scooping more warm water onto my face until I passed out in his arms.

There are many things to be said for having a good man watch your back when gunfire rains down on your life. Jens, despite his flaws and mine, managed to find a way to love me with his strength and grace. He held me while I floated in my painless oblivion, crying into my neck until help came for me.

Stretchers.

Doctors with dilated pupils.

Jamie and I going into the hospital in tandem.

Through it all, Jens.

Britta and Jens stayed with us, waiting anxiously until we were brought to recovery rooms.

When I awoke from my morphine vacation, Jens.

"Hey, Mox," he whispered. It was the sweetest sound, that man. He put his finger to his lips and motioned to the bed next to me, where Britta was passed out in her chair and bent over a zonked-out Jamie. "How're you feeling?"

My mouth was dry, like I'd been munching on a ball of yarn.

Instinctually or through years of practice and study, Jens knew me. Before I could say a thing, he wrapped my fingers around a cup of water and was helping me sit up so I could drink. His hand was rubbing feeling into my back, and he leaned me against him to support my weight.

No matter what we'd gone through, or the amazing amounts of unexpected and self-inflicted stupidity that would befall us, I knew more than ever that we would get through it together.

"I love you," I whispered, silent emotion choking me up. "I love you, Jens. I love you."

I can't count the number of times I said it, or the number of times he kissed me, but numbering the stars in the sky always seemed a little pointless to me.

Jens was my star. My constellation. No matter where I was, I knew he wouldn't have to find me – he would already be there by my side. Not because he had to, but because he wanted to. He cherished me, and I loved him.

29

FOSS WITH A GUN

*W*e were on our way the very next day. Once Jamie and I had rested and been given the bare minimum of all clear from the doctor who warned us to do as little activity as possible, we were packed into an SUV Elsa whistled for us.

Leif and Elsa took turns driving. Jens would not leave my side for even a second. He held my hand and rubbed my back, kissing my hair every other minute to reassure either me or him, I wasn't sure.

"I'm alright," I told him after half a day of his manic hovering. "I'm not going to have a breakdown, and I highly doubt you'll be able to stop another car accident."

"Aren't I allowed to want to be near you just because?"

"You're worried."

"Well, you almost died. I think I have the right to worry. I'm your crappy guard and your boyfriend. Double whammy for worrying."

I fished for a change of topic. "We're driving at normal

speed, here. You're really sure Pesta won't be able to find a new body and attack us before we get to the portal?"

Jens gripped my shoulder and then rubbed it. "Positive. She has to use a willing human subject that crosses over into Be. We've got Huldras watching the portal to make sure no humans cross over. And the transformation takes time. That kind of magic can't be rushed. We'll be at the portal in a couple hours. She hasn't got a prayer."

"For how long?" I asked, finally voicing the hard questions we never discussed. "For how long will she leave me alone? I'll destroy the portal, sure. But she's still out there."

Jens kissed my temple. "She'll leave you alone for a while."

"For how long?" I prodded, unwilling to wave off my hunches just so I would feel better for the moment.

Jens swallowed. "That siren holds a grudge. Their kind always did, but she's the worst. She'll go away for a while. Regroup. When she starts trying to build portals again, she'll go for your bones, for sure. The vendetta against your family runs deep." He cleared his throat, and I could tell he was gearing up for something big. "But there won't be enough with just you, so she'll go for our kids."

"My kids'll have my nomadic childhood, then," I stated flatly, laying out the long and short of it. "Running and never being normal."

"*Our* kids, and yes." He forced a smirk. "And like anything that comes from us would ever stand a chance at normal. I mean, come on. It's us."

I couldn't even smile at the fact that Jens wanted to have fictional kids with me. "That's the size of it?" I stared lifelessly out the window at the haze of white blurring past me. A small part of my heart I didn't know existed cracked off and floated in the black abyss where I kept the bad things buried.

Jamie heard where I was going, and had something to say about it. *No, syster. Don't do that to Jens. Don't say it. Not now. We'll find a way.*

I ignored Jamie. "I won't have kids, then. Cut her off at the source."

"Shh." Jens kissed my temple for the fiftieth time, but this one he did with his eyes closed. The pain that should have been mine alone was his, too. "I can't handle any more heartbreak today. Maybe not for a month. We'll figure that part out later. Give me time to sort her out."

"It's okay, Jens. Not a big deal. I won't miss what I never had."

His hand went over my mouth, staving off whatever nonsense I had yet to spill out. "No more. Give me time. You just concentrate on how tall you want that white picket fence."

We were quiet the entire rest of the way.

When Elsa motioned to the exit, my heartrate began to pick up. There had been so much talk of destroying the portal, but actually doing it was an entire other thing. Even though we were not expecting opposition, I was still nervous.

The sight that greeted me nearly took my breath away.

"Foss!" I called, pointing to a band of Huldras, their husbands and the beacon that was Foss.

Twenty strong, they stood together in front of the portal in full snow gear with their game faces on. As they came into better view, I saw ugly black guns in their hands.

179

Long ones and short ones, ones for hunting and others for defending. Despite my need to appear totally with it, I whimpered when I saw a handgun in Foss's grip.

I looked around as we drove into the fold, my mouth agape. In a wide ring around the portal lay obliterated bits of every kind of animal that was indigenous to that region. "Oh! What happened?" I exclaimed, my hands covering my mouth in shock.

Elsa turned to me. "I bet it's Weres, baby doll. Dozens and dozens of Weres waiting to jump on us. Did I tell you my sisters would take care of this, or what?"

"No joke," I commented, amazed at the devastation nature had suffered all because Pesta wanted what she wanted at any cost.

When we pulled up, Foss was at our door, helping us out one by one, except for Jamie and I, who were not ready to move just yet. "Took you long enough," he said by way of a greeting.

I shouted past him, my intimidation factor lowered by the fact that I couldn't really get out of the van without assistance. "I'd like to know which idiot whack job thought it was a good idea to give a Fossegrimen with a brain injury fresh off the farm from Undraland a loaded weapon?!" I found Liv's guilty eyes and yelled. "You? Seriously? Are you asking for trouble? Do you have a death wish? Or do you just not give a smack about anyone but yourself?"

"What right do you have to speak for Foss? He's not your real husband!" Liv shot back, though I could tell I'd hit my mark. She trotted away from me and stood near her sisters, chagrinned at her lapse in judgment.

"Oh, you'd better run!" I shouted, angry as all get-out.

Jens grinned at me as he hopped out of the van and stretched. "I would tell you to calm down, but that was kinda sexy."

I continued to grumble, no doubt unsexily. I held out my hand expectantly to Foss. "Give it."

"I've been using it all morning," Foss argued, gripping the gun like it was a treasured pet.

My mother had a death glare she did not often invoke, but when she did, we knew not to cross her. Turns out, that little gem was genetic. "Give me that gun, or so help me, you don't want to know what!"

"I was getting the hang of it just fine." Foss handed over the weapon, and I in turn passed it off to Jens as if I was handing him a poisonous lizard. Jens checked the safety and then pocketed it.

I pointed in Liv's direction. "That girl who's got her hooks in you? No."

Foss glanced at Liv and turned back to me. "What about her?"

"No. Just, no."

Foss chuckled under his breath. "I missed you, too."

I tried not to let my stern expression break, but it was no use. I took my crutches from Jens and moved awkwardly to the exit of the SUV, sitting on the edge of the seat. "Your head!" I blurted out. "I'm so sorry we left you. Are you alright?"

"I'm fine. Let's do this." Foss held my elbow while I got situated and Jens fished around in his red pack for the rake that stirred up so much friggin' controversy.

Liv sidled up beside Foss, her swagger recovered and in

full swing. "A little brain damage only improves a Fossegrimen."

I snapped at Liv. "'Be gone before someone drops a house on you!'" When in doubt for your insults, consult the *Wizard of Oz.*

"You're a mess!" Foss exclaimed, taking in the scope of my injuries. He motioned to my leg that was already irritating him. "Did Jens do this to you?"

"Pesta," Jens groused, sifting through the bag like he was looking for lost keys at the bottom. "But thanks for that vote of confidence. Remind me to beat on you later."

"You look terrible," Foss observed.

I did my best to turn my body so I could hug him. "I missed you, too." I pointed to the floor of the SUV. "Sit. Let me look at you."

Foss rolled his eyes, knowing we couldn't do anything until Jens located the rake. He pulled off his ski cap and showed me the bandage over the right side of his shaved skull.

I hissed. "Does it hurt very bad?"

"It's fine. Itches more than anything."

Liv jumped on the opportunity to sneer. "I thought you were supposed to be his wife, not his mommy."

My bark was a little overzealous. I blame the pain meds. "Don't you talk about his mother!"

Foss placed his hand on mine, a flicker of appreciation shining through. "You're worried. I'm okay." He let me check his wound with all the patience of a two-year-old. "Quit doing that annoying thing you do. That scared face. It's unsettling."

It was my turn to roll my eyes. "Yes. The caring thing

that's so annoying. It's my one joy to irritate you. Job well done on my part." I looked into his eyes and saw that his pupils weren't dilated. I exhaled. "You're you, for better or worse. I'm sorry I wasn't there when you woke up."

Foss shrugged. "It's fine. I understand." A note of concern drifted through his harsh tone. "You... you're okay, then?"

"No," I answered succinctly. I don't know why I told the truth; I just didn't have it in me to lie.

Foss examined the resigned look on my face with a hard expression. "About time you admitted it." He leaned over and pecked my lips. It was on the border of romantic and friendly, and like everything was with him, it left me confused. Heat rose in my cheeks, and Foss cracked half a smile at me.

Lucy! This is not proper! Jamie scolded me.

I heard Liv's intake of breath, but Jens addressed it. "You'll get used to that." Then in warning to Foss, he clarified with, "*Only* that. Understood?"

Foss ignored Jens and kept his voice between us. "Liv tells me you saved my life."

"Again," I corrected him. "I saved your life *again*."

He looked from side to side, ensuring no one overheard him. "Thanks."

Despite my impending task, I lifted an eyebrow. "Did that hurt a little? Being the minimal amount of nice like that?"

He didn't fall for my shtick. Instead he wrapped his arms around me and pulled me between his open knees, engulfing me in a hug that had my chin resting on his shoulder. He was so much taller than me; I was used to my

183

head leaning on his chest when he held me. This cheek-to-cheek hug was different, and the tenderness threatened to squeeze too much emotion from me. He turned his head and pressed his lips to my cheek, whispering into my skin, "Never doubt that I love you."

I heard that, Jamie groused.

When I pulled back, I pecked Foss's lips again. My husband held my gaze with a look that said more than he would ever admit to aloud, and I nodded to let him know I understood. "I'm glad you're alright," I told him, shivering when a gust of icy wind blew into the car.

"Thanks to you." Then Foss stood. He took the rake from Jens, who looked like he wanted to weaponize the tool against Foss. "Let's finish it."

I nodded, taking Jens's hand and holding onto Foss with my other arm. My leg wasn't broken or anything, but I decided on humoring the doctor who told me not to walk on it for a couple weeks. Jamie was a real stickler for not being in pain.

The snow was two feet deep, so it made for slow going.

Foss was crabby because of the cold. "Well it's a good thing Pesta isn't here. You're taking forever! Jens, just carry her. I'm gonna lose it if we keep going at this pace."

"You've got like, twenty more feet. Chill," I ordered.

I heard a snort a little ways behind us, and then a gunshot. No matter how many of those you hear on TV, it's nothing compared to the real thing, especially when the last gun you heard was used by your own hands to murder your best friend.

I whimpered, and Jens stopped our progression to hold

me. "It was just a Were. The Huldras can keep us safe until the portal's finished."

I nodded into his black winter coat, wishing fear for my life was the real problem.

The portal was just like the others. It was taller than necessary for a human; I could tell Pesta was used to dealing with the towering Undrans. The structure was terrible and intimidating, as the others had been. But being this close, close enough to slip through, brought to me a new level of apprehension. The portal was completed and fully functional, with a blue glow emanating from the center. "I guess she had enough bones with that Mace guy, huh."

Jens swallowed. "Uh-huh. Let's be done with it."

I dropped Jens's hand and took the rake from Foss, holding up the tool with a reluctant and pounding heart. "Some of these belong to my parents," I said to Jens. He was the only one there who had known them. The other portals had ancestors represented who had been alive decades ago that Pesta had dug up, and were not known by us. This was different.

There was a femur with a pin in it. I closed my eyes when I realized it belonged to my dad. He'd broken his leg once when he'd been a teenager. I opened my eyes and began counting the femurs, knowing there should be six. I frowned when I only found four. Two were whiter, indicative of their freshness. The other two belonged to my dad.

"Where's my mom?" I choked out, emotion gripping me around the throat. "There's only four femurs here!" I counted the pelvises, but again only made it to two. "My

185

mom's not here!" I turned and clung to Jens's jacket. "Does that mean she's alive? Is my mom still alive?"

Jens looked like he might be sick. "No, honey. Your mom's dead. If her bones aren't here, then Pesta did something else with them."

"No!" I shouted. "Pesta needed all the bones she could get to build this portal! She would've used them if she had them! Mom!" I screamed, not hopeful that calling out for her would actually do anything.

Foss was stern when I was on the edge of losing my mind. He gripped my chin and sneered into my face. "Your mother's not here. Now take the rake and tear down this portal. We can deal with the rest later." When I took too long to gulp down my anxiety, he growled, "Finish it!"

I extracted myself from Foss and lifted my hand to touch the bones, but pulled back when I realized my dad wouldn't want my memories of him to include this. It was the closest I'd been to him since he'd been taken from me, and the grief washed over me anew, forcing out a solitary sob like a rough pat on the back. I sucked down my sorrow and stored it away for another day.

Today was for my dad – for both my parents, really. There'd be plenty of time to break down after the fact.

I took the rake, and with great care, knocked the bones down, starting with the ones composing the crest of the arch.

Without a word between us, Jens knew what to do. He caught each bone before it hit the ground, treating them with the utmost respect for the death and the resonating pain I carried with me every day. "We'll burn them properly. Have a eulogy and everything for them," Jens commented as I moved to the ones on the left side, knocking them down one by one.

The portal flickered, but as with the others, it did not go out and would not until the last bone fell.

The bones on the right side were newer, and the color whiter. They must've belonged to Charles Mace, poor guy. Though I didn't know him, I treated his bones with respect, knocking them carefully down for Foss to catch.

First the femur, then the humerus. I was halfway down the row when the portal turned from its bluish hue to a brilliant purple. "Um, is that supposed to happen?" I asked them.

"Hurry and destroy it!" Foss yelled, his fear giving birth to mine.

I pulled back the rake to swing at the other bones like a baseball bat, but before I could deliver the blow, a man's hand reached out from the ethereal purple pool and grabbed my jacket.

No one saw it coming; there was no precedent for it.

The hand yanked me forward, rake and all, and pulled me into the portal.

The last thing I heard was the sound of Jens and Foss roaring my name in unison.

30

LIMBO TO LIMBO

*M*y brain struggled to keep up as my body morphed like Jell-O through the portal I had almost destroyed.

I was shaking like a leaf, trying to assess my new surroundings and not have a total freak-out. I stood on a rocky floor with no walls and no ceiling that I could see beyond a dark, murky fog that blocked out everything about a quarter mile out from where I stood.

"Goose? Do you not recognize me?"

The voice cut through all the confusion, giving me something to cling to I quasi-understood. I sounded small as I turned to the man standing next to me, the sound going out into the abyss that surrounded us and not echoing back off any surface. "Uncle Rick?" I questioned.

True enough, it was my Uncle Rick. Gray beard, dark skin, sparkling gray eyes and orange cardigan – all six and a half feet of him. My jaw dropped, but I made no move toward him.

The indulgence in his eyes he had toward me was back, renewed since I last saw him. "Is that all the love you have for me? I'm an old man, after all."

When he reached out to touch my arm, I stumbled backwards. "N-No! You're not here! I'm not here! I... I hit my head. I'm crazy." This made far more sense than anything else.

He retracted, rethinking his approach. He stroked his beard like he'd done before knocking one of my pawns off the board during a game of chess. "I can certainly see the merit in presuming insanity. But I can assure you, I'm quite me, and you're every bit the you I've always adored." He pointed to the leg I couldn't put much weight on. "Perhaps a little worse for the wear, but all the pieces still add up to my favorite niece."

I couldn't respond. I was too shocked. I turned on my heel and hobbled toward the portal to go back out to the world I understood.

"Goosy, wait," he called.

I paid him no mind. I tried to exit out the way I came, using the rake as a sort of crude crutch, but Alrik quickly blocked my way. "Let me out! You're not real, and I'm dreaming. I'm stuck in one of Jamie's dreams. He'll find me! He'll bring me back and wake me up. Jamie!" I cried out to the open air that was shrouded in black just a few meters out from where we stood. "Jamie!"

Uncle Rick waited with his usual air of patience when he knew I was doing something fruitless or stupid. "Darling, I am me, and you are you. I'm the one who snatched you from your world and brought you through the portal to the Land of Be."

I looked around at the cloudy blackness that made me feel like I was on a rocky road in the middle of foggy nothingness. "This is the Land of Be? I thought this was supposed to be everyone's grand retirement."

Uncle Rick pointed down the stone path to a point of goldish light in the distance. "The actual Land of Be is that way. We're in Limbo. This," he said, motioning around us, "is Limbo. I was not satisfied with simply destroying the portal. It takes much planning, but portals can always be rebuilt. I would not take you on such a quest for a temporary victory. You should know that by now. You've played chess enough times with me."

I decided to give in and accept that I was where Alrik said I was. That he was really alive, and he hadn't really abandoned me for Be. There was a plan, an ace up his knitted orange sleeves. "Jens and I were just talking about that. About always being on the run because Pesta'll never truly stop." I bristled when conflicting judgments fought within me. I stabbed my finger in his direction, keeping a healthy distance between us. "We're not friends. For all I know, you could be another Mouthpiece. If you think I won't shoot you again, you're wrong. I killed Pesta when she was Tonya, and I won't hesitate to run you through."

"Dually noted, dear. I assure you, I have no trace of Pesta in me." He wrinkled his nose in distaste. "If she ever tried, I would run myself through on my own, with no prodding from you."

I wanted to believe him. I needed someone to make sense of things. Before I knew it, I was hugging him, the rake wrapping around his back. "It's really you, then?" He was warm, and despite his towering height, I fit in his arms the way I always had.

"For better or worse. It appears you're stuck with me yet again. I shall try not to be such a disappointment in this life."

I recalled our earlier conversations and grimaced. "You're not a disappointment. Just a constant riddle I gave up on figuring out."

He touched my nose. "That's the thing about riddles. The best ones keep on going."

"Only if you don't like sleep," I amended, "which I do." I looked around, trying to get my lay of the land. "Um, so where are we, exactly?"

Uncle Rick held his hands out at his sides like a tour guide. "This is the pathway to Be. Most people assume you cross over, and you're in, but most people don't know your mother." His slate eyes shone with pride, and I couldn't help but lose a little of the chip on my shoulder. "Your mother is the only one who's ever made it out of Be with her hand and her soul fully intact. Most people dismissed her escape as legend, but I know your mother. I know you. I would never dare underestimate a Kincaid."

I grinned. I couldn't help it, the charmer. "You're playing me, but I don't mind it. Anytime you want to sing her praises, I'll gladly let you. My mom was incredible."

"That, she was. You see, Goosy, most people cross over, spend a few moments looking around and assume the only way is forward." He pointed down the massive hallway shrouded in black clouds to the small golden light at the end. "Don't follow the light, dear. It leads to Be. A very few have second thoughts, I've observed, but the way back is sealed."

Panic began to settle in over me. "And you pulled me in here, knowing I couldn't get back out?" Flashes of the life I always wanted but would never have ricocheted through my mind like so many painful bolts of lightning, each one sizzling a scar of loneliness I feared would never be healed over. "Why? Why would you do that?"

Alrik put his hand on my shoulder in that friendly ally way he'd tricked me into the mission in the first place all those months ago. "But there is a way out. You came into Limbo with the rake, which is the tool your mother used to break herself out decades ago."

"So I'm not trapped in here?"

"I can't imagine anything worse than a soulless Kincaid girl. I would never let you go into Be." His eyes sparkled with the indulgence I'd missed. "We have to fight for our freedom first, though. I daresay you were born ready for a fight of this magnitude." He leveled his gaze at me. "We have to kill Pesta and take her broom."

I took a step back. "Come again? What makes you think I could do something like that? Just because I killed her Mouthpiece doesn't mean…"

"It means you're the only one she hates enough to let close. She will find you here, and she'll come after you. We'll kill her and take the broom." His voice hushed to a whisper. "With the broom, we can set the souls free. It's how she grants a few of them clemency to roam the earth inside bears and other beasts. If we have the rake and the broom, we can set the souls to rest, and go back into the world without forfeiting our arms to her."

I scoffed, throwing my hands out in exasperation. "And she's just going to bring the broom into Limbo with her? Come on. I bet it's buried in Be somewhere, and I'm not going in there to dig it out."

Alrik smiled in that paternal way that was hovering between sweet and the patronizing kindness of a much wiser schoolteacher. "She needs it herself to cross over from Be to Limbo."

"Oh." My brain raced to poke at any holes in the plan. "If she can get out, why doesn't she use the broom to bust herself out instead of using a mouthpiece?"

Alrik rubbed his fingers on his thumb. "Magic. Lots and lots of magic from all the tribes in Undra locked her in here. It was either that or kill her, and some were opposed to eradicating an entire race. Pesta was the only one willing to work with us. All the other sirens were put to death. She volunteered to let us lock her in here in lieu of dying."

"I like when you say fancy words like 'in lieu'. Makes me stand up straighter." We were beginning to feel like us again, despite our grim surroundings.

"I shall attempt only the most intelligent vocabulary, then." He turned back to face the light. "The broom will work for us, but it only grants her access between her two realms." We stood in silence a moment while he waited for my brain to catch up. "You must have truly wounded her when you killed the Mouthpiece. I have you here, plus the rake she's searched decades for. I would think she should be upon us at any moment."

"When Harold came to, he told me Pesta entered him through his mouth." My throat turned into the Sahara, and

I worried the words would be stuck inside me forever. My voice was quiet, and I dreaded the person I was to be able to utter such words. "I shot Tonya in the face, so maybe that has something to do with it."

Alrik was quiet, letting my words settle instead of trying to cheer them into something they were not. "Your choice was wise for battle, but harsh to carry for a lifetime. I admire you, though I do not envy the decision you had to make. You're stronger than perhaps even I realized."

The melancholy was sealed when I responded with a glib, "Lucky me."

"When Tonya came through the portal, I tried to reason with her, but her mind was made up."

"How did she even hear about the portal? I've never seen a commercial for one."

Alrik sighed. "The Mouthpiece. He crossed over and coaxed her to enter the portal not long before he was killed. The poor child was a besotted mess and quite suggestible. She's been the only human to enter Limbo. The Mouthpiece booked a room at a motel nearby for her, and she waited there a couple days until the portal was complete. She told me she visited the spot every day until it was ready for new tenants."

My mouth was hanging open. "I had no idea she was so sad. All over a little house fire?" Picturing Tonya so despondent was awful. To lose a spark like she had? Utter tragedy.

"And losing her best friend," Alrik amended. "She wasn't thinking rationally. She'd told me of her therapist who recommended she listen to the Mouthpiece and go with him. I can only assume he'd been bewitched by a

Huldra. He did everything to sway her, including having relations with her."

"Man Friend was drinking the Huldra juice? Ack! Oh, now I'm pissed. They were disgusting together!" I thought back on him, wondering how I could've missed signs he was being controlled. "His eyes were dark, so I didn't notice his pupils. And he gave off a creeper vibe, so I didn't go near his hands to see if they were cold. Maybe I should've." My eyes widened and my volume climbed without meaning to. "Wait a second. What Huldra would work with Pesta? It was her idea to have them banished from Undraland!"

Alrik nodded. "Indeed. I fear I don't have that answer."

I cleared my throat and scratched the back of my neck, searching for a change of topic. "Hey! I don't feel the laplanding headache. That must mean they're still nearby."

"Oh, I don't doubt that, but we're not in a place that can be quantified, so the bond has no bearing here. If you tried to talk to Jamie, you would not be able to find him. He's most likely been trying to reach you since you crossed over."

"Weird, but nice to have a break. This laplanding thing? When I'm a real queen, that'll be the first to go."

He looked down on me as if I was a child telling him I would build myself a rocket ship to the moon out of candy bar wrappers. "How very nice."

My voice quieted, and I spoke the thing I'd been afraid to think on too often. "I've got elfin blood in me, right? I mean, you did that forehead thing back when I first crossed over to Undraland, plus my dad. You said it was you adopting me, and Undra adoptions change the person's DNA. So I'm a wind elf, plus a water elf, right?"

"Indeed. You have your mother, your father and a little bit of me in your blood."

"I still don't understand why any of you didn't teach me your magic. Why not train me? Maybe I could've spelled Tonya with a Huldra whistle or defended myself with the water Kung-Fu you do."

Alrik gripped the back of my head and planted a kiss to my forehead. "Because your mother wanted you and Linus raised as humans. Magic leaves traces that can be tracked, if you know what to look for." He gazed down on me with love. "Being human has served you well, dear. You killed the farlig and Circhos, and those are only two of the ways you were able to rise above without relying on magic. You're human. I wouldn't change you for the world."

I frowned. "Still. Even for party tricks. Would've been cool to learn how to make a squirt gun with my fingers that actually worked or something."

He smiled softly. "If we make it out of this, I'll be sure to teach you that." He held up his finger before I got too excited. "Only that."

I slapped my hands together and shook out my arms. "Okay, so what's the plan? Pesta comes through the light over there and, what? We just duke it out to the death? Rake versus broom?"

"That's the idea. Walk with me, Goosy." He proffered his elbow to me, and I looped my arm through it like a true lady. I limped along with him as my crutch, and he kept his pace slow enough for me to keep up. Alrik was a solid foot taller than me, so I always felt like a kid instead of a proper woman next to him. I think that's probably how it's supposed to be with uncles. He drew my attention to the light we were walking toward. "Stay to the path, dear, and don't go too near the portal to Be. The hands are stuck to the wall, but they move on occasion. It won't do to have one of them grabbing at you."

"What?" I looked around, but on either side of me black fog obscured anything that lay off the path. As we neared the portal, the fog around the glowing gold portal became easier to see through.

Arms. Tens of thousands of arms were nailed to the mud wall. They were affixed firmly at the elbow, but the hands themselves moved slow, like butterfly wings opening and closing on a flower. The fingers curled at me, beckoning me forward in their macabre way that made a scream build in my throat like vomit.

Alrik appeared almost bored at the sight. "The arms Pesta collects. Did you ever wonder what she did with them?"

"I... um... I really don't like this," I confessed, nervous at whatever might jump out at me beyond the haze. I looked up and saw that the wall went up higher than I could see through the fog. Several stories high at least, and the mud walls stretched into nothingness on either side of the portal, giving no end to the number of arms Pesta collected as her prize. "This is disgusting! Who the smack thinks of something so sick?"

"Indeed." Alrik went back to the matter at hand. "The trick is to grab her before she sees the two of us. She knows I'm here. She had a good laugh about it when she came out to snatch up Tonya, but sensing you're here will need to be confirmed. When Pesta comes out, we must wrestle her away from the gateway that leads into Be. If she pushes us through, there's no coming back with your soul or your arm intact."

I clutched the rake close to me. "Okay, so job one: grab the broom. Job two: kill Pesta. Job three: don't go into the light."

"You've always been a quick study." He smiled down at me, shifting his robes like smoothing wrinkles from a sheet. "Do you recall how sirens die from the bedtime stories you and Linus enjoyed?"

I wracked my brain, knowing I should have been sussing this out without his prodding. "Bucket of water to melt the witch?"

Alrik chuckled as if my jokes were appropriate, given the impending battle we were to fight at any moment. "I'll be sure to buy you some ruby slippers when we finish this. No. You take a siren's power by destroying her hands. Hence, Pesta's obsession with hands. Then you kill her as you would a human." He snapped his fingers, and a bead of water bubbled from the tip and trickled down his knuckle. "Sirens do all their magic with their hands. Her trophies nailed to the wall are a statement that we're handing over our power to her. Powerful magic, but antiquated delivery method."

I blanched. "Um, I don't exactly have my hand-severing tools on me. Gross, Uncle Rick."

"I shall handle the severing, courtesy of the knife Jens simply had too many of. Do you think he'll be upset I borrowed it for so long?"

I smiled. "I think he'll manage."

He reached inside the pocket of his orange cardigan to give me a glimpse of the blade. "No one ever suspects a man in elfish robes to be carrying a weapon."

"Excellent point."

"I want you to gather up Pesta's broom when she releases it." Despite the conversation, he smiled. "You called me 'Uncle Rick'. I've been 'Alrik' to you since our falling out on the ledge in Bedra."

I looked away. "You know I don't like to fight with you. You did what you did, and you are who you are. I don't think there's anything anyone could do to change that, and I was stupid for trying."

We walked in silence until we reached the door that was pure light. I wanted to touch it, but Uncle Rick pulled me back. "Not that close, dear. There's no returning from that door with your soul or your right arm. Best not let temptation fester." He watched with quiet intensity as the light gave off a faint heat that colored it gold. "Once she's finished, we tear this gateway to Be down with the rake and the broom. One tool destroys, the other frees. The rake for the portal, the broom for the souls. Then the souls shall be free to rest, and we can take the broom to go back to the world. Then we tear down the human portal, and it's finished."

"Step four, step five," I agreed, though I doubted the simplicity with which he stated the events. I removed my jacket and cast it to the ground, since I'd gone from icy weather to a comfortable warmth. I rolled up the sleeves of my long-sleeved t-shirt and cracked my knuckles in antici-pation of the plan's execution.

"This door gets its light from the bones of the sirens it

was constructed from." He observed the doorway to Be with a look that suggested an utter loss in the faith he had in his people. It was like he was looking at something unredeemable in its sadness, and I wondered what the world had been like with so many powerful creatures roaming Undraland so long ago.

The lights began to shift from gold to white. Suddenly gold burst from the center as if glitter and sunlight were mixing and exploding like a powder keg out at us. I yelped and hobbled back, Alrik standing before me to shield me with his larger body.

I gripped the rake, but almost dropped it when a bare foot crossed over into Limbo.

Then came a knee and a body clothed in a white seventies-style flowerchild dress.

It was the brown curly hair I'd gotten my waves from.

It was the mouth whose words could cut through my shtick and tricks to find me buried beneath.

It was her.

My mother turned toward me with yellow eyes like Harold's and a missing arm.

31

MONSTER MOM

I screamed.

I'm pretty sure. The prolonged high-pitched horror had to have been coming from me. My mother certainly wasn't screaming.

She was foaming at the mouth as she clutched onto an old wooden broom with a raggedy golden straw base.

Yellow eyes and a gait that suggested feral war instead of a maternal greeting told me mama was home. Only it wasn't her. Pesta was using the body she stole from my world to taunt me, to torture me into cowering.

It was working.

Tears streamed down my face as Alrik stepped to the right so my monster mom could get a glimpse of me with the rake. She growled and hissed, fuming with unbridled aggression.

I wanted to run to her, and in fact started to, but Uncle Rick clotheslined me. I fell backwards, the wind knocked out of me as I gasped out more sobs of agony. The rake punched me across the face, and I scarcely had the where-withal to hold onto it when my mother came hurtling toward me.

Her movements were jerky and impulsive – nothing like the dancing we'd done in the kitchen while we made Thanksgiving dinners. She sprinted toward the rake I was clutching, fervor and hunger in her yellow eyes.

Again, I screamed. Probably. My brain kept skipping and twirling with sickness as terror upon horror toppled over me while I cried.

I had nothing to fight with. Wrestling Tonya was one thing, but my mother? The agony was too great to even lift my head up off the ground.

"This is not your mother!" Alrik cried out. He inter-cepted my mom and threw her on the ground, but she sprang back up in the next second with zealous energy. "Pesta took her soul long ago. This is just a shell with a rabid soul inside!"

I watched my uncle fight with his surrogate sister, the same anguish that tortured me twisted the calm in his eyes to the point of non-existence. It was hand-to-hand combat, and Uncle Rick was winning, but hesitant to do so. As much as he wished us to not lose in the final round, the emotional torment tore at us, making fresh wounds that would one day scab over into hideous scars if we were lucky enough to survive.

My monster mom screeched that high-pitched grating metal sound as she launched the broom back through the portal of light as if throwing a javelin.

"Don't look, Lucy!" Uncle Rick commanded as he whipped out his knife.

The last thing I saw before I obeyed was the determination in my uncle's eyes. My heart clenched and sank into my churning gut that roiled with regret as I shut my eyes.

There was screaming and a sound like a pin piercing a balloon. The slow pop of air leaking out told me he'd sliced through her lung.

My mother faltered and wheezed. I heard more punching and slicing, opening my eyes just long enough to watch my sweet mom buckle onto her knees, blood blooming like abstract red flowers all over her white gown. Her wild brown curls framed her heart-shaped face just as I remembered, and I saw what everyone commented on so many times growing up.

I looked like my mother. Peach complexion. Curly tangles.

The same look of shock and loss that tore at my face echoed itself onto her. She was gasping for breath as panic constricted my lungs.

My mirror self collapsed onto the gray rocky floor of Limbo. After all the times I fought for closure about my mother's death when I had no body to bury, I finally saw with my own terrified eyes the graphic evidence.

I turned onto all fours as vomit and tears poured out of me.

Uncle Rick was shouting something as the gold light turned white again, bursting with gold and false beauty as the woman I would live the rest of my days in hatred of waltzed through the portal like a tall, two-legged prancing pony.

Translucent skin I could see veins with glittery fluid flowing through and silver hair that sparkled like it had been dunked in twinkling stars paraded in front of my vision that was tunneling with hatred. I seethed like a bull, not bothering to wipe the dregs of puke from my mouth. She was nearly seven feet tall with a snub nose, round face and thin lips. She looked to be made of malice and pure muscle. She was wrapped in a shapeless knee-length silver bag dress.

Pesta looked down at my mother and my vomit and laughed.

BURN AND SCREAM

*S*omehow I had the sense to clutch onto the rake when Pesta lunged for it. She thought it would be as simple as snatching candy from a baby.

Thanks to her, I was no child.

I moved up and forward simultaneously, rake in hand like a sword. I swung it at her head in a blind rage, determined somehow to remove her head with it. I bashed her temple with the iron end, but other than dazing her for a second, my force had no lasting effect.

"Oh, little girl. The fun I'm going to have with you. Slow down for me." Silver dust trickled out of her mouth on the last sentence, much like the gold dust of the elves, so I knew it was evidence of her using her magic. Pesta's voice was dangerous. Every word she spoke brought forth a magic that slowed my muscles until I felt like I was coming at her while fighting through water. I had heard my uncle tell me bedtime stories about the power of a siren's voice, but until I heard her speak, I grossly underestimated the effect.

Her broom was ready, and she came at me, delivering a crack to my forehead that sent me flying.

My only weapon at that point was the stubbornness that was always my strength and weakness. My fingers clutched the rake, refusing to relinquish the prize even through my siren song-drugged state. A trickle of blood dripped down my forehead onto the rocky floor.

Her laugh was vindictive and beautiful, and I hated her for it. She cackled at Uncle Rick as he moved in between us, her tone telling him she thought very little of his valiant attempts to save me.

Uncle Rick's knife was ready. In a downward motion, he fought to slice down through her chest.

Pesta clicked her fingers and then sang another command for us to slow down. The action released a magic that delayed our reflexes, and she was able to fend off Uncle Rick's attack. The levity was gone now, and she regarded him as if he was an annoyance that needed dealing with. She dropped the broom to punch him across the face. "Alrik the Wise. I've long anticipated feeding off your soul. Oh, how the mighty have fallen right into my web." Then she stage-whispered, "I bet you taste delicious. The best are the ones with the most fight in them. Your Hilda was an absolute feast." She kicked my mother's body.

Pesta moved toward my supine form that was still struggling to right itself. She smelled like rotting bodies and defecation. She bent down by my head, smiling down at me with a falsely maternal glow. "Dear girl. What to do with you?" She cast a glance to Alrik, who was moving toward us too slowly to be of any use. "Your mother hated the sirens, as did your father. Perhaps you need a new mommy." A purposeful gaze crossed her face, a decision she was debating now made in full.

Pesta kissed her thumb and rubbed it from my hairline down my forehead, breathing hot air on it as Uncle Rick had done back in Tonttu before the Fellowship of the Rake was formed. Her touch was warm and had a tacky feeling before the sizzle set in. I screamed at the burn her touch left, writhing in slow motion against the pain and the woman. She laughed, amused at my ineffectual fight.

I thought she would end me right then and there, but she stood and moved back to Alrik, who was shaking with rage.

"Oh, Alrik. Sit down, love. You had to know I wouldn't be satisfied with merely killing her. Where's the pomp? Where's the circumstance? You'll get a good show. Don't worry."

I sat up in slow motion as Alrik fell to his knees, weighed down by the gravity of her voice. Silver dust spat out of her mouth when she used her mind-control power. I heard my scream at his impending doom, but I was too far away and too slow moving to do anything that might save him.

His knife was lax in his hand, and fear like I'd never known crept under my skin like so many spiders fighting their way through my veins to birth out of my dermis.

Pesta strutted before him, her seduction one of death, not sex. She grabbed onto his orange cardigan and hoisted him up, breathing haughtily in his face. "Such a brave struggle the fly gives the spider. But in the end, you're still only an insect. Though I must say, I did enjoy the fight."

I gasped as his garment began to burn through, her hands searing his clothes where she touched them. She dropped him, cackling as he collapsed like a ragdoll before her, my sobs of horror and fear alerting her that she had an audience.

The gleam in her golden eyes was sheer merriment at making me watch her destroy my last remaining family member. She slapped one hand to either side of his face and squeezed, grinning with childish delight as Alrik groaned while his face sizzled.

"Let him go!" I shouted, climbing to my feet that felt like lead. I could smell my uncle's skin charring as I tried with all my might to rescue him at my snail's pace.

Pesta gave me a piteous laugh as she lifted him by his burning face and dragged him over to the portal.

"No!" I screamed.

Though Alrik's feet had no fortitude with which to move, at the edges of my vision, it registered that his hand was gripping the knife with strength that belied his limp and moaning state.

My pleas picked up to a theatrical begging to distract her. "Please! Take me instead! It's me you want. I had the rake! It's my mom that made you look like a fool! Leave him alone and throw *me* into Be!" The tears were real as the siren turned her head toward me. "I've been through too much. I *want* your world. Mine is cruel and ugly. I need you to take me!" I begged.

"Stupid girl. Patience. After the trouble you've caused me? I'll take my time with you."

My blood boiled, but I kept the pathetic expression intact as my uncle fought off the slow-motion mojo and seized his moment.

His knife was steady.

Her screams were operatic.

The blood was beautiful. Silver and gold light poured out of Pesta's left hand like a waterfall of stars and glitter, spilling out onto my uncle and bathing him in glory.

The knife twisted, retracted and stabbed into her stomach.

Pesta's haughty expression jerked with the edge of the knife, contorting to pain, and then panic.

My uncle was fierce as her hands fell away from his face. Perfect black and red handprints were seared onto his cheeks, but the pain was secondary to the victory, as it always was with him. He whispered as she spat glitter and stars onto his face, his complexion now glowing like that of an angel. "It's tragic you chose my family to destroy. Were it anyone else, you may have succeeded."

Pesta reared back in a last flare of life as she fought to destroy the mere elf who'd bested her. She tore at his face with her burning hands at the same time he raised the knife to stab into her heart.

As long as I live, I don't think I'll ever fully make sense of what happened next. The two twisted and writhed in agony and triumph with each other.

Stab.

Burn.

Scream.

Sizzle.

I blinked, and the knife was in Pesta's chest.

I blinked again, and with a last surge of inhuman strength, Pesta pushed my uncle into the portal.

I watched as all three of us gasped in terror.

Uncle Rick cried, "Finish it!" as he toppled through the white burst of light, the portal swallowing him whole.

REASONS

*W*hen I came to my senses on the floor of Limbo, it was with confusion and a heavy heart. My hands were coated in Pesta's blood, which had seeped out of her and crept toward me, rousing my brain with a cool sensation like gel and sparkling water popping on my skin.

The rake and broom were on the floor, mine for the keeping. The prize felt small – so much loss over such simple objects.

Pesta's eyes were closed, but her body was fighting for its last vestiges of life as she twitched. She looked like an exquisite doll bathed in ethereal light. It was tragic, and a complete waste of beauty. Sparks of light like mini fire-crackers fizzled and flew out like spit from her quaking fingertips.

I knew what I had to do.

The spell of Pesta's voice no longer had its grip on me, so I stood on wobbly legs over my tormenter. I didn't hold back my incoherent ramblings of terror as I slid the knife from her chest and slammed it through her gut to ensure she died quicker. One of her errant sparks zapped me in her feeble attempt at one last attack, and I felt a shiver in my bones that coursed through me like an effervescing change I couldn't put a label on.

That was the thing that tipped it. She was on the brink of death, but with a second stab through her ribcage, I watched as the last of her life fled from her body.

I began hacking away at her wrists. Uncle Rick needed her hands taken off to stop her power. I wasn't sure if that mattered anymore, now that she was dead, but I wasn't willing to take any chances. Sawing through sinew and then bone with Jens's knife was a horror I knew I would never be able to talk about, not even on the therapist's couch in five years.

With nervous hands still coated in the stars of her blood, I picked up her bare feet, sobbing lifelessly as I dragged her body to the portal and pushed it through, making sure none of the gold light that flared white even got close to touching me.

I crawled to my mother's mangled body. She was missing her right arm and was covered in blood.

Her eyes were no longer yellow, but there was no comfort in them, either. Her natural magic of laughter and optimism was not there. She was a ghost of her former self.

I knelt down clumsily and pulled her shoulders up in a hug. I clutched her to me as grief like I'd never known before crashed over me in fits and waves, crushing me with the inescapable reality that my mother was dead, and the therapist's couch I'd scheduled for five years from now could no longer wait.

I don't know how long it was that I screamed and wailed my agony, rocking my mother as if she was my baby. The utterance of my soul had no intelligible words, only incoherent mutterings of self-torture and regret.

Her hair didn't smell like hers. Her perfume was gone and her skin wasn't soft anymore. Her right shoulder was scabbed over with a circular puckered scar where her arm used to be. She was my mother, but not.

It dawned on me afresh as closure stitched painfully at the seams of my heart. My mom was dead, and with her, a part of me was, too.

After an immeasurable amount of time, I released her, staring inertly at the portal to Be. I sat cross-legged as I willed my heart to calm, my tears to settle. My hands and forearms were coated in stars and blood, my skin cold and tingly as I watched the gold light beckon me with its alluring beauty. Though the doorway was surrounded by arms that had gone motionless with Pesta's death, there was a peace to the macabre scene I couldn't describe.

It would be so easy to drift away. The pain would be gone if I just took a handful of steps toward the land of no pain. I would feel none of the weight that crushed my chest. There would be death surrounding me, but I wouldn't have to care anymore. I could rot along with the rest of those who'd chosen to leave their pain behind for the promise of mindless peace.

I stared down the portal with the same seriousness I'd once debated when I contemplated ending myself with the pills and vodka. I'd ended up pulling myself out of it after counting three reasons to stay alive.

Lying next to me was one reason not to. Before me in the portal was another. My dad was dead, and his bones had been knocked aside by his deranged daughter. Linus, my best friend and other half was gone. He'd died in my arms, and no amount of me giving my organs, my blood or my heart kept him by my side.

My love had little value. My love did not save the day.

I was quiet for a long time until the debate in my head turned to static, and I reached that rare place of zero thoughts.

I breathed as the stars glistened on my skin.

Slowly, like a blessing of light kissing the horizon of my mind, miniscule parts of myself came back to me.

My love helped to save Jens from his addiction to the lavender powder. That was reason one not to crawl into Be and collapse in my eternal rest.

My love saved Foss from the poisoned drink, the fire, the car wreck and oftentimes from himself. Reason two.

Reason began to trickle into my brain, bringing with it the dregs of emotion I was only just capable of feeling.

Linus. Though he'd died, I was not responsible for it. In fact, I'd fought alongside him with everything I had. Linus was loved, and in the end, his encroaching death shook me more than it ever had him. It would break him if he could hear the thoughts I was entertaining as viable options.

Linus served as a solid reason three.

Then, like shooting stars and fireworks, my brain began to open up and bloom with possibilities I had been too afraid to take seriously.

Going to London as Basil Cubbington.

Actually going on a first date with Jens.

The white picket fence.

Oh, the white picket fence and the entire life it represented. I may not have had much choice over the first half of my life, but with all the moxie and muscle I had in me, I was resolved that the second part would be every bit the *Leave it to Beaver* paradise I'd always dreamed of.

That settled it.

I wiped my hands off on my jeans, but it seemed the siren blood had dried on my hands and forearms, and would require soap or a loofa to get it off.

I stood, pulling on my jacket in preparation for my grand exit from Limbo. I gripped the rake and broom together in my sparkling fists and took a swing at the portal made from siren bones. In under a minute, I managed to destroy the portal and simultaneously set the trapped souls free.

I turned to my mother, exhausted, and lifted her by her bare feet, dragging her down the long corridor shrouded in shadow toward that white picket fence. We would go there together, and I would take her body to the permanent and peaceful home she also was never allowed to have.

When I finally reached the end of the rocky pathway, I laid her down and limped back for the dreaded farm tools so much controversy was concocted over. I carried the rake and the broom over to my mother and wound her remaining arm over them, taking the treasure back out to the Other Side. My side.

34

IMPOSSIBLY LESS

*T*he chaos that abounded when I emerged reeked of terror and frazzled nerves. I pushed my mother out first and toppled out atop her, apologizing to her body as Jens yanked me up.

"She's here! She's back! How is he?" Jens snatched me to his chest and shouted in earnest over his shoulder. He was shaking as he clung to me, his anxiety hitting its breaking point. "Lucy!" he cried, taking in my blood-soaked clothing. His hands ripped the jacket from my body faster than I could eke out an explanation. "Where? Where did you get hit? I'll fix it! I'll fix it!" He was frantic, his hands searching my body for signs of a tear. "Lucy! This... is this what I think it is?" He looked at my bare forearms and hands, which were still coated in thick glitter and stars. "Siren blood?"

"I'm not hurt," I informed him.

Britta's voice came back a sob from inside the van. "The seizure stopped! He's calmed down." I saw nothing except for Jens's jacket, which my face was buried in. Britta sounded terrified. "His eyes are opened! Jamie? Jamie, can you hear me?"

Jens continued to check my arms, legs and torso, fingering my face with his gloves to make sure I wasn't lying. "What happened? You were here, and then you got pulled through. We tried to get you, but we aren't human!"

Jens, Foss, Elsa and a handful of Huldras all demanded their questions be answered first, but I paid them no mind. I pried myself from Jens and pointed a glittery finger down at my mother. "Watch her," I instructed Foss as I wiped the tears from my face. He was the only person aside from Jens I would trust to watch over my treasure. "That's my mom. Nothing happens to her without my say-so."

I could tell Foss wanted to ask a million questions, but he locked them up for the time being and nodded, finally taking orders from me. His mom was the only person he actually loved, so I figured she'd be safest in his care.

I bent down and took the rake from atop my mom's body, shivering at the shift from warmth to freezing temperatures. My jacket felt unconscionably thin. Jens was talking to me, but I was focused on the job. "I can't tell which bones are my dad's and which are that Charles Mace guy's, so just help me gather them all, okay?"

"Lucy, what happened? You were here and then you weren't. Did I see Alrik's hand? Was it him? Was he in there?"

I ignored his questions and swung back the rake like a baseball bat. In one swish, I knocked down half the remaining bones, ignoring my regret and horror. Nothing compared to the determination with which I was driven to end this. Never again would my family be used by Pesta. Uncle Rick's soul was the last that would ever enter the Land of Be.

Jens kept asking his questions, but gathered up the bones as he did, piling them with the others.

The final swing brought out a growl that was less than human and more like a sheer animal attack. My father's bones clattered to the snow, each sound clanging my conscience with the disrespect that was trampled by the necessary means. It was awful, but victory in war was often thus. There was never triumph without sacrifice. There were no true wins without the bitterness of less and loss.

All around me in the snow was my loss. And though I had won, somehow I felt impossibly less.

I picked up the broom and slung both tools over my shoulders that would now be permanently weighted. "It's done."

Jens was still trying to get answers from me, but the explanations would only bring more conversations I was not ready for. I might never be ready for them, therapist's couch or not.

I jerked my chin toward the van. "Take me home, Jack."

35

FORMALDEHYDE AND FIDDLES

I can't say crematoriums are my favorite place in
the world, but one thing's for sure, they're quiet.
The barrage of questions didn't stop until about half an
hour after we pulled onto the freeway when they finally
realized I wasn't going to speak at all.

What happened? Is Pesta dead? Jamie asked in his
circuitous way. Apparently the entire time I'd been in
Limbo, Jamie had endured a seizure. He'd come out of it
the second I crossed back over, but he was still rattled from
the experience, sticking extra close to me to prevent us
from being separated again.

I slammed my mental door in his face, shutting him out
of any errant thoughts that were still sparking in my mind.
I'd instructed them to find the nearest crematorium, and
that was the last time I'd spoken. I still had my blood, my
mom's and Pesta's all over me, but I didn't care. Jens wiped
at my hands as we rode away but the blood was dried on
my clothes and the stars seemed frozen on my skin.

Jens fished out a fresh shirt for me so I could change at the next rest stop. "We're not stopping," I ruled. I peeled off the soiled garment that clung to my body in uncomfortable places. I handed it up to Leif in the front passenger's seat so he could throw it out the window. Everyone in the van now knew that I wore a lavender bra with pink stripes. I shoved the thermal shirt over my head and leaned back in my seat as Jens zipped up one of his hoodies on me. My jeans were a mess of glittery blood, but I didn't care enough to change them. I bent down to straighten the tongue of my left shoe and noticed my hands still looked like they'd been dipped in stars. They sort of reminded me of that same shiny glitter I'd seen in flecks on the chief's skin in Fossegrim.

Whatever.

Four hours later, the crematorium offered me the silence I craved. Foss had gone uncommonly quiet, slipping out with Liv to run an errand. Jens was seated on one side of me, and Jamie held Britta's hand at my other side. Reverence slung over our shoulders, and it finally united us off our separate frenzied paths.

Elsa helped whistle along the professional running the crematorium to get the job done right away, lumping all the bones in one go for a group cremation. He took the bodies back and prepared them while we waited, a row of misfits staring at our hands. The waiting room had stiff-backed uncomfortable faux-leather chairs, brown to match the dull carpet and beige walls.

Foss and Liv returned with a shopping bag. Liv made a point not to be annoying, for which I was grateful.

My heart was heavy, and the rest of my body felt the

same weight that pulled me downward. I still hadn't told them what happened, though they were all dying to know. I didn't have it in me. In fact, I didn't have anything in me anymore.

Foss's eyes were wary as they darted around the waiting room the Huldras had whistled clear for us. His face had a dare on it that warned everyone to not comment on what was in his shopping bag. He tried to start his sentence three times before he gave up and pulled out a brand new violin.

Something in me flickered, but I said nothing, which was the exact right thing to say.

Foss sat down on the floor cross-legged in front of me and put the instrument to his chin, twisting the pegs a few centimeters here and there to test the pitch. The persuasive powers of the Fossegrim fiddles didn't work on me because my blood was part human, but the magic worked well on the Undrans. Foss and I had shared too many passionate kisses in his orchard because Jamie got me buzzed on Gar through the bond, and Foss had been drunk on fiddle music.

Foss put the fiddle in his lap, frustrated. "I know this won't help you," he said to me. "I know Grimen magic doesn't work on you. But it's the best I can do. So you know, I don't want to hear about it."

Foss raised the violin again, and then lowered it. "I haven't touched a fiddle since… you know." He narrowed his eyes at me. "So be grateful." His commands were always a little cute. Like he could really control me. Like he needed to demand gratitude of a nice deed. Foss was an idiot, but part of him would always be *my* idiot.

When the bow hit the strings, my heart ceased its perpetual breaking out of pure curiosity. He closed his eyes and stroked note after note from the instrument, coaxing out a low melancholy that vibrated my heartstrings with every shifting melody.

After a few bars, just like the Nøkken song and the Huldra whistle, the fiddle started belting out three or four notes simultaneously. Slowly, and without my conscious choice, the grip my brain had on my depression started to loosen in bits and pieces.

Suddenly I could feel the sorrow of my fate without running from it. I could hear my sadness without being buried by it. I could see my past without breaking myself in half at every memory.

It wasn't magic. It was music.

Jens wrapped an arm around my shoulders, and I sunk into him, foregoing the space I didn't seem to need anymore. I began to breathe, the fifty-pound weight on my chest alleviating to a mere twenty.

When Foss finished his melancholy song that only at the end reached a level of closure and peace, the room was silent. Everyone had tears in their eyes or dotting their cheeks. Foss put the violin away and placed a light brush of a kiss to my closed mouth in lieu of speaking.

I whispered, "Thank you," to him, and he nodded solemnly in response.

Elsa came out and motioned to me. "It's time, *Domslut.*" She had stopped calling me "baby doll" since I emerged from the portal. Instead she addressed me with this new moniker I didn't care for either. She spoke it with reverence though, so while I wanted to be offended she was calling me a slut, somehow it felt like she wasn't really saying that.

I stood on legs that were surely a miracle; I have no idea how they held me upright. Jens caught my hand, his eyelashes wet. "No. You don't need to see that."

"I've got to make sure their bones are gone."

"I'll go, then." The dread of duty was evident on his face. Jens had been friends with my parents. I couldn't put him through that. He kept touching the spot on his neck where his pouch of lavender powder would have been and sniffing subconsciously.

Foss stood and clamped his hand down on Jens's shoulder so he reclaimed his seat. "I'll make sure it happens."

I held up my sparkly finger. "Wait. I want you to get me some of their ashes. My mom and my dad. I know the other guy Mace'll be in there too, but it's fine. He was my cousin, right? My family should be together." I took my necklace off and handed it to Foss reluctantly. "Please be careful with that." I stretched out my hand, but retracted it before I could relinquish it, a panic attack jumping atop me from out of nowhere. My breath was shallow and the walls felt impossibly close to where I stood. I shook my head like a caged animal. Linus and I couldn't be parted. The thought was too wrong for words. "On second thought, no. I can't." I shook my head and backed up to sit in my chair again, clutching my brother tight as my breathing came out in uneven gusts.

"I'll give it right back," Foss promised. To his credit, he did not mock my childishness.

I put the necklace back on and covered the heart-shaped vial to keep it in place. "No. You'd have to pour out some of Linus, and I can't... I can't." I shook my head. "I just can't."

Jamie turned and wrapped his arms around me. "Jens, hand me your bag. I seem to remember Lucy buying a vial of poison in Bedra. I'll dump out the poison, and we'll put your parents and Charles Mace inside with your brother."

Jamie was kind, as always. He didn't rat me out by telling them I'd bought lavender powder. He saved me from myself, and saved a bit of my family in the process. I loved him.

Jamie kissed the top of my head. "I love you, too." He fished through Jens's bag for several minutes until he brought out the cylindrical vial with a blue glass swirl wrapped around it. The fluorescent lights overhead illuminated the sparkle of the lavender glitter inside.

Jens caught a glimpse of the vial and let out a strangled cry I wished I could save him from. Without a word, I'd broken his heart. I could hear it in his tone and see it when he slipped out of his chair and bowed down on all fours, a dog on the floor at my feet.

Foss glared at Jens and snatched the glass vial from Jamie. He stomped to the snow and dumped it out in one angry shake. I half-expected him to stomp back in and shout, "You're grounded!" at me, but he marched straight past me and followed Elsa to the back room.

I sat in my chair, my head down and hands in my lap as Jens punished himself on the ground.

Jamie patted my back twice, but did not try to prod back into my brain. Neither of us wanted to be in my head in that moment.

Jens finally sat up and moved in front of me, seating himself at my feet and leaning back against my knees. Without a word between us, he picked up my hand and placed a kiss on it.

I rested my palm in his thick hair and tickled his scalp without really making myself think too hard about the lost powder, my little secret. I didn't think about Uncle Rick. I didn't think about Pesta. In fact, I didn't think about Undraland at all.

My mind was a snowstorm, a blur of white noise and cold. My parents were being burned just down the hallway. The nothing I felt was the only safe thing in my life, so I clung to it as I stroked my boyfriend's hair, silent tears sliding down his cheeks.

We'd won, but we'd lost. Oh, how lost we were.

Foss returned however long later, palm extended. "Give me your brother."

"What?" I scrunched my nose up at him.

"His ashes. I'll put them together with his parents. It's a better place to rest than alone in there."

My heart caught in my throat as Jens took the necklace from around my neck. "I'll watch him," he promised, and then went with Foss back into the behind the scenes room where they no doubt had funnels and whatnot for such things.

They came back with my blue-wrapped cylinder, and as I examined the change in the ashes, I noticed remnants of the captivating lavender glitter woven through the death, entrancing me with its beautiful swirl. My family was a beautiful thing. We were odd, had strange senses of humor and never had a home to return to, but we had each other.

Finally, we were together again. I didn't even mind that Charles Mace was in there. It was almost like we had a friend to share our jokes with. My fingers closed around the small tube as I swallowed. "Thank you."

Foss clapped Jens on the back, and Jamie stood to hug his best friend. "Brother, you did all you could."

And then Jens broke. So shocking was the sight of my boyfriend crying audibly, I snapped out of my seclusion for a moment as my heart yanked me toward the oddity.

"I didn't know! Linus was dead and I was devastated! *One night* I came back to Tomten. One night! And when I got back, they were dead! I didn't know Pesta was close! I didn't know they'd gone to her! I should've, but I didn't."

Jamie clutched Jens tighter, kissing his cheek. "Pesta waited *until* you weren't there, brother. She knew there was no way she was getting at them if you were around. There's no place safer than with you!"

"I shouldn't have taken that day off! I shouldn't have left."

Jamie's burly arms kept Jens in his cocoon of safety. He began to sway slightly, rocking Jens through his grief. "They died because of Pesta, not you. They got to see every day of their son's life because of you."

Jens whispered, "What about their daughter's?"

Jamie hugged the mess in his arms with so much love, I had no doubt Britta would be cherished her entire life long. Jamie was meant to love and be loved. He was meant for a bucketful of children and like, seven dogs. He whispered to his best friend, "Jens, Lucy's still alive. Look at her. There's still a whole lifetime of duty for you, brother. No Tom better for a job like her."

Part of me registered that he called me a job, but I overlooked it for the moment. Jens glanced over at me, embarrassed at his tears and ashamed at his seeming failure. "Lucy, I'm so sorry!" he whispered, wiping the condensation off his cheeks.

"Stop it," I crooned, taking a clumsy step closer. "Pesta's the one who killed my family, not you." I rubbed Jamie's back and stood straighter. "And Alrik and I killed Pesta, so it's done. You don't have to worry so much anymore."

Though they suspected as much, the intakes of breath all around me told me they had all needed that kill confirmed. Questions tumbled from everyone, but I held up my hands. "Let's get to a hotel, and I'll tell you everything. I can't do this here. I don't want to be here anymore. It stinks like formaldehyde and dust." I turned to Foss and Elsa. "Did you guys make sure he burned all the bones?"

Elsa bowed her head, a complete turnaround in how she normally was around me. "Yes, *Domslut*."

Foss held up his hand in solemn vow. "Every single one."

"Then let's go. I feel like I've been hit by a truck."

36

BEAUTIFUL BLOOD

*W*e split off from the Huldras, Elsa taking her team home after Liv delivered a provocative kiss to an indifferent Foss. *Women.*

Jamie used Britta as a crutch and kept his free arm around Jens as they led the way to the SUV the Huldras let us keep. Foss walked by my side, his hand on the small of my back and his arm stabilizing my janky gait as we walked through the long building. He watched the shadows around corners for false moves. I wondered when we would all stop feeling the constant press of danger.

When the icy air hit us, Jens recalled my lack of a coat. "Wait," he insisted, unzipping his to wrap around me.

"I'm okay, really. The cold doesn't bother me. Let's just get to the car."

Jens paid me no mind, but covered my shoulders in his winter jacket anyway. I kinda loved that he knew when to ignore me and when to listen. I kinda loved everything about him.

When we got to the car, Jens sat in the driver's seat, taking his job of protecting me too literally. I was a far better snow driver than he was even with one foot, but whatever. I let the poor guy have a win. He looked so worn out from the catharsis, I reckoned he needed a victory, however small.

He drove us to the nearest hotel that was not a motel and checked us in with no fear of Pesta coming for us. We stalked up to the adjoining rooms, and to their credit, the barrage of questions did not come until after the door closed behind us and we'd shed our coats and shoes.

I held up my hands as I sat at the head of the king-sized bed, hefting my bum leg up onto the bedspread. "Pesta's dead." I patted the spot next to me, and Jens slid to my side, resting his back on the headboard as his hand slid into mine. The comforter was white down and soft as a cloud. The blue walls emanated a calm vibe I hoped would seep into my pores. The hotel was a fair bit nicer than the ones I'd stayed in with my family, but I hardly had the heart to enjoy it.

Britta and Jamie sat at the foot of the bed, facing us, and Foss brought the chair to the side of the bed and propped his feet up on the mattress. "Alright. Out with the whole story now. We've been patient enough."

"Uncle Rick and I killed Pesta." All around gasps, followed by more questions, and finally the whole account spilled out of me. Uncle Rick pulling me through. Our little talk. Blah, blah, blah.

Jamie was overwhelmed, so I used the opportunity to tuck the bit about Pesta giving me her *arv* away in a box in the corner of my brain so I didn't have to touch it. It didn't matter. Pesta wasn't my mom, no matter what she'd done to my forehead. I didn't want the group freaking out about it, and I certainly didn't want it known that Pesta wasn't actually the last siren anymore. It was a good thing the *arv* didn't leave a lasting mark on my forehead, so the group would never have to know.

Now I was part siren, with Pesta's DNA mixing in with all the other mess swirling around inside me. I felt heavier, though there were so many excuses I could blame that weight in my soul on. I wondered if my blood looked like Pesta's now, and knew I would do everything I could to avoid finding out. Pesta was part of me. I wanted no part of any of it, so I pushed it to the place where all the bad things got buried and vowed never to think on it again. I would hide it from myself, which was the only way to hide it from Jamie.

Britta burst into tears when I recounted my monster mom trying to kill me and Alrik, but I was surprisingly calm. I sounded like a school teacher explaining emotionless arithmetic. I left out the part about Pesta touching my forehead. Something about that was still unsettling to me, but I couldn't put into words why. "And then I came out and rejoined all of you." There were a few beats of silence, so I took my opportunity. "I'm hopping in the shower while you all digest that." I pointed to my bag. "Britt, could you do me a solid and grab me some clean pajamas? I'm covered in siren blood, and I feel gross."

Jens hung his head, my words somehow cutting him without my knowledge.

"We're safe, guys. No one's chasing us. We can start lives here and not worry about Weres or Pesta or Be. It's done." It was meant to be reassuring, but I could hear the absence of a win in my voice.

Instead of handing me my clothes, Britta set them in the bathroom for me. She kissed my cheek, looking like she had a mouthful to say to me, but kept the cavalcade inside. She could see I was a mess.

I tried not to put much weight on my foot as I stepped into the shower.

I stood in the hot water for I'm not sure how long. It was so long that eventually I sat down to finger the new necklace that would go through life with me. The vial was heavier than my Linus heart, but then again, life carried with it more weight than it had before. I didn't think that was possible.

The way my lungs didn't totally inflate told me I was on the brink of buckling.

Jamie felt my distress and whispered in my mind, *Rest, Lucy. You've had a long day and a long life. Talk to Jens. No matter what, we're all here. We'll heal from this together.*

I said nothing to him in response, but nodded as his words peppered warmth into me in time with the shower. I pulled my knees to my chest and laid my head atop them, finally calming enough to close my eyes and take a deep breath.

That's better. Good job, sweetheart. Now wash up and go to bed. Call me if you need help.

I unwrapped the sliver of French-milled soap and started at my toes, washing the warmed skin inch by inch all the way up my body until I reached my glittery arms.

The stars blinked at me, dot and dime-sized pricks of silver and iridescent glitter and pure light stuck to my skin, immoveable in their stubbornness, clinging to my fore-arms and hands with zeal. "Britta?" I called loud enough to carry to the bed area.

Jens's voice answered me just outside the bathroom. "They all turned in for the night. I reckoned you could use a little space and a lot of sleep."

"You reckon, eh?" I teased, smiling slightly at the lingo as I stood back up under the hot flow. It felt strange and somehow right to smile again, no matter how small the motion was.

"You need something?"

"I dunno. Maybe a better soap? Some rubbing alcohol or something? Pesta's blood won't come off my hands."

"I'm coming in," he warned me, opening the door and sliding inside the cocoon of warm steam I'd built in my too-long shower. "Holy sauna, Batman. How can you breathe in this?"

"I'm part bat," I answered, holding the curtain around my body and peeking out the side. "You got something to get this off? Maybe a loofa?"

Jens rolled his eyes. "Yeah. Let me check my bag for a loofa. Did you think I was your *girl*friend?"

I batted my eyes at him. "You've got the eyelashes for it."

"That better have been a compliment," he grumbled. Then he sighed and leaned back against the door. He was showered, most likely borrowing Jamie's bathroom, and dressed in blue flannel pajamas and a black t-shirt that hugged his muscular frame like it was meant to.

"You're doing that shirt a giant favor," I confessed. Though it was an effort, I fought to reclaim a little of our levity.

He looked down as if only just realizing which clothes he was wearing. "Really? How about now?" He flexed for my ogling pleasure.

"I thought you said it was already too hot in here."

He shook his head, smiling at our flirty banter. "Man, I like you. Finish up and come on out. Leave your hands alone. We have to talk."

"You didn't have to come in here to tell me that."

"Sure, but now that I'm in here, I get to kiss you." He moved toward me and placed a chaste kiss to my lips, coaxing yet more heat into my body. "Come on out, babe." He gave me that wisp of a smirk I adored and left.

I washed my hair and finished up, my hands and arms still sparkling as I dried myself. The siren blood didn't bleed onto the towel or my clean clothes as I got dressed. It was like thick dried paint that didn't want to come off – almost like a second skin.

When I emerged, Jens was flipping through channels in bed in those pajamas that were somehow both cozy and sexy. "I missed bad TV the most," he admitted, shifting on the mattress. I could tell his back was bothering him, but he didn't want to address it. "Come watch this one with me. I think it's a reality show that's auctioning off plastic surgery to the ugliest baby." He pulled down the covers next to him and lured me to his side.

I donned a smile as we lay down next to each other, our heads and shoulders propped up on too many pillows so we could see the TV. His arm was behind me, his hand massaging my scalp. My leg draped atop his, our bare toes connecting in ways our words weren't ready to.

"I can tell we're watching TV because you're afraid to

tell me something," I commented as nonchalantly as I could. "Out with it, Jack."

"I love your body."

My eyebrows raised. "Well, I didn't expect you to say that. Um, back atcha? Why would you be afraid to tell me that?"

He turned the volume down on the flat screen, picked up my sparkly fingers and kissed them. In the lamplight, they sparkled even more brightly, illuminating the night for us as real stars would. "Every part of you, I'm over the moon for." He grimaced. "Well, truthfully, I'm not crazy about Foss's emblem on your breasts, but other than that, your body is exactly perfect. A ten in a world of fives."

"Aw, that's sweet. You too, baby. Thanks for laying it on thick. My elbows are amazing."

"So I don't want you to freak out." He continued to kiss my fingers, one at a time. The stars actually glowed and lit his face when he got close, flickering celestial patterns dancing on his golden tattoo. "What do you know about siren blood?"

I snuggled into his nook, stroking his calf with my foot. "Just that it's crazy beautiful."

"Two good words for it." He tangled his fingers through mine and held up my arm for us to both examine. "Killing a siren is hard to do. When they were roaming Undra, they were pretty powerful. Feared and revered. Their blood is sort of a marker. It was supposed to be a bad one. You know, you see someone covered in stars, you run the other way because that person's crazy dangerous. But when the sirens were offed in the massive witch hunt, the marker became a good thing. Like a battle scar that showed the world you were unstoppable. That you'd gone up against a siren and won. You met the chief in Fossegrim, right?"

"Yeah. He had a few sparkles on his hands," I recalled.

"How do you think he got to be one of the four powers? He killed a siren and wears her blood. Everyone who sees him automatically fears him. They call him *Dom*, which means doom or judgment." He turned my arm this way and that, the stars catching the light off the TV and reflecting glitter on the walls like bits of a disco ball. "You're going to carry these battle scars as long as you live. Siren blood becomes part of you. It's why Elsa was calling you *Domslut*. That's the female version."

I'm not sure how long I went without breathing, but I think I maxed out the limit on what was acceptable. "I… it won't come off? Wait, what? Are you serious?" I sat up and scratched at my skin over and over like a crazy person, trying to remove at least the top layer of dermis to see what could be salvaged beneath. "Get it off me! Get it off!"

Jamie called in my brain, *Lucy, is that you doing this? Stop!*

I shut my mental door on Jamie when I began to hyperventilate. I wanted to tear off my skin, but knew my siren blood would be seen, and I couldn't have that. I had no options, no way out.

I screamed. "She got me! Pesta's on me!" My mind whirled as visions of grabbing Jens's knife to cut the skin off my arms taunted me.

"Lucy, stop!" Jens shouted. His hands went up to calm me down.

I was frantic, and perhaps not rational. "Don't touch me! Will it get on you?"

235

"No. It dried probably a few seconds after it touched you the first time."

Jamie burst through the door, limped quickly toward us and tackled me backward on the bed, knocking the wind out of me (and himself). "It's okay!" he shouted. "It's just a scar, nothing more. She didn't win. She didn't get your right arm. She didn't take your soul."

I twisted under him and clawed at my arms, fruitlessly trying to remove Pesta from my life. "Get it off!" I screamed.

"Lucy, stop!" Jens begged. He separated my arms from each other, his mournful face pleading with me to remain lucid. "It goes down deep, probably to the bone. Baby, it could be so much worse. Siren blood is beautiful."

"She got my arms! She didn't take my right arm, she put her stamp on both!" I shouted, moisture pricking my eyes. "I killed her to leave her behind, not carry her and this whole stupid battle with me for the rest of my life!"

"Breathe, *syster*. Breathe," Jamie commanded me, mimicking deep breaths until I acquiesced. *Calm down. I'm here. The battle's over.*

Jamie was crushing me on the bed, staring me down with... not pity. No, it was camaraderie. I was his equal. Somehow through our long and tangled journey, I was a warrior, not an inconvenient human to drag along as dead weight. It wasn't just because I fought alongside all of them. It was the marks, too. I bore the marks of battle now. My body was peppered with bruises, scars and now stars.

I was a warrior. I was Lucy, Queen of the Other Side.

I could tell Jamie was reading my thoughts as my muscles relaxed under his weight. He lifted his arm off me and pounded his fist over his heart, nodding once to acknowledge the great battle we had been through, and the many more that may come throughout our conjoined lives. Then he picked up my shimmering hand, curled my fingers in a fist and pressed it to my chest. "Queen Lucy of the Other Side. Undrans will see your arms and cower in respect. You killed the last siren."

I sniffled and tried to wrap my mind around it all while I kept the dangerous thoughts tucked safely away from Jamie. After a few beats, I nodded. "Okay. I… It's okay. I won't hurt us anymore."

Without breaking eye contact, Jamie spoke quietly, lulling me with his gentle way as he traced my cheekbone with his thumb. "Queen Lucy the Fierce, it was an honor to fight beside you. You didn't need Undraland magic for any of it. You're purely human, and *that* is your beautiful thing."

I closed my eyes, swallowing down my panic and forcing words to match my pain. "I let Uncle Rick stab my mother," I confessed, my voice breaking on the last note. "There's no forgiveness for that. What kind of a person can do something so awful?" I couldn't even look at him; so deep was my shame in it all. "I'm afraid." I showed him my hands. "This changes things. It's changing me. I can feel it," I confessed, shivering at the memory of Pesta touching my forehead and the strange chill it sent through me. "Pesta did something to me in Limbo. I feel different inside. I don't know how to explain it." There was a numbing dark in me. I felt unable to laugh at the same jokes or find the levity in things I used to.

Still pressed down atop me, Jamie took my hand in his, kissing my sparkling knuckles. "You're my *syster*," he whispered. "Pesta didn't alter that. I don't fear the darkness inside you," he said, answering with love the deep-rooted questions that tore at my insides. Jamie rolled off me, pulled me up next to him on the bed and hugged me, swallowing me with the same comfort that broke Jens down in the crematorium. "You are always the one who condemns you the most. You know the reasons I could give you to absolve that guilt, and yet you choose to carry the burden." He kissed my forehead and smoothed back my damp hair. "Lucy, you can be as light as you wish, or as burdened down as you choose. Either way, no one will ever hurt you again, except for you. I'm afraid not even Jens the Brave can save you from that." He held up my arm, stretching it out like a graceful ballerina. "You have to choose to be light." He whispered in my ear, "It's time for you to play, *liten syster*. To live. It's time you put up your white picket fence and left your pain in Undraland." He kissed my cheek, and I shivered.

Flickers of laughter from nights spent playing cards with my family fluttered like a swiftly shuffled deck through my brain. Mom and Dad sending us off on countless first days of school with a well wish and, what back then felt like too many hugs, and still somehow never enough.

I wrapped my arms around Jamie, my makeshift brother. I couldn't believe I ever tired of hugs from my family. Had I known, I would have squeezed them forever, shielding them with everything I was, and now am.

I would not waste anymore of my life holding back. I squeezed Jamie with my sparkly arms, the light dancing on his neck in the room that was only lit by the lamp, the TV and me. "Thank you. I love you, big brother." I kissed his cheek, and I could tell he was grinning. "I want that life. The good one without the running and hiding and all the fear."

"Then you shall have it, darling girl." Jamie lifted me off the ground and laid me in the bed, motioning for Jens to come sit beside me. Jamie gripped my cold toes, bringing them up to his mouth to blow his warm breath on them. Since they were connected to his toes, he knew exactly how gentle to be. Jamie nodded to his best friend and left.

I decided Jamie was right. I had fought enough. Now was time for rest, and in the morning, I would play. I would laugh, and I would move on. I would find a home and start a life there.

Jens bent over me and pressed his lips to mine, his gorgeous eyebrows peaked in the center of his forehead. "You feeling better, Loos?"

Our toes connected again, and our kiss curled us around each other in a web only we knew solace in. I kissed my Tom, the tension in my body deflating in his arms. "You know? I am." I stared up at him, not sure how I got so lucky that in the midst of all the loss, Jens and I found each other. "Kiss me, Jens. I think finally I'm ready for you now."

"I'm not sure that'll ever be true, but I'll take the kiss." The beautiful and dangerous man I always felt safe with kissed me. I settled into his embrace and began making mental plans of the life that was finally on the horizon.

$\mathcal{M}$y Beautiful Thing

"HONEY, do you think you could go just a little bit faster?" Jamie begged.

Britta's careful calculation of the other drivers was a thing I found adorable. Going ten miles under the speed limit was a thing Jens and Jamie did not.

"What's the real rush? Take your time, Britt." I adjusted my knee-length black pencil skirt and tugged on the hem of my gray blouse. "I thought I was done wearing dresses when we left Undraland, but the skirts found me with a vengeance."

"I think the heels are sexy."

"Well, then you can wear them next time."

Britta, Jamie and Jens conversed about the weather and the drive, but I kept to myself for the next twenty miles until Jamie poked into my brain. *You're doing it again,* he informed me. *That quiet thing. You have to engage, Lucy. You can't keep pulling back from us.*

I'm here. I'm listening. I just don't have anything to add.

You're making Jens crazy with all your silence. It's been months, syster.

I mentally shrugged.

You can do better than this.

I bristled at the insinuation that I'd not been through enough to warrant a bit of quiet time. *You want to talk? Let's talk. How about we discuss what we're going to do when your year-long furlough comes to an end? Royalty or not, you'll be summoned back to Undraland, and I'm still pretty firm on not going back.*

I applied for an extension, Jamie shot back. *My father doesn't want me in his kingdom any more than I want to be there. Trust me, he's just making me sweat by withholding the paperwork.*

Sure, Jamie. If you're so certain it'll all be fine, why haven't you told Britta?

Jamie spoke so his voice carried to Jens and me in the backseat. "Lucy, could you explain about tipping again? I can't remember who gets a tip. Is it the cook or the waiter or the doctor?"

Jamie was almost as good at avoiding things as I was. In truth, none of us were terribly worried. I just didn't like him pushing me to talk all the time. Once his father learns I'm laplanded to Jamie, they'll have to take that into consideration and grant him permanent residence on the Other Side, of which I guess I was still queen. Jamie's marriage to Britta? Well, that was something his betrothal to Freya certainly didn't allow. There would probably be words about that, but in the end, that's most likely all it would be.

Jens glanced behind us from our cuddle nook in the backseat. "I'd like to get there sometime before dinner. Cars are starting to pile up, sis."

"Hey, backseat drivers. Shut it," I said, palming Jens's face to silence him. "You're doing great, Britta. Tell your brother where he can shove it."

Jamie turned his head to give me a simpering look at my sass. I enjoyed paying him back for his verbal comments to Britta and his nonverbal ones toward me. "Very ladylike, Lucy."

Britta was determined to get her license before the end of the month, but they were cutting it pretty close. She drifted left, nearly crossing over into oncoming traffic. Each time Jamie or Jens course-corrected her, it made her nervous, but it was necessary most times.

In the six months since the mission ended, a lot had happened, and in a wonderful dichotomy, not so much happened, either. The lots were the normal things that were so new to all of us, it felt like winning the lottery every single day. Jens bought us a large tract of land with a big farmhouse he and I occupied. Then we had a second house constructed on the property on the furthest reach of the laplanding bond's tether.

The first piece of mail addressed to me had been a thing of beauty. It was a Chinese restaurant menu, and it quickly became our favorite place to frequent. We had a key hook on the wall, a big bathtub and a welcome mat Jens insisted was just a formality. He hated having guests over. What a grump.

Jamie, Jens, Britta and I enrolled in college together. Jens didn't care what we took; he was just happy to be able to be in public with me in his visible form. Jamie and Britta were quick studies, but they mostly took the classes for the social acclimation of it all. Jamie was adorable, asking each professor as many questions as he could squeeze in. Britta was cute when she got flustered at the terminology she didn't understand. Jens was positively gorgeous when he studied with me. Furrowed brow, chewed-on pencil… all of it, I couldn't get enough of. I could picture him in doctor's scrubs, and relished the imagery.

I was… me. And for the first time, that felt like a good thing. Well, I was a subdued version of me. I was older, less carefree. Jens even commented the morning before last with a hint of sadness in his voice that I was quieter since Undraland. I had nothing to say to that.

The four of us had just completed our first semester of mostly prerequisites. I earned all As except for one B in literature (please, like I needed that to be a doctor. Unless Emily Dickinson needs her blood pressure taken, literature and I can finally part ways).

"Okay," Jens spoke up from his place beside me. His finger was twirling a lock of my hair that now touched my shoulders. "Britta, if we're late, Foss is gonna be pissed. He's not exactly friendly to begin with, and I really want this to happen today."

Britta was gripping the steering wheel and spoke through gritted teeth. "If you want me to get my license, I need to practice. I only failed it by a few technicalities last time around, and I *will* pass it this time."

"Seventh time's the charm," Jens muttered, scratching his eyebrow.

"You'll pass the test, I'm certain of it," Jamie assured his wife, his hand on her shoulder.

She shrugged off the gentle touch. "Don't distract me!" she whined, switching on the wiper blades instead of the turn signal.

"This is just not safe," Jens grumbled. "Pull over, sis. I got it from here. Lucy's still my charge, and I say no."

Three cars honked at us as they passed by. Britta was a jumble of nerves when she crawled into the backseat with me. I held her hand and rubbed her arm while I thought up questions to distract her. "I'm loving what you guys did to your bedroom. It's growing on me."

Okay, that was a lie. Their room was horrifying. Jamie and Foss had made an iron shield to hang up on the wall that Britta and I had painted a cheery sky blue. Over the doorway was hung a large sword, and Jamie's family crest was emblazoned on a huge breastplate that hung over the headboard. All it was missing was a cell, and the scene would be complete. As tired as I sometimes got watching movies late at night with Britta, I made sure never to fall asleep at her house. The guest bedroom was even worse.

Luckily Jens had taste dissimilar to his best friend and let me do the house, painting the rooms alternating olive and lavender with gold accents to keep his Undraland feel to the place. Our room was a haven, and I adored every inch of our two-story slice of Heaven. Foss had agreed to help me paint a calming constellation on the ceiling over our bed when he stopped being a jerk. So, you know, never.

Foss was as he always was. Try as I might, I didn't really want to change him much. He didn't hit me anymore, thanks to the Huldras peeling back his Fossegrimen curse to a tolerable level. We even reserved a room in our house for him to stay in when he comes to visit. He liked it better when we headed out to stay with him instead, but I like him on my turf. He prefers a kingdom, but I'm in no mood to be his servant ever again.

My darling husband bought a ranch about half an hour away. It was just enough space for us to live peaceably with each other. He employed a great many ranch hands who have the patience of Job, not correcting him too often when he treated them like servants who must obey, instead of as employees with a choice.

You're doing it again, Lucy. Britta's been talking to you, and you're doing that barely there grunting you picked up. Engage! Jamie scolded me.

Jens closed the time gap and pulled into the courthouse only five minutes late. He grinned at Foss, who had his arms crossed over his chest and a surly look on his handsome mug as he tapped his foot on the steps of the courthouse expectantly. "Hey, Foss, oh King of the Ranchers," Jens called to him, saluting with two fingers.

I held up my hands to stop everyone. "Can't bring in your knives, guys. No concealed weapons in a courthouse."

This was met with unhappy protests and cagey glances around the parking lot. We had left Undraland and eminent danger, but the anticipation of violence was engrained.

Foss was in no mood, which is to say, business as usual.

"I love that you think I have all the time in the world to just wait around for you people."

I got out and helped Jamie extract Britta from the car. "Oh, you're so important," I said, shoving my long black opera gloves onto my hands and rolling them up my glowing star-spangled arms. "How will the cows know to stand where they've been standing all morning and eat grass? How will the earth turn without you there to bark at it?"

Foss glowered at me. "I wouldn't mock the man who feeds you."

I grinned. "Did you bring me a present?"

Foss grimaced. "Why would I do that?"

My face fell. "I thought you knew. In my culture, when you get a divorce, the man brings the woman a gift to signify all their happy years together."

Foss scratched the back of his neck and glanced around uncomfortably. "Oh. I didn't know. How about a cow? You can have one of my cows." He finally met my gaze and realized I was teasing. "I think I'll send it over in the middle of the night and have it delivered to your living room." He shook his head. "'For all our happy years together'? We've only been married less than a year, and a lot of that was unhappy."

"Unhappy?" I teased, walking up to him with my let's-have-a-fight swagger. "Since when have you ever been unhappy?" I reached up and pinched his nose, gratified at how much progress he'd made that he didn't shove me. "Come on, darling husband. It's time you were rid of me once and for all."

Foss stomped into the building, but Jens proffered his

arm like a gentleman. He was extra sweet to me that morning. I was treated to such niceties as breakfast in bed, my choice of music in the living room, and even a back rub when he noticed me massaging a crick in my neck from too much studying the night before.

"You sure about this?" Jens asked, opening the door for me and his sister.

I nodded. In reality, I didn't know why it had taken Jens asking me in carefully chosen words to realize I didn't actually have to be married to Foss anymore. Of course I knew it, but the part of me I didn't like to examine too close still felt reluctant, even as my husband stood impatiently in the lobby. When the elves had drawn up our paperwork to cross over to the Other Side, they had put me down as having a Fossegrimen husband. I was legally married on paper, thanks to the efficiency of the Undraland office.

I didn't want Foss like that, but...

No. No buts. I wasn't willing to think about my reasons for hesitating. They were childish and selfish. Jens. I wanted to be with Jens. Obviously.

So, you know, maybe I shouldn't be married to his friend anymore.

I kissed Jens's cheek and detached myself from him. When I agreed to come in this morning, I didn't have the heart to tell him I'd gone with Jamie four times already, but didn't have the guts to go through with it. Seeing Jens's insecure and soft-spoken plea made me realize I was being silly. Foss was never mine to begin with. There was no point in holding onto him like I was. Besides, Foss wouldn't up and leave without talking to me first. We didn't need a piece of paper to tie us together. We had Undraland.

Foss was dressed in dark gray slacks and a green dress shirt. He was so rarely out of his ranch gear; it was strange to see him so put together. Of course, I picked out all his clothes, so I wasn't terribly surprised to see the combination, but he was handsome all the same.

He waved off Britta and Jamie, but met Jens's eye and postured, extending his hand in formal greeting. "We'll be out soon," he said, giving an unspoken command for Jens to give us a little space to get through the process.

Jens nodded easily, but I could see the hesitation he wanted to voice. "Sure. We'll be out here."

The judge's chambers had an outer room with blue vinyl chairs and a clerk at a desk who granted unenthusiastic couples entry when it was their turn. Foss led the way to two chairs near the back, motioning for me to sit down.

When Jens was gone, Foss's body language around me was different. He was looser and given to touching me when he normally might not. His arm slung around the back of my chair, his too-long legs stretching out as he tried to make himself comfortable in a world where everything was just a little too small for him. We sat in silence for several minutes before he spoke. "You're still doing that quiet thing I hate."

I shrugged.

"How are you doing with all this?" He motioned to the divorce papers he had in his hand.

I sat with my shoulders hunched forward, protecting my emotions, lest he see them and laugh. "Oh, you know. Fine."

"Jamie told me you tried to file your paperwork a few times, but couldn't go through with it." He pinched a lock of my hair between his thumb and forefinger, addressing it instead of me directly. Now that he was in my world, he knew it was no big deal to come across blonde hair. I thought he would lose his fascination with mine after the first month here. But still his fingers found my curls entrancing, winding themselves through my tresses he only loved more the longer they grew.

"Jamie has a fat mouth." I batted Foss's hand away. "Quit it." I huffed. "Yes. I tried to file before, but something always came up, so I put it off. Nothing more complicated than that."

"Women get stoned for leaving their husbands where I come from."

I glared at him. "You want I should stay married to you? Have you readied the skipping rocks?"

He crossed one leg over the other. "No. I was just saying, it's very different here."

"How about this, next time you want to make a little chit chat, steer clear of subjects like stoning me, okay?"

"You're nervous," he observed. "You always pick fights with me when you're anxious."

I harrumphed. "Yeah? Well, you only pick fights with me when you're awake. It's how I know you're breathing."

He chuckled, and the sound was somehow a comfort. "I feel strange about it, too, and not just because marriage is more permanent where I come from."

We sat in silence a few beats before his hand found its way back to my hair. I relaxed a little and leaned against him, resting my head between his chest and his shoulder.

"It's good we're divorcing. It was all pretend anyway. I can't believe Jens held back as long as he did." I didn't know why I was still trying to convince myself.

"Jens is in a tough spot. He's in love with you, but he's also bound to you. He has to tread carefully with these kinds of things so he doesn't spook you and make you both completely miserable."

My palms were sweating, so I wiped them off on my skirt. "Yeah. I just didn't realize this would be the thing that spooked me."

With his free hand, he reached over his torso and stuck two fingers in my palm for me to hold. He caressed the well of my palm with his middle finger. His deeper voice was low and soothing. "You weren't a bad wife, Lucy."

I squeezed his fingers. "You weren't a terrible husband." I stroked his wrist with my thumb. "And you saved my life too many times to say a simple thank you."

Foss nodded. "You, too. You saved us all."

Foss kept a rubber band around his beefy wrist, and I lightly snapped it. It was part of his Anger Management class, snapping the rubber band whenever he got too worked up. I appreciated the tool, but really I just like playing with it. Jens and Foss went to weekly meetings together. Foss took Jens to Narcotics Anonymous, and Jens took Foss to Anger Management. It was kinda sweet to watch them go off on their man dates and come back a little better off every time.

The clerk called the only other couple in the room, and I stiffened knowing that we were next. Foss could sense my apprehension, so he kissed my temple. "We don't have to do this if you don't want to."

I plastered on a good representation of a smile as I spoke. "It's fine. We should get divorced. Now you can go off and marry one of those women who tours the ranch and gives you the glad eye. Don't think I don't see how they look at you. Ranger Bob with his trusty steed."

"Lucy?"

"Just don't pick someone annoying. I mean, we all have to hang out with her, so maybe do an IQ check first."

"Lucy," Foss admonished my conversational dodging.

His voice was so sincere; I couldn't look at him. "Don't. Don't be nice right now. Don't make me feel," I whispered. "I can't take it today."

His breath in my ear was so quiet, I knew it had to be something that would threaten my resolve. He didn't like being openly sweet to me. "I do love you."

I nodded as I stared in front of me, a lump forming in my throat. "Yep. You too. You know, with the love stuff." I touched my heart, but was still unable to look at him, afraid of falling into his abyss and chickening out again on filing the papers. "Let's get this over with."

Our names were called, and we stood. He held my hand to communicate that any strength I was lacking could be borrowed from him, though I could sense he was wavering, too. I handed the paperwork to the clerk, who checked to make sure everything was in order and then waved us through.

The judge's chambers were straight out of every TV show I'd ever seen. Leather chairs, big ominous desk, matching, regal-looking books on the bookshelf, African-American man in a black robe who looked like he wanted everything expedited and as little conversation as possible.

We handed him our papers, and he silently checked them over. "You're here for a termination of your marriage?" He leafed through the papers until he found the one he was looking for. "That seems to be in order. Well done. I don't appreciate people coming into my chambers and wasting my time with half-done paperwork."

Huh. I didn't know judges called their offices their chambers. I thought that was a TV thing.

"Reason for divorce?"

"Irreconcilable differences," I answered quickly. That was a lie. We were too similar. We had too much fight in us to play nicely with others. We were proud and hated limitations. Foss was a hard worker, and I liked to think I was, too. Twenty credit hours plus keeping an eye on the three new Undrans took a fair amount of determination. We valued family, and fought hard to keep what belonged to us, ours.

I looked up to find Foss's eyes on me. He had been conversing with the judge, and now it was my turn. I answered the few clarifying questions. No, I didn't want alimony. No, I wasn't going to keep his name, since I never took his in the first place. No, we didn't need mediation to split up our assets. It was all there, clean and simple. Had there been a drive-thru, we would've been done in a flash. No, we didn't have any children to fight over. No, I don't want fries with my divorce order.

We signed papers, shook the judge's hand and left the office, hand in hand. Foss pulled me aside in the waiting room before we rejoined the others. He kept his same low tone to keep his niceness from being heard. "For what it's worth, I don't regret it."

I couldn't look up at him. "For what it's worth, neither do I." I should have felt lighter, but somehow my shoulders felt weighted with adulthood. Twenty-one never felt so old.

I turned to push open the door, but Foss caught my arm. Without a word, he spun me around, tilted my chin up and kissed me. It was the same closed-mouth nips we occasionally blessed each other with, but this one felt like a parting of ways. I hugged his middle, my face buried in his chest, clinging to the solid anchor I wished I didn't need, but knew I'd never fully shake.

We didn't speak. We didn't need to. Talking was where we got ourselves in trouble, so instead we swallowed the things we knew to be true, accepting the change in our relationship that would always leave me confused.

Foss linked his fingers through mine, and I could feel the calluses from playing his fiddle. Occasionally he brought his instrument when he visited us, playing calming compositions to soothe me when I slipped back into the inevitable melancholy. There was a time I stopped talking for a few weeks when we first started building a new life together in my world. Foss played for my stoic demeanor until emotion finally surfaced. Though he couldn't control me with his music (nor could he control me any other way), it was his pledge to me. No matter what our legal status was, we were soldered together like two misshapen pieces of junk metal that needed each other to be useful.

I was bound to quite a few people, now that Undraland was behind me. Jamie and I would never be rid of each other, though I'm not sure either of us cared anymore.

We'd learned to respect each other's walls and play in each other's dreams. He was the big brother I'd never had, but always wanted.

Though I was bound to Britta through her marriage to Jamie, I would have tied myself to her regardless. She was the best of the most important things you could want in a girlfriend. Britta was loyal even when I was wrong. She was both gentle and vicious at just the right times.

Foss moved to open the door that lead out to the lobby, but I stopped him. "Wait. Um, this belongs to you." I reached to the nape of my neck and fiddled with the leather lace that held his ring just over my heart. The knot was impossible; certainly it wasn't because my fingers were trembling that I couldn't get the knot undone. I huffed. "Do you have your knife on you?"

"You said no knives in the courthouse," he reminded me. "Are you sure you don't want to keep it?"

I nodded. "I'm sure. It's your ring. Save it for the next Mrs. Foss. The real one." I tugged at the lace again, flustered at the emotions that rose up in me.

"Hold still. I got it." With fingers that were rarely gentle, he slowly undid the rope that had started out feeling like a noose, but over time had become a sort of treasure to me. Being around Foss had been a similar journey.

Lucy, if you don't want me to know this, put up your wall. This is just painful to watch, Jamie said in my brain. *You remember Jens, right? He's pacing the floor out here. He's a jumble of nerves over this, so choose your path and be done with it.*

I cringed and tried to push Jamie out. It was harder to do when my emotions were so all over the place.

I held up my hair, grateful Foss couldn't see my face as I tried to remain completely motionless so he wouldn't sense my trepidation at being truly without him. I felt the knot release its grip on my psyche, and the ring fell away into Foss's palm. He clutched it in a fist he pressed tight to my breasts. His lips swept the back of my neck, and I released my hair to fall around his face. He inhaled, and I exhaled.

"That felt like a goodbye kiss," I whispered.

"Is Jamie gone?" he asked, his thumb reaching down and tracing my hip.

I nodded with trepidation. The hair on my arms stood, knowing I was about to make a choice I shouldn't.

"Then, no. That wasn't goodbye." He shook his head against my neck and turned me to face him, that unconcealed longing in his eyes tugging me forward. "One more, and then we can be done."

I didn't agree aloud, but my answering lips against his was response enough. I can't imagine many couples make out seconds after their divorce, but that's exactly what we did. Foss and I were never on the right path. We were all wrong, but he tasted like comfort during a confusing time in my life.

His thumb traced my lowest rib over my blouse, and I fisted my fingers in the shirt collar I'd bought him. We pulled each other closer, indulging in the last moments of our gratuitous relationship. This kiss was hard, but his lips were soft. I fought with everything in me to keep the wall up so Jamie wouldn't feel the fire Foss always managed to kindle inside me.

When the kiss finally hit a head, we slowly melted

down from the moment, going back in for the occasional "one last kiss" a few more times. "You're going to be a hard habit to quit," I remarked, emotion too thick to hide in my voice.

He touched his lips, steadying himself. "I think it's time." He drew me in and held me in his firm grip, restraining me from leaving just yet. His love was always tinged with a little force, but he was learning to be gentle with me. "Goodbye, Lucy."

I nodded, but the words were stuck inside me. "Yup," was all I could manage before the emotion bubbled to the surface.

Foss let me go. It felt all kinds of wrong and right. He straightened as he slid his ring back on his finger, and then moved beside me to open the door. His eyes looked up at the ceiling to avoid my face as if I was an embarrassment to him. "You're crying. You look disgusting when you cry."

"Shut your smackhole," I jabbed, wiping the pinpricks of moisture from my cheeks.

"You shouldn't show Jens you're upset. It's like, the happiest day of his life." He grumbled under his breath, his personality obliterating any forthcoming regrets or second thoughts I had concerning our divorce.

I swiped at my eyes again with my glove. "Better?"

Foss shook his head and huffed disparagingly in my face. "What do you want me to say? You're still a little ugly. Give it a couple seconds."

I guffawed. "I can't believe I was actually sad to divorce you! You're so mean!"

Foss shrugged, unfazed at my accusation. "You love me. It's your one redeeming quality."

I mimed barfing all over his chest, and then I traced a filthy curse word in the fake vomit.

He responded by rolling his eyes, turning me to the door before him and smacking my butt as I passed through. He'd started doing that a few months ago. Jens was not pleased.

"Knock it off!" I demanded, slamming my elbow back into his solar plexus. His "oof!" at my force was mildly satisfying.

Our anger reached its usual crest, and we both chuckled a little at the confusing nature of our broken and bruised relationship. He bumped his fist to mine, both of us breaking into soft smiles at the dysfunction.

Jens stood as we walked into the lobby, his hopeful expression nearly breaking my heart. "Is it... Did you... Is it done, then?" he asked, his cagey gaze laced with a note of hesitation. He was a rocket before the blastoff.

At my nod, he let out a shout of relief and disbelief that he could finally have what he wanted with no strings attached. I watched invisible bonds untie themselves from Jens, making him look younger, without the cynicism, sarcasm and worlds of survival that were bred in him. The serious people around him in suits cast disapproving looks at his outburst, but he paid them no mind.

When Foss tried to shake Jens's hand in a manly passing of the baton kind of way, Jens laughed and brought the big bull in for a hug and a kiss on both his cheeks. "You're suddenly the most beautiful man I've ever laid eyes on," Jens declared. "Other than that roguishly handsome beast of a man I saw in the mirror this morning."

Foss was not amused. "I've got things to do." His

portable gray cloud was darkening to black, and I knew it would be best if he was left alone. "See you Friday for rock climbing?"

I nodded. "Of course. Wouldn't dream of breaking tradition." I'd insisted they socialize and get some sort of modern education. Their retaliation was that I had to learn better survival skills. Every Friday was rock climbing, followed by a self-defense class with Britta, and then topped off with an evening of kayaking. I think I preferred weightlifting class with Professor Vin Diesel. Foss was relentless on Fridays, always pushing me harder. I loved him and hated him for it, but that seemed to be our way.

Foss cast us a two-fingered wave, got into his green pickup and sped away, breaking two traffic laws before he got to the main road.

Even though it was only ten in the morning, I wanted to take a nap. I was suddenly hit with a semi-truck worth of exhaustion.

Jens had other plans. He pulled out four tickets from his pocket and waved them in my face, his eyebrows doing that dance I loved. "Feel like crappy hippie music?" he asked, knowing what my answer would always be.

"Seriously? Yes!" My smile revived for the occasion. I couldn't think of any better way to celebrate my marital freedom than with the live music I knew I would love, and Jens would loathe.

I shook off the feel of Foss's lips on mine. I shook off the divorce. I shook off the scars, the deaths, Pesta and the whole of Undraland. I fiddled with the vial at my neck, and did my best to shake off the grief that I'd been married and divorced, and my family hadn't been there for any part of it.

I could feel Linus pushing me forward, so I let myself fall into Jens's arms. I melted like soft taffy against his solid chest, and the world felt right again.

"There you are. I've been missing the you that's you. I hate seeing you so withdrawn. I knew this would help." Jens's grin split his face like he'd been sucking on a wire coat hanger. "You ready for it?"

We stepped out into the sunshine, new possibilities dancing as we set to explore more of the Other Side. I'd never seen my world for what it was until Jens showed it to me. We put down roots. We got a mailbox on a post that went into the ground – not a box on a wall, like the ones we'd used in the apartments my family had frequented. We got address labels printed in actual ink, so you know it's permanent. Jens, Jamie and Foss built me a white picket fence in all of its fifties sitcom glory, and I loved the great men in my life for it.

"I'm not sure I'll ever be ready for you," I admitted. I kissed him on the steps of the courthouse, letting Jamie and Britta pass us so we could slow the world for a few breaths to enjoy our moment. For everything he'd given me, the only thing Jens seemed to need in return was for me to see him, so he could shed his identity as the invisible man.

I ran my hands through his thick hair he'd halfway brushed for the occasion, pressing my forehead to his. He delivered one simple kiss to my suggestible lips before whispering, "You're okay with this? You're doing alright? You're sure this is what you want?"

I sifted my fingers through his, nodding as I held tight to our connection. "I'm sure. I've always wanted to make out with a garden gnome. Way sexier than the pink flamingo lawn ornaments."

He grinned at my shtick, too happy to properly jab me back. The golden tattoo on his cheek shifted as he spoke. "I love you, Loos. I'm so happy right now. Remember this moment. I have no sarcastic comebacks."

His smile was charming, gorgeous and contagious. "I love you, too. You're an amazing thing, you know."

His hand squeezed mine. "You're a beautiful thing."

Wherever I went, I had my guardian gnome at my side. I was surrounded by magic, but in the end, I'd remained just enough me to build a life without it. I'd been kind, cruel, swelled with peace and crashed with violence.

I was human, and that was my beautiful thing.

The End.

Love *The Other Side*?
Leave a review here!

LUCY AT PEACE

BOOK SIX IN THE UNDRALAND SERIES

Are you ready for the *Undraland: Blood* series? Join Lucy, Jens and the Merry Band of Thieves as they get sucked back into the adventures of Undraland.

Enjoy a free preview chapter of *Lucy at Peace*

JENEVE

"*How* ow about this one?" I asked Jens of the brown blouse. It was so much fancier than anything I usually wore, but these were extreme circumstances.

"When did I become your girlfriend in all this?" Jens complained, flopping on the bed and rolling onto his back. "It looks fine. I don't know why you care so much. It's like, the twentieth outfit you've picked out. I'll say it again: you look great." His voice was deadpanned, which made me want to dress him in my brown blouse just to make him understand that people care if they look stupid or not.

"I want Jamie's sister to like me. It's important that we get along."

"Well, what you're wearing is fine for that. Just be yourself."

I rolled my eyes at my light blue Transformers t-shirt that hugged me in just the right way to provide optimum comfort and non-annoyingness. "You're such a guy."

He threw up his hands in exasperation. "Exactly my

263

point! May I be excused from girl time? You know, I have a sister in the house right down the path from our very home that you can do all this with."

I frowned, remembering that brown washed me out a little. I threw the blouse onto the pile of discards. "Britta's nervous enough as it is. She's the sister-in-law now. This is the big conversation day, and I don't want to add to the things Jeneve's upset about."

Jens sat up, slapping his left hand atop his opposite palm every fifth worth to punctuate his point. "Look, tonight's going to be fine. We already sent word that Jamie and Britt eloped. They already know. Jeneve's just invited us to come to hang out. Sure, she'll be a high-maintenance pill, but so what? She affects our lives zero when she's not here. The whole of Undraland affects us zero. It's one dinner, and then it's over. Wear jeans and a t-shirt, like me. It doesn't matter if you get along with Jamie's sister. Jamie doesn't get along with his own sister. Just be there for Britta after the fact, and you're golden."

"Oh, I have every intention of making Britta look like the gem she is so Jeneve can report back to King Johannes that his son is getting along just swimmingly on our side. I just don't want to give Jeneve more ammo to hate me. Last time we were there…"

Jens stood and moved over to the large window of our bedroom, looking in the distance to Jamie and Britta's colonial that rested on the furthest edges of our shared property. Jamie and I had established quite the tether to our psychic laplanding bond, allowing us a whole mile of space before the headache started.

The best part about killing the bear at the same time

Jamie did was that, well, we didn't get eaten by a bear. The worst part was the laplanding nonsense. If there was ever a person who could make the whole business not as terrible as it could have been, it's Jamie.

We'd had many conversations about how best to give each other space, and had even built up the door between us and stretched it to a whole hallway that we could walk down to hang out with each other or not. Sure, when emotions got intense, they seeped under the door, but Jamie had gotten married and been having sex with Britta. While I could feel the swing of his emotions (and admittedly, heard some of the thoughts and seen a few images I'd not care to discuss), we were handling it.

Jens shoved his hands in his back pockets, pressing his tailbone and stretching his spine as he spoke. "Jeneve hates me for turning down the offer her dad made me to marry her. She doesn't want me; she just wants what she can't have. Plus, you're a queen, and she's only a princess. Big time jealousy there. She's never going to braid your hair, Loos. My sister will, though, so that's the horse you should bet on."

I guffawed. "Here's a tip on women from me to you: don't refer to my best friend as a horse. How about this one?" I asked, pulling out a plain white blouse from the back of the closet. I didn't dress up often, so those clothes were really just ornamental.

Jens groaned. "I'm gonna die in this room. This is it. This will be the thing that kills me slowly. Give me back the farlig fisk. I'd fight that beautiful sea monster all over again with my hands tied behind my back if it'd get me out of this."

"If this is you being helpful, you're not."

Jens whined like a petulant two-year-old being told to wait while mommy stood in the lengthy return line at the boutique. "I'm not trying to be helpful. I'm trying to get this to end!" He rolled his shoulders back. "She's here. That's Stina's Porsche."

"How did they even become friends?" That little tidbit still astonished me. Undrans feared the Other Side (otherwise known as my side, where somehow I'd convinced them I was the queen of this universe) because Huldras roamed free. Their mind-controlling whistle got them kicked out of Undraland. It surprised me to no end that Jeneve had only been to the gate that led to our side one other time, and her first friend had been with the vindictive Huldra who hated me and wanted Jens. Actually, come to think about it, they had a lot in common.

"Stina hangs out by the gate sometimes and catches Undrans as they come out to the Other Side. Even though Jeneve's too scared to cross all the way over, they got to chatting it up across the gate, apparently." He walked over to me, picking up my hand and kissing my knuckles. "Wear exactly this. Jeans and a t-shirt. It's you, and it's what I want. That's what they'll hate. That you don't have to dress up, and you're still a queen." He sucked on my lower lip like I was a piece of delicious candy. "I'm wrapped around your cotton-blend sleeve. Let Stina keep her heels and short skirts. Let Jeneve have her fancy court dresses. You own me."

I don't know how he could get me to blush time and time again like a little schoolgirl, but Jens was a master at making me do the inner hair-twirl. I tossed the blouse into the pile and stood up on my toes to kiss him. "I stinking love you. You know that, right?"

"You'd better." He nipped at my lower lip, his hands squeezing my waist, making me feel dainty and treasured. "I just sat through an hour of dress-up Barbie for you. You owe me, Mox."

I lost my witty response in his kiss, my fingers reaching under the hem of his black t-shirt and tracing my favorite ripple on his sculpted abdomen. The third one on the right side. It was divine and a little ticklish, so I got to seduce him, seduce myself and torture him in the process. It was a solid win all around.

"Let's go." I pulled away from him, grinning at his whine of frustration that I'd started up the engine only to kill it mid-motor.

"That was cold, Loos."

I made my way out of our spacious lavender-painted bedroom and down the hall, attached to his hand. We always came as a pair, stuck in some way like magnets, or the really good kind of Velcro that never gets crap in it when you wash it too much. Jens was permanent, and that fact gave me much solace in our quaint little white picket fence life together.

He squeezed my hand as we neared Jamie and Britta's home that was laid out the same as ours. Finished basement, big kitchen with a dining room off to the side and a big living room with a fireplace right when you opened the front door. Three bedrooms upstairs, and a whole lot of love filling each crevice and corner.

Britta greeted us at the door we usually just walked right inside with a courtesy don't-be-naked-please knock and a shout through the house. Her grin was wide and cracked with distress and unhappiness. Her mouth said, "Come on in, guys," but her eyes said, "What took you so long?" She wore an ankle-length brown maxi skirt, a cream blouse and her signature two brown braids on either side of her head. She was adorable, as always.

I wrapped my arms around her. "Backup's here, babe. Show me to the ex, and then take me to the sister."

Britta hugged me tight and held on for four seconds before letting go. "I'm never more grateful for our friendship than when we have to go see Jeneve. I love you. You know that, right?"

I grinned, relaxing at the knowledge that the most important thing in all of this was getting Britta to like me, which she did. "I love you, too. Jamie totally married up. Lucky guy, if you ask me."

She kissed my cheek and smiled up at her brother, who did his best not to be insensitive. "You look nice, Britt." His grin turned devious. He always grew in attractiveness to me when evil prank Jens appeared. "Let's go mess with Jamie."

His grin died when Stina came around the corner, her short skirt revealing her very long legs that matched her cat-like smile. "Hey, baby. Good to see you again." She ignored Britta and me, attaching her lips to Jens's cheek. Then she made it her business to stand in between us, lording her six-and-a-half feet over my five-foot-seven.

"You ready to go?" Jens asked, not bothering to return Stina's greeting.

"Sure. Thanks for delivering this to Jeneve. I'm just

swamped all weekend, so I don't have time to wait for her to come to the gate."

"Yeah. What is it?" Jens took the clothing store bag from her and peeked inside. His eyes widened and then narrowed at Stina, and he shut the bag quickly.

Stina laughed. "It's just some stuff from our side that she might like. The few times we've talked across the gate, she seemed cool, so I thought I'd send over some lacy thongs, good bras and things she can't get in Undraland." She put her hand on Jens's bicep. "Oh, Jens. You've seen my thongs before. You can't be that embarrassed."

By nature, I'm not a violent person. I had to keep reminding myself of that fact every time Stina opened her lipsticked mouth. I wasn't sure why or how we'd become friends with her again. The last time I'd seen her, I'd gotten into a fist-fight with her smug smile. A few apologies to the group, a few times helping us with her Huldra whistle, and Stina was back in our lives. Yay.

"Fine. Whatever. Jamie can give them to her." Jens shouted through the house. "Jamie, you ready?"

I answered for my laplanded buddy. "He's trying to find his garden gnome hat." I shouted up the stairs. "I saw you put it in your second from the top drawer last time. It's probably buried under your socks."

"Thanks! Found it," Jamie reported, and then stumbled down the stairs a few seconds later. He was in full Undraland mode, wearing beige pants, a white shirt and his red garden gnome hat. He'd even shaved with a razor that morning. I knew because he'd nicked himself, and by proxy, nicked me. Have I mentioned how much I love being laplanded to my boyfriend's best friend? That's prob-

269

ably because I don't love it. I threw up my wall so I could have a mini freak-out when I felt the small slice. Then I stopped the tiny prick of blood and shoved the image of the sparkle from my mind before Jamie caught wind of it.

Pesta, the evil siren, had put her *arv* on me, which meant that I now had siren blood running through me, mixing with my genetics and making me, in part, her daughter. The thought was horrifying, so I made it a point never to think about it. No one knew, and I hoped to keep it that way for as long as I lived. That's realistic, right?

Jamie and Britta slid into the backseat after loading a couple bags in the trunk, while Jens pried Stina's red painted claws off of him and shut himself into the driver's seat.

I was in the front passenger's seat, belted in place with a demure smile on my face. "So, how's your girlfriend?" I asked in a sugary sweet voice.

Jens palmed my face as he shuddered. "I've never called her that before, so don't you start. Jamie, if I haven't said it before, Jeneve's got terrible taste in friends." Then he looked in the mirror to his sister, who was twiddling her thumbs nervously. "So if Jeneve doesn't shine to you this time around, it only means you're doing it right."

Britta nodded, and Jamie placed his hand on hers to stay her nerves.

I loved watching them be sweet to each other. When Jens removed his hand from my face and started up the car after Stina drove away, he knocked the outside of his fist to mine. It wasn't quite the same as hand-holding, but it was Jens, and I would take it.

Read *Lucy at Peace*,
the next book in the series.
An *Undraland: Blood* Novel

Sign up for my newsletter and
view my other books at
www.maryetwomey.com

Undraland: Blood Novels

Lucy at Peace

Lucy at War

Lucy at Last

Linus at Large

Terraway

Taste

Tremble

Torture

Tempt

Treat

Temper

Tease

Trap

Faîte Falling

Ugly Girl

Lost Girl

Rich Girl

Stupid Girl

Broken Girl

Untouchable Girl

Stubborn Girl

Faîte Falling: Faîte Rising

Common Girl

Blind Girl

Savage Girl

Dangerous Girl

Find your next great read and sign up for the
newsletter at www.maryetwomey.com

Mary also writes contemporary romance under
the name Tuesday Embers.

View her books at www.tuesdayembers.com

Made in the USA
Columbia, SC
28 August 2018